"ALONE AT LAST"

Kate announced as she returned to the kitchen.

"Rita's gone?" Jason asked as one of his hands caught hers. "Your friend is nice. I like her."

Kate raised her eyebrows. "Not too much, I hope."

Jason laughed and pulled Kate down to sit on his lap.

Kate frowned playfully. "You're supposed to say 'I only have eyes for you.'"

"I do," he said with a warm smile.

"It might be nice if you said so."

"I just did. But if you insist, I'll say it again. I only have eyes for you," he murmured softly against her ear. "And I plan to look at you all night long...."

ABOUT THE AUTHOR

The inspiration for a novel can sometimes be
something as simple as a show on TV. And that's
just where Sandra James got her idea for *Stronger
by Far*. After watching a documentary on missing
persons, Sandra was haunted by the idea of a
heroine who was compelled to find her missing ex-
husband. The result is a highly charged
Superromance, filled with adventure and intrigue.
And, as always, Ms James has drawn upon the
love and warmth of her husband and three
daughters to create characters who will touch
every reader's heart.

Books by Sandra James

HARLEQUIN SUPERROMANCE
205–A FAMILY AFFAIR
249–BELONGING

Don't miss any of our special offers. Write to us at the
following address for information on our newest releases.

Harlequin Reader Service
901 Fuhrmann Blvd., P.O. Box 1397, Buffalo, NY 14240
Canadian address: P.O. Box 603,
Fort Erie, Ont. L2A 5X3

Sandra James

STRONGER BY FAR

Harlequin Books

TORONTO • NEW YORK • LONDON
AMSTERDAM • PARIS • SYDNEY • HAMBURG
STOCKHOLM • ATHENS • TOKYO • MILAN

Published September 1987

First printing July 1987

ISBN 0-373-70277-9

He grimaced, but the nose of the plane inched down. He might be a fool, but he wasn't stupid. Kate might think differently, though, especially when she heard about this...if he ever made it back to Texas.

The man beside him pointed and grunted another order.

The valley yawned before him, like a giant beast eager to close its jaws around him. Seconds later a haze of gnarled tree branches whipped by the window.

His breath came jerkily. There hadn't been time to plan the approach. He was coming in too fast. Losing control...

Kate. Toby. Jason. Images flashed before him like clips from a movie. His life. His past. It would be different this time. If only he had the chance, he would make it up to them. All that he'd done, all that he'd failed to do.

The ground rushed up to meet him. Closer. Ever closer...

Please, just one more chance....

PROLOGUE

THE SUN BLAZED DOWN on the twin-engine Cessna. The plane streaked eastward, a glint of silver against the deep blue sky.

In the cockpit, a man stared straight ahead. His blood pounded in his ears. He could scarcely hear the drone of the engines for the thunder of his heartbeat. Beads of sweat rolled down his face, but inside he was cold—as deathly cold as the steel of the gun jammed into his ribs. A dozen thoughts and images collided in his mind. Only one managed to break free, flashing like a yellow warning light. Hijacked!

His eyes flitted toward the radio. At the same time his hands tightened around the yoke. The plane banked sharply, then was abruptly righted. A garbled curse rent the air. The pistol clattered to the floor. Two men grabbed for it at the same time, but only one emerged victorious.

For the second time in less than a minute he felt the steely hardness of a gun barrel pressing into his ribs.

"Do not try that again," the man beside him warned. "Once we are on the ground, I have no need of you. Remember that." Black eyes gleamed. There was a flash of white teeth. "You understand, *sí*. So you will land this plane now, there in the valley ahead." A vicious jab of the pistol punctuated the command.

Kate managed to keep her smile in place, though, while Mrs. Harding waved and exited the shop, but it vanished the second the door had closed. Rita Grant chose that moment to emerge from the back room. Rita was not only Kate's partner but also Kate's closest friend.

Thirty-two years old to Kate's thirty-four, Rita was a small, vivacious woman with the most gorgeous shade of honey-blond hair Kate had ever seen. Rita, too, had been divorced fairly recently, and it was while the two were at a crossroad in their lives that they had decided to open the boutique. As they had anticipated, their first year in business had been the hardest, but at long last, things had begun to look up.

Rita's blond beauty was a direct contrast to Kate's striking darkness. Tall and slender, Kate wore a simple gore-skirted dress of palest gold. The style was discreetly feminine. Her hair was a rich shade of mahogany, parted in the center and drawn into a prim heavy knot that rested on the nape of her neck. On Kate, however, the severe hairstyle was anything but puritanical. Instead it drew the eye to her high cheekbones and finely formed features, and lent her an air of classic elegance. Her emerald eyes added an exotic mystique.

Taking advantage of the lull between customers, Rita leaned against the counter, her eyes on Kate's troubled expression. She nodded toward the store window and the array of skyscrapers framed against the backdrop of a blazing Texas sky. "Don't tell me the heat's getting to you," she commented.

Kate smiled faintly. "Me? A native Texan?" Though Rita had made the move years earlier, Kate still occasionally teased her about migrating south from the wilds of northern Minnesota. Typical of August, though, the temperature outside was blistering. She could almost see

CHAPTER ONE

IT WAS THE END of a long week; a typical Saturday at Creations Unlimited, a busy Dallas boutique that specialized in high-fashion women's wear. Kate McAllister was ready to drop on her feet, yet she couldn't help but be grateful for the distraction the customers provided.

Where Kate was concerned, the day was anything but typical. All week, in fact, she had been battling the strangest feeling that something terrible had happened, or was about to happen. But she managed to mask her unease as frothy layers of chiffon floated gracefully into a waiting bed of tissue. She slipped the cover over the gaily patterned box and handed it to Mariel Harding, the wife of a prominent Dallas plastic surgeon.

"Thank you, Mrs. Harding," she murmured. "I'm sure your daughter will look lovely in the dress."

"I'm sure she will, too." The woman flashed a beaming smile. "But then my Lucy looks good in anything."

True, Kate agreed silently. Mariel Harding's daughter often accompanied her mother into the shop. The girl was perhaps nineteen, with shimmering blond hair and a stunning figure. She was beautiful, charming and spoiled as only the daughter of wealthy parents could be.

Lucy reminded Kate just a little of herself fifteen years ago, but thank heaven she'd lacked the self-important ego Lucy possessed.

the heat shimmering in undulating waves above the asphalt surface of the street.

But the vague, nagging feeling inside Kate had nothing to do with the heat. The tingle of apprehension simply refused to be denied. She'd already checked on Toby twice in the past hour. The last time she'd phoned Nancy, the neighbor who kept Toby until Kate arrived home from the shop, she'd sounded just a little miffed at the interruption.

Relax, she told herself for what seemed like the hundredth time that day. *Just relax. Today is no different from any other day.*

But it was, and she knew it. She didn't know how, but she did.

Aware of Rita's speculative gaze on her face, she tried to brush the sensation aside. "I know this is going to sound a little odd," she began rather sheepishly, "but have you ever had the feeling that something was about to happen?"

Rita laughed. "Sure. In fact, it's what I keep praying for, and dreaming about every night," she proclaimed with a gleam in her eyes. "One of these days, a rich, handsome man will waltz into my life and carry me away from all this drudgery."

"A valiant white knight with a shining suit of armor?" This time Kate's smile was genuine, though definitely not envious. "Follow the yellow brick road, Rita. It's probably the only way you'll ever find such a man."

If Rita detected a hint of cynicism in her partner's voice, she paid no mind. Instead she wrinkled her nose prettily. "Actually, I was hoping he'd find me."

Kate said nothing as she paused to rearrange a rack of leather handbags. Part of her wished she could be as nonchalant about men as Rita. The other woman en-

joyed dating. But then, Rita and her ex-husband had
parted on friendly terms. As Rita put it, they found they
made better friends than lovers. She often joked that she
and Dennis should have tried living together first before
taking the final plunge into a lackluster marriage. But
Kate knew that no matter how much Rita laughed and
joked, her morals would never allow her to settle for a
live-in arrangement. It was Kate's opinion, however, that
Rita was probably better off without the elusive story-
book romance she craved. Her own sheltered upbringing
hadn't prepared her for the cold realities of life, but Kate
had learned.... Oh, yes, she had learned.

"Speaking of men..." In that very unsubtle way she
had, Rita steered the conversation backward. "When are
you going to let me fix you up—"

"With the friend of a friend?" Kate's thoughts veered
unerringly toward her son. "I already have a man in my
life, thank you."

Rita made a face. "Not a six-year-old, silly. Though I'll
admit he's handsome enough with those huge green eyes
and wavy blond hair. But even knowing the lady-killer
Toby will someday be, I mean a real honest-to-
goodness—"

"Don't say it!" Kate interrupted, but this time her
laugh was forced. "I get your drift."

Rita immediately regretted her impulsiveness. She
probably knew better than anyone why Kate preferred to
steer clear of men, but a marriage that had ended on the
rocks after a dozen years wasn't the only reason, or so she
speculated.

Rita and Kate had been through a lot together, start-
ing with Kate's first year in college. She'd shared Kate's
happiness when she'd walked down the aisle with Greg
McAllister, shared her fears when her husband was

drafted and later fought in Vietnam, shared her sorrow when Kate stood before the newly dug grave of her father.

She had squeezed Kate's hands, encouraged and praised while Kate labored to bring her child into the world, and blinked back tears of happiness at first sight of Kate's son.

Yes, she had seen Kate through good times and bad. But despite the way she had seen Kate grow into a strong, self-contained woman, there were times when Kate's eyes took on a haunted quality that made Rita's heart ache.

"I'm sorry, Kate," she said, biting her lip. "But you know I worry about you."

Kate shook her head, aware of Rita's concern. Even if she had wanted to, she had no time to fit a man into her life. Opening the boutique, and making it financially viable, had taken a tremendous amount of time and energy this past year, energy she had willingly put into it.

The only daughter of Michael Anderson, a real-estate broker, money had been the least of her concerns while she was growing up in Bradley, a small town northwest of Dallas. She'd lost her mother at a very young age, and consequently, her father had showered her with everything money could provide, and much of his time as well. Yet somehow Kate had grown up rather in awe of her hard-working, business-minded parent.

In retrospect, however, Kate had been remarkably unworldly, in spite of her appearance. She had been perfectly content to let first her father, and then Greg, do most of the decision-making for her. Even when Greg had started McAllister Air Express, that had been his triumph, not hers.

Now, for perhaps the first time in her life, Kate was proud of herself. The reins of control were in her hands, and she was determined to make a good life for herself and Toby, and she finally had the confidence to do it.

"There's no need to worry about me," she attempted to soothe Rita. It was true that she had dated no one since her divorce, but that suited her just fine. "Right now, I'm far more concerned with building a stable home for Toby. He took the divorce very hard."

Rita gave her an odd look and settled on the stool behind the cash register. "But don't you ever get lonely?"

If she did, she wasn't sure she'd have admitted it, even to herself. "I've only been divorced a year and a half," she reminded Rita.

"So have I!" the other woman protested, then grinned sheepishly. "Well, closer to two, I guess. Anyway," she went on, "since it seems like we'll both be spending the evening alone, why don't you pick up Toby and the three of us can go out for dinner?"

Tempting as it sounded, even more tempting was the thought of a refreshing shower and a nice, cold glass of iced tea in the comforting surroundings of her own home. Maybe it would ease the prickly state her nerves were in.

"Thanks, anyway, Rita," she started to decline. "But I think Toby and I will just—"

Suddenly the door to the shop opened. Both women turned at the same time. A tall, chestnut-haired man stepped through the door. Loose-limbed and lanky, he was dressed casually in khaki-colored slacks and shirt.

Despite the blast of heat that accompanied the man's entrance, Kate felt an unmistakable chill run down her spine. And suddenly she knew what was behind the niggling unease that had plagued her all week.

"Greg," she whispered. She knew by the expression on Jeff Coleman's face that she was right. Her head swam dizzily, and for a moment she felt as if she were suffo-

cating, but she recovered quickly. "What is it?" she asked before he'd even reached her. She scarcely recognized the ribbon of sound that was her voice. "Tell me, Jeff! His plane—"

Jeff shook his head quickly, grasping the hand she flung out beseechingly. It was ice cold. He squeezed her fingers, painfully aware of what was in Kate's mind. Many, many times, he'd seen the fear that darkened her eyes whenever she watched Greg's plane take off. And as Greg's operations manager, he'd also received too many anxious phone calls the second Greg's flight was even minutes overdue. But it was Greg who had told him that Kate's father had died when his twin-engine Cessna crashed shortly after takeoff, and it wasn't until then that he'd really understood Kate's fear.

"We don't know anything for sure yet." He tried to reassure her, then hesitated, wondering if he was doing the right thing. Still, he realized he had no choice. Kate held a quarter interest in McAllister Air Express, and she'd once been Greg's wife. It really didn't matter that they were no longer married.

Kate's fearful eyes were focused on his face. Her skin was nearly colorless. "His plane," she repeated, her voice thin and raspy. "You think it's crashed, don't you?" The tight constriction in her chest threatened to rob her of breath once more. "Jeff...Jeff, tell me!"

Jeff's eyes closed briefly. Lord, but he wished he were anywhere else just now! He'd always liked Kate, and even Greg's bitterness over the divorce hadn't managed to change that. She had been through so much, and although he liked Greg as a friend, and respected him as his boss, he knew damned well Greg hadn't made things easy for her. He couldn't help but feel protective toward her.

"I came to the shop because I didn't want to drop this on you at home, with Toby around." He paused. "Is there somewhere we can be alone?"

His expression was apologetic as he glanced at Rita, who hovered anxiously behind Kate. "It's okay," she told him quickly. "Rita is a friend, a very good friend." Rita echoed the sentiment, then belatedly Kate introduced her partner to Jeff. She added with a weak smile, "I have the feeling this is one of those times when I'm going to need all the support I can get."

With a silent but vehement concurrence, Jeff watched as Rita flipped the sign at the front of the shop to Closed. The three then moved quietly to the small office Rita and Kate shared in the rear of the building.

When they were seated, Kate's eyes never wavered from Jeff's face. "Tell me what happened," she requested, her voice filled with quiet determination. "Everything, Jeff."

He grimaced. "There's not much to tell. Greg left Thursday for Mexico City. I know he arrived okay, checked into a hotel that night, and stopped by our office at Hidalgo Field yesterday morning. He intended to make another pickup in Veracruz, stay the night and return around noon today." There was a brief but significant pause. "He never made it, Kate. Not even as far as Veracruz."

Hard as she tried, Kate couldn't stop herself from shuddering. Greg had been making runs to Mexico for several years now. Kate knew enough of the country to realize that the terrain between Mexico City and Veracruz was treacherous indeed. There were mountains, rain forests. It would be only too easy for a plane to go down...and never be found.

She closed her eyes and took a deep, cleansing breath. Jeff's voice sounded very far away. "Before I had a chance to check further, this arrived for you." She opened her eyes and saw him shove a small package toward her. "Special delivery."

Kate accepted it with a frown. "But what does this have to do with Greg's plane disappearing?"

Jeff was silent for the longest time. As Kate stared across at him, icy tendrils again trickled down her spine.

"Maybe nothing," he said finally. "Maybe everything." He hesitated for a moment. "I don't know, Kate. Call it crazy—hell, call me a lunatic! But why would someone send *you* a package at the McAllister Air Express office? As far as everybody knows, the business is Greg's baby."

He was right. While it was no big secret, very few people were aware that Kate was still a silent partner. "Maybe it's personal," she said.

"Personal?" Jeff grimaced. "Somehow I don't think so. I've got a bad feeling about this whole thing, Kate. Greg's plane disappearing, and then *that*..." His gaze dropped to the soiled yellow package Kate now held in her hands.

Kate's gaze followed his. "There's no return address." A heavy knot coiled deep in her stomach as she noted the markings in one corner. "This originated in Mexico, Jeff."

The feeling of dread intensified. Kate had to force herself to open the envelope.

A small photo dropped onto the desktop. She found herself staring at Greg, but it was a Greg she scarcely recognized. The background was vague and blurred, but he was sitting on a filthy cot, his head and shoulder propped against the wall. His face was battered and bruised, his blond hair matted and greasy. Her mind whirled giddily as she saw that his eyes were closed. He could have been sleeping. Passed out. Or maybe he was...

"Kate." Jeff's voice was gently prodding. "There's a letter."

Kate's eyes slid to a small square of paper that had fallen beside the photo. She unfolded the letter, her stomach clenched with fear.

Greetings, *señora*. As you see, we have your husband. You want him back, you pay us fifty thousand American dollars. Be in Mexico City by 10:00 p.m. on Monday. Stay at the Hotel Cordoba. We will contact you there. *You* bring the money—no one else. No tricks, no *policia*, or you will never see him again.

"He's been kidnapped," she whispered numbly. She picked up the photo, staring at the swollen face she scarcely recognized as Greg's. "He looks half dead," she choked. "My God, Jeff, do you think he's—" But no. No! She couldn't say it. She couldn't even let herself think it.

Jeff had already reached across and removed the letter and photo from her grip. He sucked in a harsh breath and dropped back in the chair. They stared at each other, and Kate read his mind only too well.

Her soft mouth was set stubbornly. "He's okay, Jeff. I have to believe that. *We* have to believe it."

Jeff wasn't convinced, but he didn't let on. "I wish I could say it was a hoax. But somehow I don't think so. The Hotel Cordoba is where Greg always stays." He paused. "What are you going to do, Kate?"

Kate had risen and began to pace the small room. Greg was hurt, perhaps very badly hurt, but she clung to the conviction that if he was dead, she'd have known it, just as she had known that something was wrong. At any rate, she had to find out what had happened to him. "I'm going after him," she said quietly. "What other choice is there?"

Jeff's eyes narrowed. "I'm not so sure that's wise," he cautioned. "In fact, I can't help but wonder why the hell they want you to deliver the ransom."

Her lips twisted in a faint semblance of a smile. "Why else? Insurance. Maybe they plan on kidnapping me as well if I don't pay it." Her gaze moved back to the letter. "There isn't much time to get the money, even if I had it."

Jeff looked confused. "But your father..." He faltered as Kate shook her head. "I'm sorry. I just assumed he'd left you—"

"He made some bad business deals just before he died. What little was left went into Greg's company," she explained tonelessly. Her stomach knotted as a feeling of dread descended. Greg had been so bitter during their divorce, it had surprised Kate when he insisted she retain her quarter interest. Circumstances being what they were, she wasn't inclined to argue. Since Greg had retained the majority holding in the company, he made all the business decisions, and Kate was content to keep it that way.

But several months ago she'd seen him very briefly when he'd needed her signature on a loan. He was in the process of expanding the business, and everything was mortgaged to the hilt. "He doesn't have it, either, does he?" she asked, her face pale.

She knew even before Jeff spoke what the answer would be. "As far as liquid assets go," he told her grimly, "he's in bad shape. We might be able to sell off a couple of planes and some equipment, but that will take time."

And time was the one thing they didn't have. The kidnappers wouldn't hold Greg indefinitely. And God only knew how long it would take her to raise so much money.

"What about the government? Either ours or Mexico's?" Rita's worried gaze traveled from Jeff to Kate. "Isn't there something they can do?"

"By the time someone in Washington, D.C. or Mexico City got around to doing anything, he could be dead." Jeff winced when Kate's face whitened. "Kate, there's something else," he said slowly. "Even if they could help, I'm not sure we could contact the authorities in either country."

She stared at him. Good Lord, what more could possibly go wrong? Her lips barely moved as she spoke. "Why?"

Jeff shifted uncomfortably. "The last few runs he's made to Mexico, he's been acting—" his shoulders lifted helplessly "—I don't know what else to call it but strange. I don't think anyone else has noticed it but he's been jumpy while we're loading and unloading, supervising the whole operation himself. It made me wonder if he isn't involved in something..."

"Illegal?"

He nodded.

Kate closed her eyes. She would never have suspected Greg of doing any business that would land him on the wrong side of the law, yet he was so cocky, enough of a daredevil to think that nothing could go wrong.

"Do you have any idea what kind of cargo he was carrying? What he was bringing back?"

"Oil rigging supplies going down. On the return trip, I'm not sure. The shipments are always boxed and crated.

There's no telling what's really inside.." He threw up his hands. "It could be anything! And I don't have any idea if the kidnapping is connected with the cargo he was carrying. Either way, it doesn't look good."

He glanced over and saw her stricken expression. "I'm sorry, Kate," he said quietly. "But we have to be realistic. If Greg is alive, and we don't know that he is, he may not stay that way for long."

"I know." Charmer that he often was, Greg's smooth-talking ways wouldn't do him much good now. It was left to her to be calm. Rational. She had to think of something—anything!—that they could do to free Greg. Calm and rational? Her thoughts suddenly mocked her. Those were the two things Greg had accused her of *not* being the day she'd told him of her decision to end their marriage.

But this wasn't doing anyone any good. Not herself, and certainly not Greg. She forced herself to rise, and began to pace around the small room. "We've got to think of a solution," she muttered. "We may not have the ransom money, and we may not know what kind of trouble Greg's in, but we can't just leave him down there. Not when we don't know what the people holding him may do to him."

"Short of hiring a commando team to blast him the hell out of wherever he is, I don't know what to do," Jeff said grimly. "If the ransom isn't paid, there's no telling what might happen."

It took a moment for his words to sink in, but when they did, Kate ceased her pacing and stopped dead in her tracks. "That's it." She expelled a slow breath, and as her eyes met Jeff's, a faint ray of hope began to flicker inside her. "That's it, Jeff," she breathed.

"What?" Both Jeff and Rita turned in their chairs to gaze at her with startled eyes. "You want to hire someone to get him out of there?'' Jeff sounded totally bewildered.

"Yes. No." She sat on the edge of the desk and bit her lip, her thoughts churning wildly. "I mean we won't have to hire him…exactly. I think I know someone who would be willing to go in and try to get Greg out."

Jeff's heavy brows met in a frown. "Who?"

"His name is Jason Davalos." Even as she said the name, an image cut across her mind. Jet-black hair above a leanly configured face, eyes that should have been as dark as obsidian, but instead were a strange, tawny color—almost gold. Even after all these years, she saw him as clearly as if it were yesterday…and an all too familiar ache unfolded deep inside, the force of which stunned her. She'd thought she'd conquered old ghosts long ago. But did a woman ever forget her first lover?

She hadn't been a woman, Kate reminded herself harshly. She had been little more than a child who'd always gotten what she wanted…and she had wanted Jason Davalos. The only problem was that she'd had no idea how to hold on to him.

Dimly she became aware that Jeff's eyes were trained on her face. "That name sounds familiar," he said slowly. "Friend of Greg's?"

She hesitated. There was no need to tell Jeff everything. "He used to be," she said slowly. "He and Greg grew up in Bradley, and they served together in Vietnam. As far as I know, Jason still lives there."

"And you think he can find Greg and get him out?" Jeff tried not to sound too skeptical. Slim as he suspected Greg's chances were, he wasn't sure this was the answer, either.

Kate was only too aware of what was going through his mind, but she tried not to dwell on it. "They were in the same para-rescue unit in Vietnam," she explained. "Greg did some of the piloting for Jason. Jason was part of the ground team that went in after downed pilots and wounded soldiers. After his discharge, he joined the Drug Enforcement Administration for a few years." She raised her eyebrows. "Greg once said Jason spent most of his time in Mexico. And if Greg happens to be involved in something illegal..." She drew a deep breath. "I think it would be to his advantage to have someone like Jason on our side."

"But we don't even know where he's being held." Jeff dragged his hand down his face wearily. "It could be in Mexico City, or it could be in Veracruz, or somewhere in between. Mountains, jungle...who knows? And who knows if this friend can even find him?"

"Jason may well be the only chance we have; the only chance Greg has." If he was still alive. She stubbornly brushed the disturbing voice aside. "When they were in Vietnam, Jason sometimes went into the interior for days on end, surviving on not much more than his wits. He's also fluent in Spanish, since both his parents were from Mexico. And with the time he spent there with the DEA...I can't think of anyone better suited to try to find Greg."

"But the kidnappers want you there on Monday. Chances are, they'll probably want the ransom then, or soon after. That doesn't give you much time, Kate."

"Then I'll have to try to stall them awhile, to give us a chance to find Greg." *If* Jason agreed to help. Granted, Jason and Greg had been best friends for years, but that had been a long, long time ago.

But if Jason was unwilling to help Greg...that was something Kate refused to think about. "I'll go see Jason first thing tomorrow morning." Quiet as her voice was, there was no mistaking her conviction. "If he agrees, we'll leave on Monday."

Jeff stared at her. "We? As in you and Jason Davalos?" At her nod, he straightened abruptly. "Wait a minute, Kate. You can't go traipsing all over Mexico trying to find him! Why don't you let me go?"

"Because you're needed right here. I don't know the first thing about running the company and this isn't the time to shut down, not with money as tight as it is. Besides, you read the note. *I'm* the one they want to deliver the money." Her expression grew more troubled. "I wish I could leave sooner, but with the banks closed, I don't see any way around it. I'll need money for expenses, and I have a little saved for emergencies. This wasn't the type of emergency I'd expected to use it for, but maybe it will be enough to appease the kidnappers."

"I'll take care of things here at the shop." Rita's eyes were worried, but she knew Kate well enough to realize that there would be no dissuading her once her mind was made up. "I'll be glad to take care of Toby, too." She cast a doubtful look at Jeff. "But I think Jeff is right. You'd be better off staying right here at home."

"We don't have any choice," she told the two of them firmly. "We can't leave Greg down there, not knowing what will happen to him if we don't agree to pay the ransom. This is the only shot we've got."

A taut silence settled over the small room. "I suppose you're right," Jeff relented. "I just hope we're not asking for more trouble."

Trouble? Once again Jason's image drifted into her mind. She shivered at the prospect of facing him again after all these years.

She had the vaguely unsettling feeling her troubles had just begun.

CHAPTER TWO

LATE SATURDAY NIGHT, Kate sat on the edge of Toby's bed. Sunday was normally a day reserved especially for the two of them to be together, and it was indeed a rare occasion when Kate didn't spend it with her son.

Toby was a six-year-old bundle of energy—easily distracted, just as easily pleased, but usually not a problem child. Greg had made little time for his son, but nonetheless, Toby revered his father. As a pilot, he was regarded as something of a hero by his young son. Consequently the divorce hadn't been easy for Toby. In typical child fashion, he wondered if he'd done something wrong. Kate had explained many times that she and his father weren't mad at anyone, least of all Toby. It was simply better for all of them if they no longer lived together. She knew the youngster didn't really understand, but she was also aware that he secretly hoped she and Greg would reconcile someday.

"You said you were going to Bradley." Clad in light cotton pajamas, Toby looked up at her. His bottom lip quivered. "Why won't you let me come with you?"

Kate sighed and started to reach for him, but he pulled away.

"Why, Mommy? Why can't I come?" His voice wobbled traitorously, but his wide green eyes were accusing. "You said you'd take me there. I want to go to the little candy store you told me about. The one where they make the peanut-butter fudge.''

The one where Jason had once bought her a huge chocolate candy kiss...and then followed it up with a far more delicious version of the real thing.

That was why she'd never taken Toby to Bradley. Since she'd sold her father's house there after his death ten years ago, she hadn't returned. There was no need. Still, that wasn't the only reason, she admitted reluctantly. There were too many memories in Bradley. Memories of her father, and just as many of Jason. But those of Jason were far more disturbing. The last few months, though, Toby had grown especially curious about her child-hood—where she had lived, what she'd liked to do, the schools she'd attended.

''I'm sorry, Toby.'' Her eyes conveyed her regret. She tried to ruffle his silky blond hair, but again he evaded her touch. ''If I could take you with me, I would. But this is something I have to do alone. Before school starts, I promise—''

''Hey, Toby.'' Kate glanced back to see Rita peeking through the door. ''I was just thinking,'' she offered in a casual tone that didn't fool Kate in the least, ''maybe the two of us could go to Dinosaur Valley State Park tomor-row.''

Kate mouthed a silent thank-you over her shoulder when Toby's face lit up.

''Wow,'' he breathed, ''that sounds neat-o.'' His eyes darted eagerly to his mother's face. ''Can we, Mom?''

''I can't go with you,'' she began.

His hesitation was fractional. ''That's all right. Me and Rita—we'll have a swell time!''

He sat still for Kate's good-night kiss, but as soon as it was delivered he bounced several times before sliding beneath the covers.

Rita was waiting in the living room when Kate slipped from Toby's bedroom. Home for the two McAllisters was a long, brick, ranch-style house, the epitome of middle-class America, complete with a two-car garage that housed Kate's station wagon. She'd bought the house after she and Greg split up. With a young boy on her hands, she'd had no taste for apartment living. She wanted Toby to be able to run and play freely. Greg had kept the fashionable split-level house on the outskirts of Dallas, and Kate was very glad he hadn't insisted she stay there. For her, it had ceased to be a home. For years, it had been little more than a battlefield.

"Well?" Rita asked when Kate dropped down onto the sofa. After closing the shop, they had picked up a pizza to take home. Rita had also stopped at her apartment to change her dress for a loosely cut top and jeans. Now she sat with her bare feet curled beneath her. "Is he ready and rarin' to go?"

"Is he ever." Kate chuckled. "Though that might not have been the case if you hadn't come through when you did."

Rita laughed and held up her index finger. "First rule I learned as an aunt—when all else fails, resort to bribery." Rita's older brother lived in Fort Worth, and had two daughters and a son who weren't much older than Toby.

Kate shook her head and smiled slightly. "Sounds like a great rule, as long as the parents don't find out. Although this parent isn't complaining. At least not yet," she added dryly.

Rita smiled, but then a rather pensive expression entered her eyes. "Kate." She hesitated. "I don't want you to take this the wrong way, but are you sure you know what you're doing? I mean, going off alone to try to track Greg down..."

"I won't be alone," Kate reminded her. She felt her heart speed up unconsciously as she added, "Not if Jason agrees to help me."

"Do you really think he will?"

"I hope so. Jason and Greg were very close when they were younger. And then there's Vietnam. I suppose it has something to do with being smack dab in the middle of a war zone. Greg told me once he trusted Jason as he'd never trust anyone in his life." Kate's smile held a touch of wistfulness, and something else Rita couldn't quite identify. Then she said softly, almost to herself, "Jason will help, I'm sure of it. And we really don't have any choice. I can't let Greg down."

Rita opened her mouth, closed it, and opened it again. "That's what bothers me, Kate. I guess I feel like you're, well, you're really going out on a limb for him, and what did he ever do for you?"

"I was married to him for nearly twelve years," she reminded the other woman very gently. "They may not have been the happiest years of my life, but I can't pretend my marriage didn't exist."

Rita snorted, a distinctly unladylike sound. "Happy? That man made you miserable! Especially the last few years. Oh, I know you're too loyal to say anything against him, but he was never there when you needed him. Where was he when your father died? Why, he didn't even bother coming home when he found out. In fact, he didn't show up until after the funeral. He wasn't there when Toby was born, either. As usual, he was off flying on some job!''

There was no point in denying Rita's accusations. Kate had agonized too long, and too hard, over the same questions herself. She'd been devastated when her father died, and Greg was nowhere around. He'd taken a summer job in Alaska ferrying supplies between the peninsula and the islands off the Alaskan coast.

The same thing had occurred when Toby was born. For years, she had excused his behavior by telling herself that Greg was hard-working and wanted to make a good life for his family. But she couldn't stop herself from wondering if she'd ever really come first in Greg's life, and it had taken her a long time to realize she hadn't. Greg was a risk-taker, a thrill-seeker. He had no room in his life for a wife and a son.

Still, he'd been there when she needed him most...during the lonely months when Jason was no longer a part of her life.

Kate's hands formed a white-knuckled grip in her lap as she fought the treacherous pull of the past. The lingering shadows of memory no longer haunted her, but she had no desire to step back in time. The day she had left Greg she'd promised herself that brighter tomorrows were just ahead.

She made that same promise once more.

Her voice was quiet but clear when she finally raised her head. ''Knowing that Greg is in trouble, I couldn't live with myself if I didn't do something to help him,'' she told her friend.

''But this whole thing scares me. Thinking of you off in the wilds of Mexico!''

Kate's lips curved in the first genuine smile of the evening. ''It's perfectly civilized, Rita.''

"Except when someone just disappears like Greg did!"

Kate's smile withered. "That could happen anywhere. And it's all the more reason to make sure we find him— and find him quickly."

Rita gazed at her with wide, troubled eyes. "Kate," she said tentatively. "You aren't still in love with Greg, are you?" She bit her lip. "I mean, you're not secretly hoping that the two of you can get back together if you manage to get him out of this whole mess?" She gave her a long, slow look. "Are you?"

"I don't love Greg anymore," she answered finally. Her expression was pained. *Tell it like it is, Kate,* an inner voice chided. She had never really loved Greg the way she'd loved Jason. She'd felt comfortable with him; he was steadfast and dependable, at least at first. He'd made her laugh when she'd thought she would never laugh again. And when Jason left her she had needed so desperately to feel wanted again. Greg was the one who was there for her; to comfort her, to hold her, to love her as Jason had never loved her.

Kate hesitated a moment. "I'll admit our marriage wasn't perfect, but I'm as much to blame as Greg."

The other woman's mouth tightened. "At least you tried to make it work."

So had Greg on occasion. It had been just enough to keep Kate thinking their marriage could succeed. And, she added silently, she had also been afraid. Afraid of failing, afraid of coping with life completely on her own, with no one else to shoulder the burden. Then when Toby had come along, she had stayed with Greg out of a sense of duty, and the hope that their son would bring them closer.

But Kate had eventually realized that many of the storms she had weathered—her relationship with Jason, her father's death, the deterioration of her marriage—had shaped her into a woman who was far more confident and self-sufficient than she had ever dreamed.

"Don't blame Greg for everything," she repeated. "We both made mistakes and—and there are things you don't know about."

Rita folded her arms and gave her an oddly penetrating look. "Then maybe you should tell me," she said quietly. "There's something else bothering you, isn't there? It's not just Greg being kidnapped."

A heavy silence descended. "Yes and no," Kate admitted at last. "But you're right. It's not just Greg." She drew a deep breath. "It has to do with Jason, too."

Rita murmured something encouraging. Kate smiled shakily, then began to speak very softly. "Jason and I... We were married once."

Rita's eyes widened. "But when?" She looked utterly confused. "I mean, you were barely twenty when you and Greg got married. Were you childhood sweethearts?"

Kate shook her head. "My father worked in Dallas, but we lived in Bradley. It's a small town, the kind where everybody knows everybody else. Greg's family moved there when I was about ten." Her eyes held a twinge of sadness as she paused. "Greg had this friend..."

"Jason?"

She nodded. "I'd known Jason, or at least known of him, since I was younger than Toby. His parents had a small farm outside of town, just down the road from my father and I. Dad always used to wonder how they managed to keep their place afloat, but they were proud and hard-working. Jason's parents didn't speak any English, though, and they kept pretty much to themselves. Jason and Greg were three years older than me—both big-brother types. Neither one paid much attention to me..."

"Until the ugly duckling grew into a swan," Rita guessed astutely.

Kate's laugh was shaky. "That's a good way of putting it. I wasn't very worldly in those days. Jason had gone off to college, but then his mother died. His father had passed away the year before. Anyway, he had a younger sister to raise, so he dropped out of school and worked the farm. That happened the summer after I graduated from high school. I hadn't seen him for ages, and our housekeeper sent me over with a basket full of food."

As she spoke, her fingers traced idle patterns on the fabric of the chair. A circle, a square, the outline of a tiny heart.

"I'll never forget the way he looked that day, so fiercely proud yet vulnerable. Crazy as it sounds, I think that's when I fell in love with Jason Davalos."

"You started seeing each other then?"

Kate sighed. "I went back the next day, and the next..." She smiled mistily. "It was wonderful, Rita. Being in love with Jason felt so—so right." Her smile died. "But then I got pregnant. We ran off one weekend and got married. My father was furious. He knew I'd been seeing Jason but he never dreamed it was so serious. In his eyes, Jason was fine for a friend—"

"But not good enough for a son-in-law."

Kate's lashes drifted shut in silent assent. Her fingers were laced tightly in her lap. "Daddy started telling me Jason was no good, that he'd never be anything more than a dirt-poor farmer."

Rita looked horrified. "Kate, you didn't let him get to you!"

She swallowed painfully. "Rita, I was so confused. I thought Jason loved me, but he seemed so different after he found out I was pregnant. Sometimes I felt like I didn't know him at all. My father wanted us to live with him, but Jason refused. Daddy wanted him to go back to college, too, but Jason was too proud to accept any money from him."

She shook her head in poignant remembrance. "I felt like I was being torn in two. I couldn't please Jason. I couldn't please my father. Jason was constantly after me to stand on my own two feet, while Daddy.." She shook her head in a telling gesture.

Rita's mouth tightened. "Good Lord, Kate! No wonder you were confused, with the two of them badgering you like that!"

Kate leaned her head against the back of the sofa. "It turned out that Jason married me needlessly anyway," she recalled tiredly. "I had a miscarriage during my fourth month. While I was in the hospital, Daddy saw a lawyer and started divorce proceedings on my behalf." She shuddered. "I'd never seen Jason so angry. He walked out and I haven't seen him since. I guess I thought he'd be back, and together we could make my father see.." She inhaled tremulously. "The next thing I knew, Greg told me Jason had sent his sister off to live with an aunt in New Mexico, and he'd enlisted in the army."

Rita raised her eyebrows. "I suppose Greg was there to pick up the pieces?"

Kate hesitated, then nodded her agreement. "Married and divorced, all at the ripe old age of eighteen, and married again not much more than a year later." Her voice was faintly textured with bitterness. She turned her head to look at her friend. "You didn't know I had such a sordid past, did you?"

Rita's reply was a long time in coming. "It's never too late, Kate. You should remember that. Maybe it's time you and Jason set things right."

And so speaks the voice of an incurable romantic, Kate echoed silently. Then she frowned. It wasn't like her to be so cynical.

As for she and Jason setting things right...Once, a long time ago, Kate might have believed they could. But time, and circumstances, had convinced her otherwise. As far as she and Jason were concerned, their marriage had been a mistake. A mistake from start to finish.

IT WAS AFTER NOON on Sunday before Kate pointed the nose of her car toward Bradley. She had slept little the night before. Greg's kidnapping still seemed a bizarre nightmare, and her stomach was tied in knots.

She had tried to phone Jason shortly after Rita had left, but no one had answered. And when there had been no answer again this morning, she wasn't sure if she was relieved or dismayed. With a silent sigh, she turned her attention back to her driving.

The countryside was awash with wildflowers in vivid reds, blues and yellows. Flat, grassy plains gave way to gently rolling hills. It was a vista that seemed in constant motion; up and down, a kaleidoscope of colors and shapes that caught the eye. But Kate was oblivious to the vast Texas panorama just outside the car window.

Throughout the forty-five minute drive, it preyed on her mind that she hadn't been able to contact Jason yet. What if he was out of town? What if she couldn't track him down? What if he had moved?

Her decision to bypass the heart of the small town wasn't a conscious one. But as she turned onto the old highway that circled Bradley, she told herself she had neither the time nor the inclination to explore old haunts, to deliberately risk confronting any more of her past than she had to. The prospect of facing Jason again was all she could handle at the moment.

Her head was aching when she finally pulled onto a long gravel road. Dust flew out from behind the car as she drove past a cluster of outbuildings. Several horses grazed peacefully in the paddock near the barn. When Kate came to the end of the private road, she stopped and leaned her arms tiredly against the steering wheel.

The tiny frame house that had once stood at the top of the gentle hill was gone. In its place was a rambling, low-slung building of whitewashed adobe with a flavor that was distinctly Spanish. Finally she gathered the strength to get out of the car and approach the house. She stepped through the graceful arch of the entranceway into a small courtyard. A profusion of colorful, well-tended flower beds caught her eye. A woman's touch.

The thought had scarcely registered when one of the double doors swung open and someone stepped out of the house. Blazing sunlight fell full on the woman's face. Kate caught her breath. Jet-black hair combed back from a high forehead had been pulled into a loose ponytail that emphasized high cheekbones, almond-colored eyes and full red lips. The woman was young, quite young, and very, very beautiful.

Kate's heart lurched. Jason's wife?

At precisely that moment the woman caught sight of her. She gazed at Kate with dark, startled eyes.

Her mind still reeling, Kate stepped forward. "I—I beg your pardon." She pushed a lock of hair away from her cheek, feeling grimy and disheveled before the woman's obvious youth. The dark-haired beauty didn't look much more than twenty. "My name is Kate McAllister," she began once more. "I'm looking for Jason. Is he here?"

The woman shook her head, and the look in her eyes changed to one of frank curiosity. Kate was aware of keen eyes traveling over her limp, white linen jacket and slacks.

She tried again. "I really don't mean to intrude, Mrs. Davalos, but it's—"

A burst of laughter was the last thing she expected to hear. This time it was Kate who appeared startled.

"Please!" The young woman laughed pleadingly. "If you call me Mrs. Davalos, you'll make me feel old before my time."

Kate frowned, amazed that she sounded so calm. "But aren't you Jason's wife?"

"Heaven forbid! It's bad enough to have him for a brother—" the woman rolled her eyes exaggeratedly "—let alone a husband."

Kate stood stock still. "Wait," she breathed. Her eyes widened in mingled amazement and recognition. "Rosa—you're Rosa!"

The woman looked puzzled. "Yes, but how did you know—"

"I'm Kate McAllister," she repeated, hoping her name would register. "I used to live about two miles down the road on the Anderson place. The last time I saw you, you were about five years old and running around in pigtails."

Rosa's mouth dropped open. "You're the Kate who threw Jason into a tailspin all those years ago. *Now* I remember."

A tailspin? That was nothing compared to the way he'd made her feel. Kate smiled weakly. "How is he?"

She found herself on the receiving end of a long, curious gaze. "You're the only one who's been called Mrs. Davalos, if that's what you mean."

It wasn't, but knowing that Jason hadn't remarried gave her a peculiar kind of satisfaction. She cleared her throat to cover the awkward void. "Is Jason here?"

Rosa shook her head. "He left early this morning for a cattle auction. He won't be back till later this evening." She shrugged. "About seven or eight o'clock, I'd say. What did you need to see him about?"

Kate hesitated. "I'm afraid it's rather personal. Jason and my ex-husband used to be good friends, you see…"

"Wait…McAllister." The other woman frowned, then snapped her fingers. "That's right. You're married to Greg McAllister."

A dull flush crept into Kate's cheeks at Rosa's disapproving tone. "Was," she corrected briefly. "We're divorced now." She paused. "I'm surprised you remember Greg. You couldn't have been very old."

"I don't remember much." The girl's friendly manner withdrew. "But I know all I really care to about him."

The eyes that gazed back at her were tainted with wariness. Kate heaved a mental sigh. If this was any indication of Jason's reception….

She studied the oval-shaped face for a moment, then came to a quick decision. "This is very important, Rosa." With a minimum of words, she explained what had happened to Greg, and why she had come.

Rosa's expression was grave when Kate had finished. "How awful," she murmured. "If I could get Jason back any sooner, I would. Honestly," she added quickly, as if she was afraid Kate didn't believe her. "But he's in Fort Worth and I don't know how to get hold of him."

"It's okay," Kate said gently at Rosa's guilty look. She made a feeble attempt at a laugh. "I tried calling last night and again this morning, but I didn't get any answer. To tell you the truth, I wasn't even sure I'd find him here. I haven't been back to Bradley for quite a while, and I—I thought he might have moved," she ended lamely.

"We were both out last night, and I was in town this morning. As for Jason leaving..." Rosa shook her head. Kate was relieved to note that a little of the wariness had left her face. "He was born and raised on this land," she said simply. "It may seem strange, but it's a part of him."

Her eyes narrowed against the glare of the sun, Kate made a slow, sweeping assessment of the surrounding landscape. Here and there the sun glinted off a meandering stream. A coat of burnished gold covered the knobby hills, which stretched as far as the eye could see, blending with a cloudless blue sky.

Strange? No, it didn't seem strange at all. There was a wild and rugged beauty to the scene, a raw, untamed quality that was as much a part of Jason Davalos as the land he owned...to which he belonged.

"Why don't you come in and have something to drink? There's really no point in driving all the way back to Dallas. Now that you're here, you might as well stay."

The invitation was unexpected, but Kate hardly relished the idea of making the forty-five minute drive a second time. "Do you think Jason will mind?" she asked slowly.

Rosa shrugged dismissively. "Don't worry about Jason. If he gives you any trouble, just leave him to me."

A prickly feeling ran down her spine. Kate wasn't sure she liked the sound of that. Jason had always given her goose bumps, and while it had once been an extremely pleasant sensation, that wasn't the case now.

"I don't want to impose," she began, but something of her thoughts must have shown in her face.

"It's no bother. Really," Rosa told her firmly. "I'll just set an extra plate for dinner, too. Nick won't mind, either."

"Nick?" Kate sent a curious glance sideways as they turned and started toward the door.

"A friend," the young woman said quickly. Kate thought she detected a faint shadow cross Rosa's face, but it was gone so soon she decided it must have been her imagination.

The interior of the house was blessedly cool and refreshing. In the living room, wood-plank floors and ceilings beamed with pine created an effect that was as natural and soothing as the desert hues of the decor. The furnishings were a combination of old and new; the modern sofa blended with the more traditional chairs and pine tables.

"Have a seat and I'll get us something to drink." Rosa pointed to the sofa. "Is lemonade okay?"

"Sounds great."

Rosa returned a moment later with two tall, frosty glasses. She handed one to Kate, then sat down across from her.

Kate's eyes trailed around the comfortably furnished room a second time before they returned to Rosa. "This is really nice," she murmured warmly. "Jason seems to have done very well for himself."

For the first time since she'd extended the invitation, Rosa's smile seemed a little forced. She traced a finger around the rim of her glass. "Must be a big improvement over the last time you were here. Were you expecting the same rickety old shack you left behind?'' There was no malice in either the words or the tone, but there was a challenge there nonetheless.

"I really hadn't thought about it," Kate said truthfully.

"No." Rosa's voice was cold. "I don't suppose you had."

Kate sat back and met her gaze calmly. "Is there something you'd like to say?"

"Yes. Yes, there is, now that you mention it!" Rosa's dark eyes flashed. "Our tiny little house didn't compare to the fancy one your father owned up on the hill, did it? Jason couldn't give you everything your little heart desired, could he? He just wasn't good enough for you." She jumped to her feet. "Well, look around you, *Mrs.* McAllister, because things have changed. Jason is every bit as respected in this town as the next person, and no one looks down on us now!"

Kate stared speechlessly. She hadn't expected such an outburst from this sweet-faced young woman. In one distant corner of her mind, she recognized that Rosa's outspokenness and spirit were traits she herself hadn't possessed at the same age. *Things have changed,* Rosa had said.

They had, indeed, Kate acknowledged in a silent salute to the other woman. But so had she.

She placed the half-empty glass on the table. Her chin lifted, not in a show of defiance, but of pride. "Let me tell you something, Rosa." Kate delivered the words into a tense, waiting silence. "The tiny little 'shack' that once stood here was a home, a *real* home—not because of how big or small it was, but because of the people who lived in it. Your parents saw to that. As for Jason and I, whatever problems we had were between the two of us."

She met Rosa's eyes unflinchingly. "But make no mistake. I was never—*never*—ashamed of being his wife and living here with him."

Rosa simply stared at her. Then her gaze slid away, and her eyes closed. Her slender shoulders slumped and she dropped into the chair once more. "Oh, Lord, I'm sorry." She bit her lip, her apology mirrored on her face. "I didn't mean to say that—I shouldn't have said it! But you coming here after all this time has, well, it's like opening up a can of worms, to be perfectly honest. Jason went through so much after the divorce."

Had he? she wondered silently. "Don't apologize." Kate tried to lighten the intense moment. "It isn't often that a woman gets to take her big brother's side."

They both laughed tenuously. This time it was Kate's eyes who lowered first. "Did Jason...do you know if he's felt that way all this time? He thought I was ashamed of him?" Much as she wished to end the discussion, she had to know.

Rosa bit her lip and nodded silently.

Kate smoothed the pleat in her slacks. "I see." Her voice was almost a whisper. "I didn't realize—"

"Oh, he's never come right out and said so." Rosa had guessed what was on her mind. "To tell you the truth, I can't even remember the last time he even talked about you."

Kate drew in a sharp breath. That hurt—far more than it should have.

"Jason's never been the type to bare his soul," Rosa continued. "In this case, action really does speak louder than words. I never realized it until I was older, but it wasn't hard to figure out that it was despair over losing you that drove him to leave Bradley. He spent the next three years in the army, then two more with the DEA...

He visited me at Aunt Alicia's in New Mexico whenever he could, but in all that time, he never came back here.''

Each word was like a step deeper into her soul. Jason's reasons for staying away from his home were anything but foreign to Kate. She understood in a way that surpassed even Rosa's understanding.

"My Aunt Alicia could never figure out why he wouldn't sell the farm. As young as I was, I knew he'd return eventually and we did—nearly ten years ago. Lord, this place was a mess! Fences down, weeds sprouting everywhere you looked." She shook her head. "The first thing he did was tear the old house down and build this one. Little by little, he's bought up the surrounding land. We're running cattle on most of it now."

She paused, and added softly, "You were right, Kate. Jason may not be rich, but this place has turned out better than anyone ever thought. He *has* done well for himself.''

Oddly, it was an observation that offered little comfort. Kate was glad for Jason, but it was an unwelcome reminder of the shortcomings of her own life. Two marriages. Two divorces. But at least she had Toby, thank God.

Almost as if she had read her mind, Rosa came over to sit next to her. She hesitated only a second before laying a hand on the older woman's shoulder.

"I'm sorry, Kate, honestly. I had no business judging you when all I know is Jason's side of the story." At that, she made a face. "Right now, I'm not sure I even know that very well." Gently she squeezed her shoulder. "Let's not talk about you and Jason anymore. Let's talk about you, or me—or even the weather!"

This time Kate was only too glad to comply. She welcomed the chance to get to know the woman who had once been her sister-in-law. And there was much to like, Kate discovered as the afternoon progressed. Rosa was warm and vibrant, outspoken and buoyant. Yet she possessed a wisdom that was unusual in someone so young. She also had a knack for making Kate talk in a way that few other people had ever managed. Rosa soon learned about Toby, and about Rita and the business.

Kate couldn't help but notice Rosa's absorbed interest when she spoke of the boutique. "You must be a budding fashion designer," she teased as she helped prepare dinner.

Rosa pulled a stainless-steel bowl from the cupboard. "I wish," she said with a sigh. "I might have the drive and ambition, but I just don't have the artistic talent."

Kate tipped her head to the side. "How do you know unless you try?"

"I did," came the glum reply. "I went to art school when I was eighteen. I lasted about two months before I was told to drop out or flunk out."

"What have you been doing in the meantime?"

She shrugged. "I've got three years of college under my belt."

"That's great!" Kate wondered a little at Rosa's rather blasé attitude. "Any plans after you graduate?"

"Graduate?" She chuckled. "That may or may not happen in the next century." At Kate's puzzled look, she went on to explain, "Jason always complains that I'm majoring in hodgepodge and minoring in potpourri. He thinks business administration is what I should be setting my sights on." She made a face. "He also thinks I've never outgrown the urge to play dress-up. *I* think the only reason he wants me to finish college is because he never could."

Kate winced inwardly. Not wanting to pursue that line of conversation, she backtracked slightly. "So you like the fashion scene?"

"I like working with clothes and material. Matching things up, pairing accessories and things like that," Rosa admitted. She began to shred lettuce into a bowl.

"Then why not get a job in one of the department stores in Dallas? You might have to start at the bottom, but that way you'd know if you like it well enough to make a career of it."

Rosa paused in her work. Slowly she lowered the lettuce to the counter. "I've thought of that," she said.

Kate frowned at her tentative air. "What's stopping you?" At Rosa's sudden silence, comprehension began to set in. "Jason," she murmured, as much to herself as to Rosa.

The woman hesitated, then shook her head. "Being some kind of career woman...I'm not sure it's the most important thing in my life." Before she could say more, the doorbell rang. "That's probably Nick." She wasted no time in moving toward the front door.

Kate understood her hurry when a slender, dark-haired young man entered the house. So this was the Nick that Rosa had mentioned earlier. But a friend? He was more than just a friend, Kate judged silently. As Nick pulled Rosa into his arms, she wisely turned away from where she'd been watching near the kitchen doorway. Kate began to set the small pine table with the plates and cutlery Rosa had put out earlier. She didn't turn around until she heard a tiny cough behind her. Beneath the olive tint, Rosa's cheeks were faintly pink. The blush of love, Kate thought with a curious catch in the region of her heart.

"Kate, I'd like you to meet Nick Montoya. Nick, this is Kate McAllister. She—'' Rosa halted fractionally "—she knows Jason. They go a long way back.''

Kate murmured a hello. The hand she extended was immediately clasped in a firm male grip. With their dark, shining hair, snapping black eyes and small, slender build, Nick and Rosa looked a little like brother and sister. But the kiss they'd exchanged was anything but familial, she reminded herself.

"You and Jason know each other?'' Nick asked as he slipped his hand through Rosa's.

Kate nodded. "I grew up here in Bradley.'' She glanced at Rosa and decided to spare them both as much embarrassment as possible. "Jason and I were married once.''

"Married? Jason was married?'' He sounded rather shocked.

"It was a long time ago,'' Kate offered gently. "I was just out of high school then.'' When his eyes sought Rosa's as if for confirmation, Kate smiled pleasantly. "I'm surprised Rosa recognized me today. Jason and I weren't married long, and she was only six at the time.'' She then proceeded to bypass the uncomfortable moment by pointing out to Rosa that the potatoes were boiling over.

Kate soon discovered that she liked Nick Montoya almost as much as she liked Rosa. He had been working as a ranch hand for Jason the last six months. He was a bit on the quiet side, but there was clearly no holding back when it came to his feelings for Rosa. Both love and pride shone in his eyes whenever they touched upon her, and there was no doubt that Rosa returned his feelings in full measure.

Seeing the two of them together made Kate feel both heartened and just the least bit envious. When was the last time a man had looked at her the same way Nick looked at Rosa? Still, she couldn't help but tease them just a little.

Kate helped clear the table, but Rosa insisted she sit and enjoy her coffee while she took care of the dishes. Nick quickly jumped up and grabbed the dishtowel.

"You two make such a great team," she told them when they'd finished. "Any wedding bells in the offing?"

The smile was wiped clean from Rosa's face. Nick's expression turned grim. Kate bit her lip. "Sorry if I said something wrong." She glanced from one to the other. "It's just that the two of you seem to care so much about each other."

Rosa looked ready to cry. "I'm sorry," Kate said again. Were her teasing hints about marriage really so terrible? She felt so helpless.

Nick saw Rosa into the chair she'd occupied at dinner. He stood next to her, one hand on her shoulder. "Don't be," Nick said briefly to Kate. "Rosa and I—we *do* love each other." His eyes flashed angrily. "And we *would* like to be married—the sooner the better."

Kate frowned. She guessed Nick to be perhaps the same age as Rosa, twenty-one or so. "That's a problem?"

Nick's laugh sounded bitter. "Only if you have a brother like Jason."

Jason again. Suddenly she was beginning to see. "He doesn't like the idea?"

"No." Rosa wore a pitifully sad expression. "He thinks we should wait, so we know if we're right for each other. But we both know already!" There was a painful catch in her voice. "I love my brother and I want to have his blessing, but sometimes I think if Jason had his way, we'd never be married."

Nick's hand tightened on her shoulder. Rosa reached up to lay her fingers lightly over his. "Nick was, well, he was a little wild for a while."

"I ran with a bad crowd after high school," he injected flatly. "One night things got a little rowdy and we stole a car. I spent some time in the county jail because of it. It's not something I'm proud of, but I've paid my dues." His mouth tightened. "I'm *still* paying where Jason is concerned."

"Nick, please!" Rosa looked at him imploringly, then glanced back at Kate. "Jason's not the tyrant he sounds, honestly. I know he only wants what's best for me."

"Then why doesn't he let *you* decide?" Nick snatched his hand from Rosa's shoulder. It balled into a fist at his side. "He doesn't like me, Rosa, and he can't stand the idea of you marrying me. We both know it."

"Then why did he give you a job when no one else would?" Rosa sat up straighter. Her eyes sparkled angrily. "He's giving you the chance to prove yourself, Nick. Can't you see that?"

"Oh, I can see all right." There was a cutting edge to his voice. "I see that he doesn't think I'm good enough for you. I can see that the only reason he gave me a job is because he was afraid you might run off with me. He only wants the chance to wear you down, to prove to you how right he thinks he is about me. He's probably just waiting for me to quit so he can show you what a failure I am!"

Kate scarcely heard Rosa's angry voice and Nick's retaliation. A fleeting sense of déjà vu overtook her. Glimpses of her own past flashed before her like clips from a video. She heard a quavering voice telling a stony-faced man that she was carrying his baby; saw a tearful young girl weeping on his shoulder before a pair of hard male arms enfolded her with tender urgency. Her father's face swam before her. His angry shouts resounded in her brain, his and Jason's as they argued and fought....

She didn't realize she had risen until her shoulder connected with the doorframe. She closed her eyes and fought an almost hysterical impulse to laugh. How ironic. No, how fitting, that her return to Bradley had led her straight into a situation that was amazingly like the one she'd left behind so long ago.

Suddenly the screen door burst open. Across the room, Kate's eyes snapped open. Nick and Rosa's argument dropped off sharply as a figure filled the doorway. Kate froze as the man stepped into the room.

It was Jason.

CHAPTER THREE

THEY SAW each other at the same instant.

Kate's first thought was that the man before her was a stranger. All trace of carefree youthfulness had vanished. In its place was a man who had seen and experienced every facet of life, a man who had fought with everything he had...and won.

He wore boots and faded blue jeans. His shirt was open at the throat, revealing a darkly tanned chest with a dense mat of wiry black curls. Crowning the uncompromising slash of his mouth was a thick, luxuriant mustache that was alien to her. Kate felt as if her stomach had dropped clear to China at the sight of him. Handsome wasn't the word that came to mind, though all of the elements were there—jet-black hair, those surprisingly light, golden-brown eyes, a rangy, muscled build. But there was an underlying hardness that told the story only too well. The years since she'd last seen Jason had left their mark.

Jason's first thought was that she hadn't changed at all. She was still slender, small-boned but perfectly shaped. And though he hated to admit it, even to himself, she was just as beautiful as ever. More, if it were possible.

But on closer look—and damned if he wasn't practically devouring her with his eyes—he detected a subtle difference. There was strength in those fine-boned fea-

tures, a strength and confidence that hadn't been there
before. He'd never seen a more sensual woman—and
here was the rub—this was a ripe, full-blown woman, not
the young girl he remembered...a woman who would always land on her feet.

Hadn't he learned that the hard way?

For one brief moment he wondered if he were dreaming, suspended in time. But as he continued to stare at
her, everything came crashing back, all the feelings he'd
fought for so long. Feelings he thought he'd overcome
surged through his veins like a dam giving way. Anger
that she hadn't wasted one minute in marrying his best
friend; resentment that because of her, he'd lost that
friend forever.

But above all, a longing that no other woman had ever
managed to match. He'd never even come close to feeling the same way he had about Kate. And it was for that
powerful surge of desire that he uttered a silent, despair-
ing oath over his own weakness.

He tore his eyes away from her and focused on Nick
and Rosa, standing near the table. "Are you two at it
again?"

Nick stiffened at his curt tone. Before he had a chance
to say anything, Rosa stepped in front of him, as if to
shield him. "Just a little disagreement." She shrugged.
"Nothing that can't be taken care of."

The younger man swore softly. "Damn it, Rosa! We've
been beating around the bush long enough. Let's get this
settled once and for all."

"Nick!" Her voice carried a warning and a plea.
"Please. Not now." With a slight tilt of her head, she
indicated Kate standing behind them.

His harsh expression softened slightly as he glanced at
her. He looked back at Rosa, then slammed out the back

door, muttering under his breath. Rosa began to follow him.

"Let him go." Jason looked at Kate, but it was his sister he spoke to.

It seemed at first she hadn't heard. Her eyes remained riveted on the door Nick had just passed through, then traveled slowly back to her brother. It wasn't until he muttered "please" that she silently pivoted and turned toward the living room.

Kate stopped her as she passed. "Thank you, Rosa. For everything." She conveyed another brief, silent message as their eyes met, one that Kate hoped would comfort. Rosa smiled back, but her eyes were bleak.

The silence in the small kitchen seemed suddenly deafening when she and Jason were finally alone.

Kate was the first to speak. Her level gaze never wavered from his. "Hello, Jason."

"Kate." By now he'd recovered from his initial shock at seeing her. He wondered what had brought her here. Not once had she ever tried to see him before. "It's been a long time."

Too long... The traitorous words spiraled through her mind and she had to bite them back. Instead she inclined her head in agreement. "Fifteen years," she murmured. "It is a long time."

His booted feet echoed on the floor as he opened the refrigerator and pulled out a can of beer. The liquid inside fizzed as he popped the top off. He propped an arm on top of the refrigerator door. His eyes glinted. "Care for some?"

Kate stiffened. She knew what he was doing, and she knew that he, too, was thinking of one particularly sordid night when her father had called Jason a useless, beer-guzzling farmhand to his face.

Her chin lifted. "Still holding a grudge, Jason?" she retorted coolly. "Somehow I thought you were a bigger man than that."

Something flickered in his expression. It wasn't anger. Perhaps it was surprise. He slowly lowered the can and placed it on the counter. "Why are you here, Kate?" he asked very quietly.

Kate's eyes ran swiftly over his figure. He seemed broader, bigger than she remembered. "I need your help." Her tongue darted out to moisten her lips. "I need it badly."

Jason stared at her for a moment, but he had to will his eyes away from that unconsciously seductive action. It was so damned provocative, yet so innocent. She'd always employed that particular gesture when she was nervous, and his instantaneous recall was a bitter pill to swallow.

It also made him want to drop his defenses at a time when he knew he'd never needed them more. "I should have known it wasn't me you really wanted to see." The hard line of his mouth matched his voice perfectly, yet he hadn't realized he'd spoken so harshly until he saw a shadow pass over her face.

It reminded him yet again that she was the same, and yet different. Her posture was stiff and unnatural. For a second he'd have sworn there was a flash of hurt on her face before that expression of cool poise replaced it.

The Kate he'd known possessed a fragile ego that had bruised so easily, far too easily for her own good. He'd wanted nothing more than to protect her...for a lifetime.

Abruptly his anger drained away. He was acting like a first-class jerk. He pointed her in the direction of the living room, and they sat down on opposite ends of the sofa.

"What's this about needing help?" he asked curtly.

There was a peculiar tightness in the pit of her stomach, and Jason's dark, unfamiliar mustache only added to her feeling of unease. It made him seem more a stranger than ever. "It's Greg," she said rather breathlessly. "He's in trouble."

Anger hardened his features. Kate wasn't prepared for the burning glitter in his eyes. "I don't believe it," he said harshly. "You want *me* to help him? Lady, you came to the wrong man. I'd as soon strangle Greg McAllister as—"

"Jason!" She jumped to her feet. "He was your best friend once. Doesn't that mean anything to you?"

Jason swore viciously. "I don't care what kind of trouble he's in. Your husband is the last man I'd lift a finger to—"

"He's not my husband. Not anymore. We were divorced eighteen months ago."

Jason was silent. This time Kate could read nothing from his expression. His eyes, so distant, so indifferent, rested on her face for a long, intense moment. Whatever she had expected with her announcement, it wasn't such a callous disregard. Didn't he understand the danger Greg was in? How could he be so cold?

"Damn you, Jason Davalos!" she cried. "I should have known you wouldn't help. You're just as proud and stubborn as you ever were." She whirled and would have run from the room, but he grabbed her before she had taken more than a few steps. To her horror, she felt the unmistakable prick of tears. With a cry that was part despair, part relief, her head dropped down to rest on his chest.

It was instinct, or so he told himself, that had made Jason reach out to her. She was upset, distraught. He saw panic in her eyes just before she whirled around. His arms closed around her, and he realized she was shaking. Filled with conflicting emotions, he felt an urge to walk away, to forget he'd ever laid eyes on her again.

His eyes squeezed shut as he struggled with himself, resting his head against her shining hair. And then all he could concentrate on was how soft she was, how much like sunshine she smelled.

The last place he wanted her was in his arms. But nothing...*nothing* had ever felt so right.

He eased his finger under her chin and gazed into misty emerald eyes. "Don't cry, Kate," he whispered hoarsely. "I never could stand it when you cried."

She could feel the slight pressure of his hand against her skin. The tip of his finger was callused and rough, testimony to the years of hard, physical labor. But his touch was soft and gentle, meant to be comforting. Even while her throat tightened at this unexpected glimpse of the gentler side of his nature, all of her senses were sharply attuned to the place where he touched her.

When Jason's gaze moved to her lips, her mouth grew dry. How could he still affect her this way? It was impossible. Unfair! After everything that had happened between them, all the pain and heartache, had she learned nothing?

But he felt it, too, this feeling of awareness that time had not erased. She read it in bleak and stormy brown eyes, and knew that Jason was as much an unwilling victim as she.

The thought offered little comfort, and hastily she stepped back. It was rare for her to cry these days, and she was a little ashamed of her display. Jason's hand left her and dropped to his side. Reluctantly it seemed, or was she merely being fanciful?

"I'm okay," she assured him, recovering quickly. Before she lost her nerve, she began once more. "Jason, will you at least listen to me? Please?" She clasped her hands before her, unaware of the silent plea in her eyes.

The silence stretched out between them. "All right," he said when she'd nearly given up hope. His face was expressionless. "But I'm making no promises."

Kate resisted the impulse to sigh with relief. She remained where she was while he resumed his seat on the sofa. Quickly, before he changed his mind, she told him of Greg's plight.

His face was grim when she showed him the ransom note and the photograph of Greg, but she wasn't encouraged by the hard light in his eyes. "Well." His mouth twisted cynically. "Greg's certainly gotten himself into one hell of a mess, hasn't he? If he's really on the wrong side of the law, he might at least have had sense enough to make sure he stayed on this side of the border."

Something snapped inside Kate. How could he be so hurtful and unfeeling? "Damn it, Jason, I didn't come all this way to have you tell me what I already know! Are you going to help me or not?"

Her reaction was a mistake. She knew it by the sudden tensing of his jaw. "What do you want from me, Kate? Money?" His lips curled cynically. "It's odd how the tables turn sometimes, isn't it? Your father always thought I was such a gold digger."

Kate couldn't believe she'd heard right. "It's not your money I want."

"That's good, because I don't have it. Not that kind of money, anyway."

With an effort, she controlled her temper. "I don't want your money," she said again. "What I want is to see Greg out of Mexico, safe and sound and home again. I know you served with the DEA. I know you were in Mexico for a while." Her eyes found his. "I'm asking you to help me find him, Jason, find and rescue him before this goes any further."

Her words fell into a taut, waiting silence. Immobile, Jason stared at her. For a moment she thought he hadn't heard. Only the coldness entering his eyes convinced her that he had.

"Does he matter so much to you?"

The question caught her off guard. "I—" she faltered abruptly. "It's the right thing to do, Jason."

His mouth twisted. "A question of humanity, Kate?"

She nodded slowly. Her eyes never left his.

"That's the only reason?"

She bit her lip, not certain what he sought from her. "Greg and I, well, we may not be married anymore, but the fact that we once were counts for something." She didn't know why, but there was also one thing she wanted to make perfectly clear. "I may not be in love with him anymore, but I can't abandon him either," she finished quietly.

"What about me, Kate? We were married once, too. What if I had been kidnapped instead of Greg? Would you turn your back on me?"

His softly voiced question shocked her, but her reply was swift and sure. "No, Jason. No!" Good Lord, she thought shakily, if it were Jason in Greg's place, she'd have moved heaven and earth to rescue him. The thought jumped out at her before she even realized it.

The conviction in her voice surprised him. He didn't really understand why he'd asked that particular question. But regardless of her answer, he wondered if he weren't just a little bit crazy for even considering going along with her.

"I don't think you realize what a Pandora's box you've just opened."

His deathly quiet tone confused her, but hadn't Rosa said something to that effect? She gazed at him uncertainly. "I know the timing may not be the best. I mean, with your ranch and all—"

"It's not that. There's nothing going on here that Nick and the other hands couldn't take care of—*if* I were to go after Greg." He cut her off abruptly, rose to his feet and crossed to the window. With the onset of dusk, the sky was a dark shade of blue. Wispy clouds just above the horizon were painted pink and violet by the setting sun.

"Then what is it?" Kate's eyes lingered on the rigid set of his shoulders, then drifted to his profile. His jaw was clenched harshly. Beneath the midnight band of his mustache, his lips were ominously thin.

When he said nothing, her heart plummeted. But before she had a chance to think further, she heard him speak.

"You don't know what you're asking, Kate." His voice was so low she had to strain to hear him. "Greg and I may have been friends once, but that was a long, long time ago."

He sounded so incredibly weary, her heart went out to him even as a hopeless ache began to throb deep in her breast. He was going to refuse her. "Jason..."

Slowly he turned to her, but his face was hidden in shadow. She could detect nothing of his thoughts. "There are a lot of bad feelings between the two of us. You didn't know Greg hated me, did you? Well, neither did I until we met again in Vietnam." He smiled grimly when he saw her start. "I certainly never expected you to die of a broken heart. But I didn't expect you to take up with Greg the minute I was out of the picture, either."

He forged ahead, his voice laced with bitterness. "Greg took a great deal of pleasure in letting me know all the little details. Imagine how I felt with my best friend throwing it up to me that my ex-wife was now Mrs. Greg McAllister."

Kate had no time to protest, no chance to defend herself. He gazed at her, his eyes cold. "The way Greg always taunted me, I used to wonder if he was jealous because you were mine first. But it didn't take me long to figure out Greg had a vindictive streak none of us ever realized he had." He gave a short, harsh laugh.

Her mind was reeling. She felt physically sick to her stomach at the realization that there had been so much bad blood between Jason and Greg. At the same time she wondered if she hadn't deliberately blinded herself, simply because it hurt so much to think of Jason. But she knew instinctively that Jason was right. There were times when Greg hadn't been able to conceal his jealousy of others. Charming as he was, he was sometimes very possessive.

She made her way unsteadily to the nearest chair. "All because of me," she whispered numbly.

Jason scarcely heard her. His mind was filled with an unwanted but unavoidable resentment. In spite of all the bitterness between himself and Greg, he'd never believed Greg was capable of such selfish cruelty. What would Kate say if she knew what else her husband had done? He was lucky—damn lucky—that he hadn't ended up in a North Vietnamese POW camp, courtesy of Greg McAllister.

Part of him wanted to lash out at her, as if through Kate he could somehow get back at Greg. But what would be gained by telling her? His expression softened slightly as he looked at her. Her face was pale, her eyes dark with pain. Kate was the one who would suffer. Kate, not Greg.

He wished he could tell himself he didn't care. But he couldn't. Damn it, he couldn't.

The anger drained from him abruptly. "It may have started because of you," he told her very quietly, "but it didn't end there, by any means. Greg made sure of that. *Very* sure."

The words were meant to be comforting. He had the strangest sensation that life—or perhaps Greg?—had pulled a few tricks on Kate, too.

"There's more?" Her lips barely moved. "More than Greg—"

"Taunting me? Reminding me of what he had that I didn't?" His voice was softly jeering, as Greg's must have been. "Oh, yes, Kate, there's more. But that's all I'm going to say about it."

She was silent for a long time. When she finally looked up at him, her eyes were dark and shadowed. "Whatever he did, was it really so bad that you'll turn your back on him and pretend he never existed?"

He shifted his gaze. "Don't bother fishing, Kate. Believe me, you don't want to know."

She flinched at his unyielding tone. "Jason, please. I—I'm scared. I'm afraid they'll kill him, with or without the ransom."

Abruptly he faced her once more. "Have you given any thought to what happens *if* and when he's found? If he's involved in anything shady, the Mexican authorities won't let him go. He could end up in prison."

He watched her closely. He thought she went paler yet, but she held her ground. "All the more reason to find him—and find him quickly."

She felt as though she were wading into a bed of quicksand, but slowly she moved toward him. She touched his arm tentatively, feeling his muscles tense at the contact. He didn't withdraw as she half expected, and somehow that gave her the courage to go on.

"Please, Jason. I know it's not fair for me to ask, but if you won't do it for Greg, will you do it for me?" Her voice caught. "For old times' sake?"

Jason wished she'd said anything—*anything* but that. If she had, he might have been able to resist. Even though everything inside warned him against it, he looked deep into her eyes. And there he saw the painful regret for all that might have been but never was, the heartrending mixture of hope and fear. He knew that if she'd asked him to go to hell and back, he wouldn't have denied her.

"How soon do you want me to leave?" He grimaced at the brief flash of relief in her eyes.

"The earliest flight is at noon," she said quickly. "I've already reserved two seats." A flash of panic seized her. Would that be soon enough? Over twenty-four hours had passed since she'd received the ransom note.

"We? Did you say we?"

Startled, she glanced up at him, bracing herself as she did. She had no intention of sitting at home, waiting and wondering how the search was going. She would go crazy before it was all over.

She drew herself up proudly. Big and brawny though he was, Kate was her own woman now. "Yes, I did. The ransom note specified that *I* was to deliver the money. I won't take the chance that the kidnappers will find out I can't come up with the ransom." Quiet as her tone was, her eyes shot sparks that fairly dared him to argue.

That was exactly what he did. "I don't give a damn what that note said! I have no idea what we'll be getting into. If they're holding him in the jungle... Good Lord, do you know what conditions are like there? This is the rainy season, the hottest time of the year. The heat is intense, the humidity unbelievable. There are no roads in places, no fancy hotels with swimming pools and a staff to wait on you hand and foot." He glanced disdainfully at her designer suit.

Her lips compressed. "I don't need a maid, thank you, and I'm just as capable as you of roughing it."

"Roughing it, hell! I don't think you realize how primitive it can be down there. And this whole thing could be dangerous. It's just plain foolish for you to come along!"

Kate's chin jutted out. "I'm going," she repeated stubbornly. "With or without you."

Jason planted his hands on his hips. "What the hell is that supposed to mean?"

She returned his menacing gaze coolly. If he expected her to be intimidated, he could think again. "It means," she told him very deliberately, "that if you object to my coming along, then I'll just have to find someone who doesn't mind."

"You can't. There isn't time."

He thought he had her there. The gleam of satisfaction in his eyes told the story only too well. "Then I'll go myself," she retorted sweetly.

If the situation hadn't been quite so grim, Kate might have laughed at the way his mouth opened and closed, then opened again. It closed with a snap, and Kate found herself on the receiving end of a brittle glare. The seconds ticked by while they stared at each other in a silent battle of wills, neither one prepared to back down.

Eventually the look in Jason's eyes changed to resignation, coupled with a reluctant admiration. "You've changed, Kate," he said abruptly. "You're—" he gestured vaguely "—I don't know. Stronger, I guess."

It was a compliment. A grudging one, perhaps, but a compliment nonetheless. If she had changed, however, it was in large part due to the man before her. But it was a change that had not come about without cost. She had paid the price many times over.

"It's funny you should say that," she returned quietly. "Tonight, when I first saw you again, I thought you were the one who had changed. Now," she shook her head. Her smile was wistful, her eyes pensive. "Now, I'm not so sure."

Exactly what interpretation might be put on that statement, Jason wasn't sure. He tried not to think about it as they arranged to meet at the Dallas-Fort Worth airport tomorrow morning; tried not to think about it as he watched her car head down the drive a few minutes later.

He'd spent years trying to forget her, years fighting the empty ache inside every time he thought about her. But there was no erasing the feeling that within the space of an hour, she'd gotten under his skin once more.

In the days to come, he suspected he would do well to remember that only a fool would fall into the same trap twice. Only a fool.

CHAPTER FOUR

HOURS LATER, Jason lay sleepless in his bed, until finally he rose to sit before the open window. He listened to the quiet sounds of the night and watched as the moon chased the stars toward the eastern sky. He absently fingered the medal that rested just above his heart—the medal Kate had given him so long ago....

There would be no peace for him this night. He had known it the moment he'd walked into his home to find Kate standing there, her eyes wide and startled and so full of expression he was sure he'd stepped back in time. So delicate. So lovely. He had seen her and desired her as much as he had all those long, lonely years ago. Years when he hadn't been able to control the fiery passion of youth and, after a while, hadn't wanted to.

He knew better now. He knew how dreams could become nightmares. How cherished hopes and promises disintegrated into cold, hard truths. Ah, yes, he knew, and still the memories unfolded like misty layers of dawn....

HE SAW HER as clearly as if it had been yesterday. He knew her, of course. Bradley was such a small town, and the Andersons had been their nearest neighbors. She'd always been a cute kid. A little shy and timid maybe. In spite of the rich, vibrant red of her hair, she'd always reminded him of a fragile moonbeam. He smiled slightly as he recalled the occasions in grade school when he'd defended her against several youngsters whose taunting gibes were far more hurtful than teasing.

It was something Jason could not abide. He'd lived with bias almost from the time he was born. There were half a dozen or so Mexican-American families beside his own who made Bradley their home. During the summer there were more, but after the harvest, they migrated from place to place, wherever there was work to be found.

He spoke no English when he entered school. He and the other Spanish-speaking children had been laughed at and ridiculed by classmates, parents and teachers alike. Later he'd heard his parents called wetbacks and far more ugly names, seen them shunned and scorned as the dirt-poor Chicanos who lived just outside of town. As a young boy, he'd tried to tell his parents it would help if they attempted to learn the language. But they were too old, his mother often told him, too set in their ways.

Greg was really the only one who had ever defended him, who befriended him when no one else would. And Kate, afraid-of-her-own-shadow Kate. He'd watched her progress from pigtails to braces to a desirable young woman. He had even been the first man she'd practiced her feminine wiles on.

It was odd how people changed. There once was a time he would have sworn Greg and Kate were different.

He wondered what would have happened if he had finished college as planned. His parents had scrimped and saved to give him what they could never have. But things were no different in San Antonio than they'd been at home, and he missed his parents and sister. He missed the old rickety house he'd known all his life. He missed the land his parents had worked so hard to keep.

His father had died first, his mother barely a year later. And Jason was bitter—bitter because life had given his mother and father so few comforts. Bitter because now, except for his sister, he was more alone than ever.

Kate had grown up in the two years he'd been away at college. It was almost as if they had never met before, and he hadn't wanted to like her. He'd seen her the day he arrived home, driving up to the drugstore in her fiery red sports car with the top down. She'd jumped out and strode inside, wearing a short blue-and-white tennis outfit and immaculate white tennis shoes that looked as if they'd come straight from the store window. He knew then that she was beyond his reach. Untouchable, just like all the Anglo girls he'd met in college, the ones who flaunted and teased, then conveniently changed their minds at the last minute. But much as he hated to admit it, he realized Kate had stirred something deep inside that he couldn't quite deny.

Jason saw her again three days later. He'd found a baby-sitter in town who could watch Rosa while he worked. He was on his way out to the fields when he spotted Kate's car heading up the drive, a cloud of dust billowing out behind. He scowled when he saw her wave gaily and hop out of the car.

"Hi, there. I was hoping I'd catch you before you left the house."

She was dressed in fashionably designed jeans and blouse. His lips thinned as he recalled the clean but well-worn overalls he'd laid out for Rosa that morning.

"Hi."

Her eyes flickered at his cool greeting. He knew he had discomfitted her, and he almost expected her to jump in her car and head home, but she didn't.

"Jason, I—I'd like to tell you how sorry everyone is about your mother...."

He scarcely gave her a chance to begin. "Everyone? Yes, everyone was so sorry the only ones who came to the funeral were the Aguillas and the Escobars."

She looked as if he'd struck her. With the sickening way his insides churned at her reaction, he had the uneasy sensation he just had. With such expressive features, Kate had always been an easy target. He was no better than any of the jealous playmates he'd ever defended her against, and he was suddenly ashamed.

"I'm sorry." Her voice trembled. "I wanted to come—honestly I did." She glanced away and then back again. "But Daddy had other plans for me," she added in a low voice. She turned toward the car, and he sensed she was fighting tears. "Here. Stella fixed this for you." She held out a large wicker basket toward him.

"Stella?"

She nodded quickly. "Our housekeeper."

Beneath the corner of the cloth, which lay loosely over the top, he saw a loaf of crusty homemade bread. It was on the tip of his tongue to retort that he needed no one's charity. Only the oddly vulnerable look on Kate's face stopped him. He stepped forward and grasped the handle.

She was tall, taller than the last time he'd seen her. The top of her head came nearly to his nose. So close to her, he detected the subtle fragrance of lemon and some other sweet-smelling scent. The gentle curve of her cheeks had the same smooth, downy texture of a sun-warmed peach. He was painfully and acutely reminded that Kate Anderson had indeed grown up, and it was for that very reason that he solemnly swore not to prolong this encounter.

Instead he set the basket on the hood of her car and peeked beneath the cloth. Besides the bread there was a generous wedge of cheese, fresh fruit jellies and jams, pickles and a variety of other canned goods. There was also a fresh peach pie—his favorite.

"There's way too much for just Rosa and me." His eyes flickered back to her. Lord, she was pretty. Why hadn't he ever noticed it before? "I'll be out in the north field getting the wheat crop in most of the day. You could come back for supper, if it's okay with your father."

His invitation surprised Kate as much as it did himself. The sudden sparkle in her eyes seemed to light up her entire face. He experienced the strangest feeling of warm satisfaction.

"Oh, Daddy won't mind. He's always telling me I should get out more." She laughed, a warm, tinkling sound that the wind carried away. Jason didn't think he'd ever heard anything so sweet and pure.

She did come for supper that day, and the next day and the next as well. Sometimes she brought lunch to him and they sat near the huge tire of the rusty old tractor. They drank lemonade beneath the shade of an old cottonwood tree, and she invited him over for a swim after a long, tiring day in the fields.

She was spoiled; unbelievably so, in Jason's eyes. It was natural, he supposed. She'd lost her mother when she was little more than a baby, and her father made it up to her the only way he knew how: a car, horses, riding lessons. Yet for all that, Kate took pleasure in the simple things in life like watching the sunset or playing with Rosa. It was almost as if she looked at life through a veil of innocence.

Shy, sweet, innocent Kate, who was always just a little uncertain of herself. Uncertain? At the thought, an unwilling smile edged Jason's mouth. He shifted and propped his back against the windowsill, his eyes still on the moon-drenched sky, watching, but seeing another time, another place.

Oh, yes, he'd known from the start she had a crush on him. She had pursued him with a tender naïveté that was as endearing as it was amusing. She had begun to flirt with him, and he couldn't help but tease back. Any time he had injected the faintest note of suggestion into his voice, the color bloomed high in her cheeks. He recalled the first time she'd sent him a glance meant to be coy. It had ended up so blatantly obvious, it nearly set him off into gales of laughter. Kate was simply too innocent to pull it off.

But as time passed, the tables began to turn. Jason was painfully aware of everything about her. Her half-demure, half-impish smile intrigued him. The slim length of her legs tempted him. He ached to trap her mouth beneath his and taste her pure, sweet fire. He longed to tangle his fingers in her hair, mold the soft swells of her body to his while he made love to her.

He saw the world reflected in her eyes, but it was a world that would never be his.

She had dropped by one evening just after he'd tucked Rosa into bed for the night. He couldn't withhold the sudden dark mood that overtook him as she stepped inside. The air was hot and sultry, and he felt as if the temperature had jumped another twenty degrees at the sight of her. She wore very brief cutoffs and a pale pink tank top that outlined all too clearly the gentle thrust of her breasts. He'd have bet everything he owned that nothing lay between her skin and the flimsy cotton covering. Kate was driving him insane and he was crazy for letting her do it.

Her welcoming smile faded as she took in his thunderous expression. "Is this a bad time?" she asked quickly.

It's a helluva time, he wanted to shout in frustration. That he didn't was more proof of his insanity. "Let's go outside," he said shortly. "It's cooler."

They sat on the creaky porch swing. Jason was curt. He was surly. He was just this side of rude.

Kate was puzzled. Over the last few weeks he'd seen her gradually emerge from her cocoon. She'd laughed more freely, talked more openly, and Jason cursed both of them as he watched her retreat into her protective shell.

Finally she stood. There was an uncertain question in her wide green eyes. "I—I think I should go."

Jason said nothing. *It's what you wanted, isn't it?* a sneering voice silently prodded. *No,* another screamed. What he wanted was to kiss and love the breath out of Kate until nothing else mattered—not her world, not his.

Kate moved a few paces away from him, then stopped. He felt her eyes on him in the darkness. "I'm sorry," he finally muttered.

She didn't say anything for a moment. Then she asked softly, "Why?"

Why? Bitterness and frustration welled up inside him. How could she stand there and pretend she didn't know? Her father was a well-to-do real-estate broker who gained both money and influence with every year that passed. Undoubtedly Michael Anderson's plans for his daughter didn't include a poor Chicano farmer. The rare times he had encountered Kate's father in the last few weeks had clued him in only too well. Michael Anderson's attitude was faintly condescending; no doubt he thought Kate's friendliness was little more than charitable generosity.

Kate moved a step closer. "Did I say something to make you angry, Jason?"

He steeled himself against the hurt he heard in her voice. "No." He forced himself to look at her, then wished he hadn't when he saw the silent plea in her eyes. *Talk to me,* she seemed to be saying. *Just talk to me....*

"No," he said again. "I'm not mad at you."

She bit her lip. "Then why are you acting like this? Something's wrong, Jason, I know it. Tell me what it is." Her voice grew more urgent. "Maybe I can help. If there's something you need, maybe Daddy—"

That was the spark that set the fire to burning. "I don't need help!" he blazed fiercely. "I don't need you and I don't need anything from anybody!"

Kate recoiled as if he'd struck her. In the instant before the fiery mist of rage faded from his sight, he saw her flinch. She stared at him, her eyes huge and wide and full of pain. He heard a sound, a sound that might have been a cry of pain if she had let it escape, and then she whirled around.

He reached her before she'd gone more than a few steps. She resisted at first, but he pulled her firmly within the protective binding of his arms.

"I'm sorry, Kate." God, how he hated himself for putting that look on her face. These last weeks would have been unbearable if it hadn't been for her. His hand trembled as he smoothed her hair. "I'm a heel—a jerk. Why do you put up with me?"

He could feel the tension in her body. Her face was buried in the hollow of his chest, but slowly she raised it to gaze at him with glistening green eyes. "No." Her voice emerged tremulously. "You're not a heel. You're just—just you."

And that was the whole damn problem, Jason despaired silently. He knew he should let her go, pretend this had never happened, for both their sakes. Both of them were simply too vulnerable right now, and with their defenses down like this . . . He couldn't be responsible for what might happen.

But the arms that should release her refused to obey. He held her more tightly, and lightly played his hands up and down her spine until he felt her relax.

"Jason?" She murmured his name against the small triangle of skin below his neck.

He rested his cheek against the top of her head. "What?"

"I've often wondered how you came by your name." She drew back to gaze up at him. "Jason isn't Spanish."

If the question had come from anyone else, he knew he'd have been immediately on guard. But there was only a frank curiosity in Kate's eyes.

"I'm named after an uncle, my Aunt Alicia's husband," he told her. "They live in Albuquerque now, but they helped my folks get on their feet when they first moved here. Aunt Alicia met Uncle Jason one summer when Uncle Jason was on his way to Monterrey. His car broke down and my grandparents put him up for the night."

"Sounds like a case of love at first sight."

"That's what my mother always said." Feeling as if he'd been smitten himself, Jason smiled down at her. He realized he was still holding her, and at the faint darkening of her eyes, he knew that she was aware of it, too.

"Can I ask you something else?"

"Sure." His voice had turned husky.

"Do you like me?" Her eyes met his, then she glanced quickly away. "What I mean is . . . do you like me the way a man likes a woman?" It came out all in a rush.

Jason's arms stiffened in surprise. Of all the things to say . . . But for once he didn't feel like laughing at her.

This time he was the one who looked away. "I'm not blind, Kate," he muttered. "And I do like you too damn much for your own good."

An eternity seemed to pass before he heard her voice again. "Then why—" her tongue came out to moisten her lips "—why haven't you ever kissed me?"

He did look at her then, and it was sweet agony not to succumb to the impulse then and there. "It's not because I haven't wanted to."

Her eyes shyly met his. "I wouldn't have stopped you."

"I know that."

"Then why?"

The muscle in his jaw tensed. None too gently he released her and stepped back, desperately needing to put some distance between them. "Do I have to spell it out?" he said gruffly. "You're a good kid, Kate. I wouldn't want to do anything to change that."

"I'm not a kid!" she flared. "I'm eighteen years old and out of school," she began.

"I doubt that! You told me just last week how your father plans to pack you off to some fancy Eastern college this fall."

"I've already made up my mind! I'll live right here in Bradley and go to college in Dallas."

Jason heaved a heavy sigh. Her father would have something to say about that.

He stood motionless as she took a tentative step toward him. A sultry breeze whispered through the treetops. The ghostly shadows of the night played around them. Moonlight trickled down from the sky, cloaking her body in shadows. Only her face was lit by a gossamer moonbeam.

He caught his breath. If she came any closer...

He stiffened when she slid her hands around his neck. "I want you, Jason," she said with only a trace of shyness. Her eyes flickered away, but when they returned to his face, she sounded more certain than ever. "I want you and I'm not afraid to say so. Why can't you admit it, too?"

"I already did." There was no way to let her down easily, but the words came out more harshly than he intended. The confused hurt in her eyes tore into his heart, and he cursed silently. "Don't you see, Kate? You're going away in the fall. I don't want to start something we can't finish." Very gently he reached up to clasp her wrists with his fingers, drawing them down between them and breaking her hold.

Kate's lips were pressed tightly together, as if she were trying very hard not to show any emotion. But it was all there in her eyes, those beautiful green eyes that glistened with moisture.

He tried again. "It's better this way, believe me. I don't want to hurt you."

She made a strangled sound. "What do you think you're doing right now?" she cried in a trembling voice.

Jason could take no more. What did it matter if he was right or wrong? Kate was hurting and he could stand it no longer.

He caught her fiercely in his arms. She hesitated only a second, then melted against him in a way that made his knees turn to water.

"Oh, Kate," he muttered raggedly. "Do you have any idea what you do to me? You turn me inside out. You've had me tied up in knots for days already." He twined his fingers in her hair and tilted her face upward. Their eyes melded for the space of a heartbeat, but that was all it took.

He knew the moment her despair turned to a budding hope, knew the instant he was overcome with a bitter-sweet resignation.

"Don't look at me like that, Kate," he warned her softly. "You're playing with fire."

Her fervent whisper touched him clear to the soul. "I don't care."

Still he hesitated. "I feel—I feel as if I'm almost afraid to touch you."

She merely smiled at his confusion, a slow, disarmingly sweet smile that took his breath away. Leaning forward, she curled her fingers around the nape of his neck and slowly eased herself closer to his lips.

His mouth took hers with all the pent-up emotion he felt in both body and mind. Fiercely, hungrily, as if he were starved for the taste of her. Softly, sweetly, with all the tenderness and caring he held deep in his heart.

Beneath his, her mouth trembled like the wings of a butterfly. He felt her start in surprise as his tongue touched hers. Then there was no uncertainty, no hesitation at all as her lips parted to await his gently swirling intrusion.

"Oh, Kate." His blood hammered in his ears when he finally drew back. He rested his forehead against hers and laughed shakily, needing to do something to lighten the intensity of the moment. The sublime pleasure that glowed on her features made him want to shout for joy.

"The truth now. You don't do this often, do you?"

She frowned up at him, but her eyes were dancing. "It wasn't my first kiss, if that's what you mean."

He chuckled, but inside he felt a rush of masculine pride that Kate hadn't been too free with herself. But even if she had, he knew it wouldn't have made one damn bit of difference about the way he felt right now.

He kissed the pouting pink lips, which smiled against his own a second later. "It won't be your last, either," he murmured huskily.

Her smile faded. Her gaze lifted to search his face. "Is that a promise?" she asked quietly.

There would be no going back. They couldn't erase the spark of awareness between them as easily as chalk on a slate. They both knew it, and it was with mingled regret and a fervent prayer that Jason lowered his head and tenderly took her lips.

It was a kiss that progressed all too quickly into a fiery storm he could barely control. Jason's heart beat the driving rhythm of a drum. A golden-white heat poured through him. His hands skimmed her back, then slid down to gauge the subtle differences between male and female. Again her soft gasp of surprise echoed in his mouth, and once more she delighted him with her response, a response that was both bold and innocent.

He tore his mouth from hers. "Kate, if you know what's good for you, you'll get in your car and leave this minute...."

Eyes that had been sleepy with pleasure slowly darkened. "You're what's good for me, Jason. I know it now, more than ever before." As if she were blind, and could see only through her fingertips, she reached up and began to trace his chiseled features, one by one.

"Besides, how can you even think of me leaving already? I can hardly think at all." She smiled when her fingers brushed the smooth hardness of his mouth.

Through the winds of time, Kate's voice echoed softly in his ear. *Let's go inside, Jason. Now...*

He tried to close his mind to what came next, but it was no use. He couldn't hold back now, any more than he'd been able to then. Again he heard the whisper of their clothing as it slid to the floor. Once more he tenderly explored the warm secrets of her body, absorbed her soft cry of pain into his mouth the instant she became his...

He remembered the joy of loving her, the ecstasy of possessing her, the wrenching pain of losing her. All of these things, he knew once more. All this...and more.

His eyes were bleak when he finally turned away from the window. No, there would be no peace for him this night.

CHAPTER FIVE

ROSA WAS IN THE KITCHEN before him the next morning. In spite of the sleepless night just past, the prospect of facing his sister disturbed Jason more than the thought of facing Kate later this morning.

Rosa nodded briefly when she saw him in the doorway, then dropped her gaze quickly. He had the feeling she was avoiding his eyes.

Quietly crossing the floor, he helped himself to a cup of coffee, then glanced at her across the rim. "Miss me already, little sister?"

He hadn't meant to goad her, he really hadn't. But he knew she took it that way when he saw her chin tilt a notch and her eyes flash angrily before she turned away.

She thumped a frying pan on the stove. "Would you like an honest answer, big brother?"

Jason ignored her sarcastic tone. Aware of a slight twinge of guilt, he noted the faint shadows beneath her eyes. She had clearly spent as restless a night as he.

"Never mind," he muttered. He sat down at the table and picked up the newspaper. Though he tried to concentrate on the fine black print before him, his mind was on Rosa.

She moved around the kitchen fixing breakfast and doing her best to ignore him. He knew from experience it was always this way when they argued about Nick. Yet every so often, he sensed her eyes on him. By the time she put two plates on the table and sat down, he felt something else was on her mind.

Finally she broke the brittle silence. "Do you need any help packing?"

He shook his head. "Not much to pack," he said briefly. "I don't expect to be gone long."

Rosa frowned. "Do you really expect to find Kate's hus—" She was careful to correct herself when Jason's expression hardened. "Kate's *ex*-husband?"

"Who knows?" He shrugged. "It won't be easy, that's for sure. If we can't locate him within the week, I doubt we will." There was no emotion in his voice whatsoever as he added, "And by then it probably won't matter."

She looked at him closely. "Why are you doing this, Jason?"

He didn't answer. Instead he got up and poured another cup of coffee. The shuttered look on his face as he approached the table again warned her the subject was closed, but Rosa paid no mind. "Is it because of Kate?"

"Kate?" His laugh was short. "Kate has nothing to do with this."

"No?" Rosa raised her eyebrows. "I think Kate has everything to do with it." She sat back calmly to await his reaction.

His face darkened to a thundercloud, as she had known it would. "What makes you think that?"

Rosa thought of the network of scars that marred her brother's back, a legacy of his time in Vietnam, a legacy that had something to do with Greg McAllister. "I know how you feel about Greg," she said quietly. "I can't imagine why you'd want to do much of anything for him."

Jason shoved his plate back. Most of his breakfast was untouched. "Greg and I were once—" he hesitated "—good friends."

Her eyes found his. "And Kate," she told him evenly, "was once your wife."

He jumped up so quickly the wooden chair crashed to the floor behind him. She stared at him openmouthed, her fork suspended halfway between her plate and her mouth.

"That's what this is about, isn't it?" he demanded. "Kate. What is it you want to know, Rosa? All the sordid little details of my marriage? Well, I'm sorry but I'm really not in the mood. Maybe you should ask Kate, or have you already?"

Rosa blinked. "I...no," she sputtered, when she could finally speak. Jason certainly wasn't meek and mild-mannered, but his violent reaction stunned her.

"What happened between Kate and I doesn't concern you."

Slowly she lowered her fork to the table. "So I've been told," she murmured, then bit her lip. "I'm sorry, Jason. I don't mean to pry. It's just that I really never expected to see Kate again, and I, well, I like her. She owns a women's boutique in the city, you know." Her eyes searched his face. "I can't help but wonder what went wrong between the two of you. And since you've never even come close to marrying anyone else..." She looked at him helplessly as her voice trailed away.

His posture lost some of its tension. He righted the chair and sent her a grim half smile as he did so. "I was too busy raising a big-eyed, button-nosed sister."

It was an excuse, and they both knew it. Still, she wisely kept that observation to herself. "Hmm," she murmured airily. "I had no idea I was such a problem child."

Jason's smile ebbed. "You weren't," he said slowly. "Until lately."

The minute the words were out, he wished he could recall them. He could almost see the barrier drop between them, a barrier that was entirely too familiar of late. A part of him longed to go back to the days when he'd ruffled her hair, tossed her high in the air and earned a toothless grin in return. Or to her teenage years when, with no one to rely on but each other, they had grown closer than ever. What had happened to that closeness?

He'd been charged with being a parent as well as a brother. Up until the last few months, he thought he'd done a credible job at both. But this situation with Nick... He shook his head.

Rosa said nothing, but her dark eyes simmered with resentment as she began to collect the soiled plates and cups from the table.

Jason hesitated a moment while she marched across the room. "Rosa," he began. "While I'm gone—"

The dishes landed in the sink with a clatter. She whirled around to face him. "No need to worry about me, big brother," she told him hotly. "Contrary to popular opinion, I'm *not* a child."

Jason's mouth tightened. "I never said you were."

"You don't have to! It's obvious in the way you treat me. You want to run my life, Jason Davalos, but I've got news for you." Her chin tilted defiantly. "I happen to be over twenty-one, and I can do what I want, when I want!"

But to Jason she sounded very much like the child she proclaimed she wasn't. "You're also very emotional and impetuous."

"Impetuous!" she echoed. An expression of disbelief flitted across her features. "Why, Nick and I have been wanting to get married for nearly six months."

"You'd better not do it the minute my back is turned, either!" He warned her. "And I don't think I need to remind you that you haven't even known Nick much longer than six months."

A deathly silence descended. The color drained from Rosa's face, leaving it pinched and white-looking, but her voice was clear as a bell. Clear but very bitter. "Did you do this to Kate, too? Try to run her life the way you want to run mine?"

Exasperated, he ran a hand through his hair. He'd let the dig about Kate pass, for now. "Damn it, I didn't mean it the way it sounded and you know it!"

"I don't." Rosa's eyes were huge in her pale face. "Tell me, Jason. If I married Nick tomorrow, how would you feel? Would you welcome him into our happy home?" She didn't bother to hide her mockery.

Jason didn't answer; he didn't have to. Why the hell couldn't Rosa see his side of it? he wondered in sheer frustration. Nick was young and hot-headed. Both he and Rosa were at an age where emotions often came first, consequences much later. Rosa might think Nick was ready to settle down, but Jason wasn't convinced.

"Damn it," he muttered again. "I can't stop you from marrying Nick or anyone else—"

"You can!" she cried. Their eyes locked across the room, and to his despair, hers filled with tears. Silently he cursed himself. "You can," she whispered again. "Because you know how much I love you."

Jason closed his eyes. He felt as if she'd just landed a blow right at the very center of his heart.

His fingers clenched on the back of the chair. Except for Rosa, he was alone in the world. How ironic it was that his parents had valued family above all else. Family, togetherness, a closely knit circle of love. If they could see what was happening between the two people they had left behind, the two they had loved most in the world.

He finally opened his eyes when he heard the screen door slam. He caught a glimpse of Rosa running toward the garage. He heard her car start and the spray of gravel a second later.

Jason's face was grim. Rosa was gone. She was probably running straight to Nick—and he hadn't even told her goodbye.

A SHORT TIME LATER, he was talking briefly with Nick and the other hands he employed, going over what would need to be done in his absence. The barely veiled hostility in Nick's eyes grated on him further, and he was sorely tempted to say to hell with Greg McAllister, and have it out with Nick and Rosa once and for all. He hated to leave now, especially after the argument with Rosa, and there was a tight ball of apprehension coiled in his stomach. He had the feeling that all hell was about to break loose where those two were concerned. He trusted Rosa, but he didn't quite trust Nick.

It was no wonder that his mood was anything but tame when he arrived at the Dallas-Fort Worth airport. Kate had phoned earlier to say she'd already taken care of the tickets. So after stopping at the airline's counter and obtaining a tourist card, he headed straight for the terminal.

He saw her when he was perhaps twenty feet from the gate. Her hair was swept up into the same severe hairstyle she'd worn yesterday, a style he didn't really care for. She was dressed in white slacks and a loosely cut, pale pink top of some gauzy material. The clothes were casual but still discreetly elegant, and clung to her soft, feminine curves in a way he didn't even want to think about. He grimaced when he realized he'd quickened his stride.

At that precise moment Kate glanced over her shoulder. She had been talking to a petite blonde who stood next to her, but it was almost as if she had sensed his presence. She turned slightly, and it was then that Jason saw him.

Any number of sensations washed over him as he closed the last steps between them. Surprise. Disbelief. Crazy as it was, he had never even considered the possibility of a child... He experienced a potent sense of loss, for standing before him was just one more reminder of how barren his life really was. The boy was perhaps six or seven; Jason couldn't be sure. His small sturdy figure was clad in jeans and a bright red knit shirt. There was no doubt that he was Kate's son—Kate's and Greg's. The hair and eyes were a dead giveaway. Yet oddly, only one thought was clear in his mind as he took in the boy's sun-streaked blond hair and bright green eyes.

The kid should have been his—his and Kate's.

Kate watched Jason approach nervously. Her heart gave a little leap at first sight of him but it plummeted as he came closer. He hadn't yet taken his eyes off Toby, and she wondered what was going through his mind. Only a moment ago he had looked angry. But now his expression gave nothing away. Last night Jason had left her in no doubt that his feelings toward Greg were anything but benevolent. How would Jason feel about Greg's son?

"Jason." She inclined her head in greeting. "I see you made it." How she managed to sound so calm and collected, Kate wasn't sure.

He gave a secretive little smile. "There was no need to worry, Kate," he said very softly. "I would never leave a lady in the lurch."

As if she didn't know. He'd married her for that very reason once, hadn't he? She focused on the mildly inquisitive look he gave Rita. "This is my business partner, Rita Grant." Quickly she introduced them and explained, "We own a small boutique here in town."

Jason nodded. Again his eyes flickered toward Toby. "Who's this young man?" he asked.

Her hand dropped to her son's shoulder. "This is Toby." Pride echoed in her voice. "My son."

While Kate looked on in everlasting surprise, Jason dropped down on one knee before the boy. His craggy features were far warmer than they'd been last night.

"Hi, Toby." The hard mouth beneath the mustache relaxed into a smile as he took Toby's hand. "Come to see your mom off on her trip?"

His tone was easy and familiar. Toby didn't seem the least bit uncomfortable with this tall stranger. "Are you goin' with her?"

"Yes, I am," Jason replied, straightening up.

"I wish I could go. But Mom says I have to stay with Rita." Toby glanced wistfully at his mother, then at Jason, as if he was the one person on earth who could make his mother change her mind. Then to Kate's dismay, his eyes filled with tears. "Can't I come, Mom? Please?"

"Not this time, Toby," she said very gently. Lord, but she hated to leave him. For the first time she wondered if Jeff and Jason hadn't been right. Maybe it would have been wiser for her to stay at home. If anything happened to Greg... If anything happened to *her*...

"Hey, Toby. I need to pick up a magazine or something to read. How'd you like to come with me to that little gift shop down there?" Jason pointed back toward the main terminal. "Your mom and I have plenty of time before the flight leaves. We could look at the planes on the way." Belatedly he looked to Kate for approval.

Kate's gaze held a silent thank-you as she nodded. In the brief second their eyes met and held, something flickered in his before he turned his attention to her son.

"My dad's a pilot," she heard Toby say proudly as they walked off. Kate cringed mentally, wondering at Jason's reaction, but his reply escaped her.

When they were out of earshot, Rita glanced at Kate. "He's not what I expected."

"Oh?" Kate gave a short, nervous laugh. "What did you expect?"

Jason and Toby had just turned the corner and disappeared from view, but Rita continued to gaze thoughtfully in their direction. "I'm not sure," she murmured. "At first glance he seems so..."

"Hard?"

"He does," she agreed. "But he obviously isn't." She gave Kate her full attention once more. "He looks, oh, I don't know. Tired, maybe. Or like he's been through a lot."

Kate hesitated. "I gathered last night that he and his younger sister haven't been getting along very well lately."

Rita sat down in the waiting area. "Maybe that's it," she mused, then glanced at Kate from the corner of her eye. "Or maybe he's—"

"Don't tell me." Kate raised a hand. "You think he's been pining away all these years."

The other woman raised her brows. "Is he married?"

"No," Kate said flatly. "But that doesn't prove a thing." Why she was so cross at her friend, she wasn't sure. And why Rita was so eager for her and Jason to find each other again was something that eluded her as well.

When the time came to board the plane, Toby's shoulders slumped visibly, but at least he was dry eyed. Jason teased him about taking care of Rita the way he took care of his mother, and instead it was Kate whose eyes glazed over with moisture when she kissed Toby good-bye.

"Say hi to Dad for me," he called after them.

Kate winced inwardly, picturing Jason's reaction. "I told him we had to fly down to help Greg on business," she told him as they followed the other passengers through the boarding tunnel. "He's used to Greg coming and going all the time, and I thought..." She stopped, then went on in a low voice, "I suppose you think I'm a terrible mother, lying to my son like that."

Jason took her arm and eased her in front of him as they passed through the narrow opening into the plane's cabin. "You couldn't tell him about Greg. It would only scare him." He shrugged. "And I wouldn't exactly call it a lie, anyway."

He smiled slightly at her. Somehow his approval made her feel better about leaving Toby, and Kate felt the tightness in her chest ease slightly.

The flight was heavily booked, and with Jason behind her, Kate was forced to take the window seat. Jason stowed her shoulder carry-on in the overhead compartment, then shoved his duffel bag under the seat. When he sat down beside her, she tried not to think about the up-coming hours in the air.

Her palms grew damp when she heard the dull whine of the engines. She swallowed, trying to allay her fear when the seat belt light blinked on and the jet rumbled away from the gate. Moments later they barreled down the runway before lifting off. *This is silly,* she told her-self as the plane climbed through layer after layer of clouds. *You're a grown woman, not a child like Toby.* But even Toby wasn't afraid of flying. He loved it whenever Greg spared the time to take him up.

Snatches of cottony clouds invaded her peripheral vision. She had to fight back the impulse to rake down the window-covering. Beside her, Jason flipped indiffer-ently through the magazine he'd bought earlier. Kate's palms began to sweat, but every muscle in her body felt as if it was encased in ice. She sat numbly in her seat.

"Can I get you two something to drink?"

Jason looked up at the flight attendant. "Nothing for me, thanks," he said briefly. "Kate?" When she didn't answer, he glanced over.

Her eyes were glued to the wide expanse of blue sky that lay outside the tiny window. She was white as a ghost.

"Kate!"

The attendant leaned closer. "Are you all right, ma'am?"

It was the unfamiliar voice that brought her back from the edge of panic. "I'm fine," she said in a raspy tenor.

Jason and the attendant looked skeptical at this an-nouncement. "Are you feeling sick?" the woman asked. "I can get you something if you are."

Kate shook her head. "I'm not sick."

"How about a drink?" Jason didn't take his eyes from her face. No, he echoed silently. Not sick. Just scared to death. He'd seen that look far too often in the rice paddies of Vietnam not to recognize it for what it was. "Maybe a double," he added.

"No! I'm fine," she said again. "The last thing I need is a drink. Then I would be sick. I didn't have anything to eat this morning," she added with a wobbly smile. "I don't need anything, really."

"As long as you're sure." The attendant looked doubtful as she retreated, while Jason merely looked angry.

Kate didn't mind, though. At least it gave her something to think about, other than herself. She took a deep, cleansing breath.

"Why didn't you tell me?"

"Tell you what?" What was he so angry about?

Jason grimaced. "That you were afraid to fly."

Kate started to glance out the window but checked herself just in time. Instead she focused on her hands, now clasped tightly in her lap.

"Why didn't you tell me, Kate?" This time his tone had gentled considerably. Strong, brown fingers stole into her line of vision to lightly cover her hands. She didn't realize how cold she was until she felt the warmth of his skin penetrate her own.

When she didn't answer, he separated her hands and held one. Kate wasn't sure what she thought he would do, but she was surprised when his fingers wove lightly through her own. She stared at his hand lying so intimately, so familiarly, against her thigh.

Rita's words came back to her. *He isn't what I expected. He seems so hard, but he's not.* This time Kate silently concurred.

"I'm not sure," she murmured finally.

"Were you afraid I'd think you were...weak?"

Her eyes drifted up to meet his. The concern she saw reflected there gave her the courage to answer truthfully. "You would have thought so once."

Jason opened his mouth to deny it, but something stopped him. Was she right? he wondered suddenly. It was his turn to stare at their joined hands, but a second later he frowned. "Have you always been afraid to fly? I don't remember it."

Why should he? Considering the state of their marriage, she had every reason to believe he would prefer to erase that chapter of his life forever.

"We never traveled anywhere together," she reminded him. Not even when they had eloped together—if running off to Dallas could be called eloping. But perhaps it was the kindness he was showing now that compelled her to explain, "I've never liked heights, but I wasn't really afraid to fly until after my father died."

Jason felt an icy shock wave come over him. "Your father is dead?" He recalled that when he'd finally returned to Bradley, Michael Anderson's house had been for sale. He had assumed that Michael had moved to Dallas.

"He was killed in a private plane crash ten years ago." Low as her voice was, she couldn't quite keep the pain from it.

"I'm sorry." He started to make a movement with his other hand, then abruptly checked it. "Ten years ago?" His eyes narrowed. "What about Greg?"

The tension that had started to ease began to seep through her again. "What about him?" She strived for an even note.

He sounded impatient. "Has he been operating his business all that time?"

Her nod was barely perceptible. "Longer."

"Longer?" If Jason had sounded angry before, he sounded positively furious now. "How did you feel about him flying?"

The air had turned suddenly brittle. "How do you think I felt?" she countered quietly. "I hated it. I was terrified that every flight might be his last."

She could feel the rigid pressure of Jason's fingers on her own, but she welcomed it. "Greg always shrugged it off. He said he wouldn't sacrifice his livelihood because of a silly phobia. But I always knew it was more than that." Her smile was bittersweet. "To Greg, a life without flying would have been like losing his arms and legs."

Jason couldn't believe he'd heard right. "Then he knew? Greg knew how you felt about it?"

Kate stared straight ahead. "He knew" was all she said.

He was filled with a blinding rage unlike anything he'd ever felt. Once before he'd had a taste of Greg's heartlessness. But he would never have guessed that Greg could be so callous and cruel to his own wife.

Jason's mouth curled. His livelihood, Greg had said. And to think that there was a time he had been willing to give up his livelihood *and* his home to save his marriage to Kate. But Kate had ended up in tears at the thought of leaving her father, and he'd given it up. In Jason's eyes, if Greg McAllister had been any kind of man he could have found another way to support his family. At the very least he could have hired someone else to do his piloting.

He leaned back in his seat, his face grim. "Looks like Greg fooled us both, doesn't it?"

He didn't expect an answer; he didn't get one. Kate continued to stare straight ahead, her lips pressed tightly together, her eyes purposely void of emotion.

Neither one said anything more. It seemed the past, where the two of them were concerned, was a terrible place to visit.

Yet throughout the long flight, cold clammy fingers clung tightly to his. Jason couldn't have let go even if he'd wanted to.

And the hell of it was, he *didn't* want to.

It seemed an eternity before they landed. Kate fell into a light sleep shortly after lunch. When the heavy plane rolled to a stop on the tarmac, he gently nudged her awake.

Her lashes fluttered, and she stared directly into his face. He was tempted—ah, so tempted—to lean over and brush his lips against hers. Her eyes were the same inviting color as the sea on a warm, summer day.

But instead he smiled crookedly. ''We're here, Kate. Welcome to Mexico.''

CHAPTER SIX

ONCE THEY HAD LANDED, Kate was more convinced than ever that the decision to come after Greg had been the right one. He wasn't dead, she was certain of it. It was almost as if she could feel him calling out to her.

Earlier that same morning, Kate had phoned Jeff to get the address of the McAllister Air Express office in Mexico City. While the company was by no means a large-scale operation, Jeff had said the office at Hidalgo Field was a mere hole-in-the-wall in comparison to the home base in Dallas. Greg's only employee in Mexico City doubled as both mechanic and clerk. Kate had planned to visit the office right away to see if she could learn anything new from this man, and Jeff had offered to phone ahead to let him know she was on her way.

Therefore it came as something of a surprise when a man tapped her shoulder just after she and Jason stepped off the plane.

"*Señora?* You are Señora McAllister?"

All around them were milling, darting people, chattering and laughing in English and Spanish alike. But the accented voice belonged to a short, burly Mexican. He wore a loosely woven white shirt and dark pants. Jet-black hair waved back from a broad forehead, and a thick, droopy mustache nearly obscured his mouth. A bright light shone in dark, obsidian eyes as she was swept by an eager, all-encompassing gaze.

She was suddenly glad of Jason's presence behind her. But then again, he didn't have to stand quite so close. She couldn't possibly be in any danger with so many people around.

"Yes," she confirmed. "I'm Mrs. McAllister." Her voice held a twinge of annoyance.

Her hand was immediately seized and ferociously pumped for all it was worth. Kate blinked when the stranger finally let go. Before she had a chance to draw a breath, Jason pinned him with a hard demand. "Does the lady know you?"

The stranger grinned. "I'm Manuel Ortega. I work for your husband."

"Ex" she opened her mouth to clarify, then caught sight of Jason's harsh expression. She stopped herself, without knowing quite why.

"I see." She smiled at him tentatively. "Jeff Coleman called you this morning then."

"*Sí.*" The man nodded.

"There was no need for you to meet us, Mr. Ortega. We'd planned to go to Hidalgo Field to talk with you."

Manuel shrugged. "It is a long way from here. I thought it would save you some time if I came here."

"That was thoughtful of you." She glanced around, then started to ask if there was someplace nearby where the three of them could be alone. But once again, Jason beat her to it.

"There's a coffee shop that way." He pointed a short distance down the crowded corridor. "We can talk there."

The coffee shop was only slightly less noisy, but it was better than standing in the middle of the crowded corridor. Here, too, however, space was definitely at a premium. Kate found herself wedged between the side of the tiny booth and Jason's body. His long legs were angled halfway across hers. He gave her a deferential smile as he slid an arm across the seat to allow her more room, but that only made things worse. Now her shoulder was nestled quite cozily into the hollow beneath his, and there wasn't a thing she could do about it. She was forced to turn her body toward his, since Manuel Ortega chose to sit across from Jason. He had only to move his head a scant inch and his lips would...

Manuel Ortega cleared his throat. "Señor Coleman said your husband was in trouble."

"Trouble" seemed much too tame a word to describe a kidnapping. This time, though, Kate jumped in before Jason. "He's been kidnapped," she said bluntly. She could feel Jason's eyes on her profile but paid no mind. "We're here to try to find him."

Ortega's eyes widened. "Kidnapped! *Madre de Dios!*" He erupted into a long string of Spanish, but Jason cut him short.

"We think you may be able to help."

"Help! But, *señor*!" Ortega's pudgy fingers spread over his chest. "I know nothing! The last time I saw Señor McAllister was last week. When he left for Veracruz on Friday. I know nothing—"

He lapsed into Spanish, and again Jason stopped him. "He never made it to Veracruz."

By now Manuel Ortega looked quite panicked. Kate was rather miffed with Jason's high-handedness, and he seemed to frighten the little man. His black eyes darted in all directions, as if he expected the police to close in at any moment.

"We're not accusing you of anything," she told him gently, but inwardly she was seething. "We just need to find out what happened the day Greg left.'' She took a deep breath. "Please, Mr. Ortega. Will you help us?"

Ortega cast a quick, guarded glance at Jason. Interpreting the look, Kate said quickly, "He's not with the police. Mr. Davalos is just a friend who's trying to help me find Greg."

After that, Manuel relaxed visibly.

"Do you remember anything different about that day?" she asked. "It may not seem important, but think of anything that might set it apart from any other day. Did Greg act differently? Was he nervous? Jumpy, perhaps?"

Ortega shook his head, his expression rather guilty. "I haven't worked for him very long, *señora*. A month—no more."

Kate's shoulders slumped. A month. Greg only made the Mexico City run once a week. This man probably didn't know much more about the business than she did.

"What kind of cargo was he carrying?" The question came from Jason.

"I don't know. He loaded it himself. I asked if he wanted me to help, but—" Ortega shrugged "—he said he could handle it."

He loaded it himself. The words touched a chord in Kate's memory. Jeff had said something to that effect. Once more her stomach tightened. Greg had his hands in something dirty, she was almost positive. And it could end up costing him his life.

Manuel's face suddenly brightened. "He had no passengers this time."

"He sometimes had passengers?" Kate prompted.

"*Sí*. Two weeks ago, he went to Veracruz. There was a man with him." He snapped his fingers. "Wait! Someone came to talk to him just before he left. It was the same man, I am certain."

"Who was he?" Her tone was urgent. "What did he look like?"

Ortega's face fell. "I don't know who he was, *señora*. He was tall." He squinted at Jason. "Like you, *señor*, but not as big."

Jason didn't look impressed. "An American?"

"No." The other man frowned. "He was very well dressed, though. In a suit. And he carried a briefcase."

A businessman. Kate hid her frustration. There was nothing so unusual in that. Greg probably carried passengers routinely on short hops like the one from Mexico City to Veracruz. In all likelihood, the man had stopped in to arrange for passage another time.

"You're absolutely sure he didn't leave with Greg?" She couldn't quite keep the despair from her voice.

Ortega nodded vehemently.

Unfortunately that about summed up the extent of the meeting's productivity. Though Kate normally wasn't a moody person, this whole situation with Greg made her feel as if she would break apart at any moment. The way Jason stuck to her like glue didn't help matters, either. A man stepped between them when they exited the airport, and though they weren't separated by more than a few feet, the second Jason caught up to her, he slid his hand under her elbow once more.

She yanked her arm away. "I didn't bring you along as a bodyguard, you know!" she muttered angrily. "The kidnappers already have Greg. I doubt they want me, too, and they're certainly not about to snatch me away from you. The way you keep holding on to me, they'd end up with you, too!"

His thoughts exactly, though perhaps she was right. Maybe he was being just a little too paranoid. Still, her imperious tone rattled his temper. If she wanted him to keep his distance, fine. "Have it your way, *Mrs.* McAllister."

She had offended him; called up that fierce male pride that she had known all too well in the past. She saw it in the ruthless thrust of his jaw, in the hard glitter of his eyes before he jerked them away from her and strode off.

"Jason." He was heading down the sidewalk toward a waiting stream of taxicabs. Kate had to run to catch up with him. "Jason!"

He halted so abruptly she barreled into him. He jerked his thumb over his shoulder and indicated an unoccupied white cab at the curb. "Is this one to your liking, ma'am?" he asked in an affected Texas drawl.

"Jason, please!" Kate didn't realize she had even touched him until his gaze slid downward. It rested on her fingers, now tightly clutching the fabric of his sleeve. In spite of the angry glitter in his golden eyes, she doggedly kept her hand where it was.

She spoke when she sensed that she had his attention. "I'm sorry, Jason." She gestured vaguely with her other hand. "This—this isn't easy for me. I don't mean to take it out on you, I swear."

His eyes finally drifted back to her face. Her lips were parted, and she panted slightly from her exertion. "It's not any easier for me either, Kate," he said after a long moment.

She knew he referred to the state of affairs between himself and Greg. "I know," she said with a faint smile. "But since we're here, we'll just have to make the best of it." He said nothing, and Kate felt a slight flush color her cheeks. Her hand remained on his forearm a second longer before she told him softly, "I'm glad you came with me."

There was no doubting the sincerity in her tone. It was reflected twofold in the depths of her eyes. But Jason was struck once more by the lingering sadness he saw there, and he strongly suspected Kate wasn't even aware of it. Still, he couldn't afford to let himself be taken in by her again.

He nodded toward the waiting cab. The driver had begun to frown at them impatiently. "We should find the hotel before it gets any later."

His coolness stung. Kate felt as if she'd extended a hand in friendship only to have him slap it away. She dug in her purse and emerged with a small piece of paper. "It's the Hotel Cordoba. Jeff said it's the same one Greg always uses when he's here. As long as the kidnappers want me to stay there, I thought we could talk to the desk clerk and see if he or anyone else remembers Greg."

Jason doubted it would do much good, but he didn't say so. He gestured Kate inside the cab, then gave the driver the address Kate had scribbled down. Her back was stiff as she sat next to him. He had the feeling she wasn't going to take this well.

"I'm not trying to tell you what to do," he said abruptly. "But when you talk to the hotel clerk, I don't think you should mention that Greg's been kidnapped."

She lifted an eyebrow. "Meaning I shouldn't have told Manuel Ortega?"

Jason said nothing, but she didn't have to hear it from his lips to know he disapproved. "I don't see what difference it makes." Her chin lifted defensively. "I had to tell him something. He'd have known it wasn't a social call. Besides, I don't think he's likely to blab to anyone, especially the police.'' She shrugged. ''He must have had a few too many parking tickets.''

''I don't suppose you had any choice,'' he finally conceded. He glanced at her as they pulled away from the curb. ''He thinks you're still married to Greg.''

Kate's heart gave an involuntary leap. Was Jason jealous? Surely not. Nor was it likely that he'd been mooning after her all these years, either, she chided herself firmly. No, that notion definitely didn't reconcile with the stony-faced man beside her.

But she hadn't imagined the displeasure in his voice just now, either.

''He must have misunderstood,'' she murmured.

Jason neither agreed nor disagreed. The atmosphere in the back of the cab was far from comfortable so Kate turned her attention to the outside world.

Mexico City was a city of many faces. Sprawled out in a mountain-ringed hollow, it was exotic, modern and cosmopolitan. Glass-and-steel skyscrapers reached toward the sky. Fancy shopping centers covered acres of land.

Her eyes widened as she caught a glimpse of an old-fashioned organ grinder. Near an open-air marketplace, street peddlers hawked everything from tacos to kitchen utensils. The scent of fragrant blossoms drifted through the open window.

A slight smile touched Jason's lips as he watched her absorb the sights and sounds of the strange new city. He leaned over to point out the twin-capped volcanos to the southeast.

''They're called Popo and the Sleeping Lady,'' he told her.

Kate glanced at him curiously. ''You lived here when you were with the DEA?''

He nodded.

"Two years, was it?"

"Yes."

"Long enough to grow attached to it," she mused.

"Oh, I don't know." He shrugged. A slight smile played on his lips. "I didn't have much of a chance to play tourist."

"Didn't you like it here?"

His smile slowly ebbed. "Yes and no. It was a change, and the work was a challenge. After Vietnam, I, well, I just wasn't ready to go home."

Vietnam again. Vietnam and Greg. Jason didn't say so, but she had the feeling there was a connection.

"I didn't really do much traveling on my own while I was here, except to visit the village my parents came from. It's north of here, near Monterrey." He was silent for a moment. "I missed Texas, though. I didn't know how much until after I came home."

There was no need to elaborate; she'd had almost the same conversation with Rosa, and she had no wish to delve into the subject further with Jason.

She decided a change of subject was in order. "Do you think you could ask the driver to stop at a bank? Preferably one near the hotel. I should exchange some currency." She glanced at the cab driver, then lowered her voice. "I also need to make a deposit."

Jason frowned. "A deposit? We won't be here that long, Kate. Not if we're lucky."

"I have a draft from my bank in Dallas."

"A draft? For the ransom?" His eyes bit into hers. "You told me you didn't have the money."

"I don't," she denied quickly. His harshness made her feel guilty, even though she had no reason to be. It also wounded her to know that Jason thought she had deceived him.

"At least not all of it," she explained in a low voice. "I had some money saved up for Toby and I..." Why was Jason looking at her so accusingly?

Her chin tilted bravely, and she went on. "There's only about five thousand dollars, but if worse comes to worst, maybe it will appease the kidnappers."

Jason deliberately looked away, not trusting himself to speak. So Kate had scraped the bottom of the barrel. He supposed it was a good thing they'd left Dallas so quickly, or she might have found herself in debt clear to her eyebrows. How far would she go in order to secure Greg's release? he wondered grimly. But then he already had the answer to that. She'd come to him, hadn't she? She must have been desperate—very desperate indeed—to look to him for help.

His features were tense as he leaned forward to pass on her request to the driver.

MODEST AND UNPRETENTIOUS, the Hotel Cordoba was small but still boasted full service. A few years past its prime, it had a nostalgic charm nonetheless. The hotel did not appear to be heavily favored by tourists, but that was fine with Kate.

Her room was sunny and airy, with a small balcony overlooking the bustling street below. But a couch and table set against one wall made it a bit cramped. Unpacking didn't take long, but the entire time she couldn't get Greg out of her mind. She kept seeing that horrible photograph, his face battered and bruised.

The telephone shrilled. Kate jumped at the sharp sound, then grabbed the receiver and gasped out an anxious hello.

There was a dead silence. Then a raspy, thickly accented voice inquired, "Is this Señora McAllister?"

"Yes! Yes!" She sank down on the bed, certain her legs would no longer hold her.

"You have the money?"

"I—" To her horror, her voice caught. She'd known the call was coming, only the note had said tonight. She thought of Jason in the room next door. They had discussed the call only minutes ago, but now her mind went blank. *Try to draw him out, find out as much as you can.* Beyond that, she couldn't remember.

"Th—the money?" she stammered.

"Sí!" the voice hissed. "You did not bring it, did you?"

She could sense the caller's anger. "I did!" she cried. "At least some of it..." When the words finally came, they tumbled out, one after another. "You wanted me here today, but because of the weekend, I couldn't even get to the bank until this morning. I did what you asked, but I had to sell some investments to come up with the rest. I had to make arrangements to have it wired."

The silence that followed sent chills to her spine. "And how soon will that be?"

The voice was very low. Between that and the accent, Kate had difficulty comprehending the words. "I'm not sure," she bluffed. "A day or two. My broker couldn't tell me for certain." Her heart throbbed fearfully while she waited. She and Jason had to buy some time to locate Greg; today was virtually wasted. But if this man refused...

"All right, *señora*." His voice came after a lengthy silence. "But no more mistakes. You have made two already, by not bringing the ransom and not coming alone."

Kate gasped.

"You thought to deceive me, no? But I saw the *señor* with you when you entered the hotel, so who knows? Perhaps he, too, will disappear." The man's scratchy laugh was menacing. "I will call again tomorrow night. Be there, *señora*, or you will be sorry."

"Wait!" she cried. "What about Gr—" But the question never materialized. The line went dead, and Kate was left staring at the receiver.

"Kate?" There was an insistent rap on the door. "Are you okay? I heard your voice and I—" Jason broke off when she opened the door. He stepped inside, his gaze on her pale face. "News about Greg?"

Kate summoned a wan smile. "Not exactly," she admitted, and went on to tell him of the call.

"Was there anything distinctive about his voice, or the way he talked? Anything familiar?"

She shook her head. "His accent was very heavy, and I could barely hear him. Everything he said was just above a whisper." She looked up at him. "Do you suppose he could have been in a public place and didn't want anyone to hear him?"

"It's possible." Jason paused. "Could you guess at his age if you had to?"

Kate sighed and dropped onto the narrow couch. "The only thing I could really tell was that it was a man's voice. He could have been twenty-five or he could have been seventy-five." She threw up her hands. "I was afraid if I told him I'd brought the entire ransom he'd demand it right now, and then where would Greg be when he finds out I haven't? But by letting him know I don't have it, I may have just made things worse for Greg anyway!"

"If he wants the money bad enough, I don't think he'll jeopardize the deal by hurting him." Jason frowned.

"But the fact that he knows I'm here with you is bound to make him suspicious, and it sure as hell isn't going to make it any easier to locate Greg before they find out what we're up to. Not if they're really keeping tabs on us."

Kate couldn't hide her frustration. "But I don't understand how he spotted me in the first place! He said he saw you with me when we checked in. This hotel isn't bursting at the seams with tourists or anyone else, but how could he possibly know who I was?"

"He already knew what hotel you'd be staying at," Jason reminded her. "And he may have checked with the airport to see what time the flights from Dallas arrived. He may have forced Greg to give him a description of you, too. Or maybe Greg had a picture."

Kate bit her lip guiltily. She, Greg and Toby had had a family portrait done about three years ago. Greg had certainly never been a gushing family man, but as far as she knew, he still carried a snapshot in his wallet. "I think he does," she said with a grimace. "Not exactly detective material, am I?"

Jason smiled slightly. "You're under a lot of pressure." His gaze softened when she glanced up at him in surprise. "Why don't you get dressed and we'll go get something to eat," he suggested. "Maybe it'll take your mind off things for a while."

IT DID A LITTLE, but whether it was for better or worse, Kate wasn't quite certain.

She toyed with her dinner that night. The food was good, not too strong or spicy for her American palate; she just didn't have any appetite. She was wise enough to recognize that part of it was anxiety over Greg.

The other part was due to the man sitting across from her. The momentary gentleness she had glimpsed in Jason's eyes was gone when they had rejoined half an hour later.

He scarcely looked at her, except when they spoke to each other, which was less and less often as the meal progressed. He seemed tense, maybe even a little angry, and he was treating her as if she were a virtual stranger.

It bothered Kate. It bothered her far more than it should have. After all, when this whole ordeal with Greg had been wrapped up—no matter what the outcome—she and Jason would go their separate ways once more. But couldn't they at least be friends?

Once they had been friends *and* lovers. Kate's stomach dropped at the thought, and she forced her mind away from that disturbing avenue.

She glanced around the room, as she had already done numerous times. The hotel was lovely. Quaint and old-fashioned, the dining room was an extension of the lobby. The walls were done in gleaming dark paneling. Lush green plant life spilled from macramé hangers and filled the corners. High overhead, a ceiling fan lazily stirred the air.

"This reminds me of *Casablanca*," she murmured. When Jason said nothing, she sighed inwardly. "If you see the waiter, I'd like another drink."

His eyes moved to the tall, frosted glass in front of her plate. "You haven't finished that one," he pointed out.

Kate reached for the glass and took a long sip from the tiny straw. The drink was fruit-flavored, both tangy and sweet. "Now I have." She smiled as she set it back on the table.

A heavy brow lifted. "You sure you can handle two? They're stronger than you think." His eyes dropped to her plate. "And you didn't eat much. On an empty stomach—"

"For heaven's sakes!" She suddenly felt rather rebellious. "I'm not a kid anymore, Jason Davalos. In case you hadn't noticed, I'm all grown up now."

He had, and that was the whole damn problem. The silky jade sheath she wore proclaimed only too well that she was all woman. Slender arms peeped out from beneath the tiny cap sleeves. A slim belt encircled her trim waist and emphasized the supple curves both above and below. The self-doubt he'd seen an hour before might have been a figment of his imagination. The woman who sat across from him was every inch the successful owner of a fashion boutique, a woman who exuded confidence and prosperity, and a certain aloofness as well.

She made him feel like he was out of his league, and he couldn't help but resent her for it. With his dark slacks and light brown sport coat, he blended in with the crowd as well as anyone else. It didn't make sense that he should feel so out of place.

But none of his feelings about Kate had ever made sense.

"I talked to the registration clerk earlier," he said abruptly. He paused while the waiter cleared their table. "He said Greg was the perfect guest—prompt in paying his bill, checking out on time... But one of the bellboys mentioned that Greg was a big tipper."

Kate frowned. "And?"

He shrugged. "I didn't think that sounded like Greg."

She was silent for a moment. "He's different from when you knew him." Her smile was bittersweet. "He's much more flamboyant than he used to be. He's always been a daredevil, but now he likes to..." She hesitated.

"Play things up? Brag a little?" He mulled the possibilities over. Had Greg changed? It didn't sound like it to Jason.

She nodded reluctantly. "He likes to talk big, especially if he's been drinking." She eyed the cocktail the waiter had just delivered and pushed it aside. She'd suddenly lost her taste for it.

"It's possible that could have something to do with his kidnapping."

Kate bit her lip. In light of Jason's conversation with the bellboy, it seemed more than a possibility. "I suppose it could. Especially if he's been flashing a lot of money around." Her gaze slid away from Jason's. "I've seen him do that a few times." Her fingers clenched her napkin. "Where do we go from here?"

Jason's eyes flickered at her quiet tone. The anxious concern in her eyes was like a rusty knife slicing into him. There had once been a time when he would have done anything for Kate. But she had wanted nothing from him then, maybe not even him...

He swallowed the burning feel of betrayal and wished he didn't feel so torn in two. It went utterly against the grain to say the words, but he forced them out. "Don't worry, Kate. We'll find Greg. Somehow we'll find him."

LATER THAT EVENING, Kate placed a call to Texas. It took a few seconds for the long-distance connection to go through, then she summoned a smile at Rita's breezy hello.

"You sound pretty cheery. Toby can't be giving you too hard a time."

"Are you kidding?" Rita laughed. "Although he did tell me you always let him have three helpings of ice cream for dessert. And you always let him stay up until eleven o'clock—"

"Eleven o'clock!" This time Kate's smile was genuine. "He's never been up that late in his life! Let me talk to him and set him straight. Eight-thirty is his bedtime and he knows it."

As it happened, Toby did get to stay up past his bedtime but it was because he was talking to his mother. Kate heard all about his day.   "When you comin' home, Mom?" he finally asked. He didn't sound overly eager to see her again. Kate wasn't quite sure if she was glad or not.

"Soon," she promised. "Very soon."

"I miss you, Mom."

A lump swelled in her throat. "I miss you, too," she whispered.

Rita came back on the line. "How was the flight?" she asked in friendly concern. Rita knew how much Kate hated to fly, so she was the one who usually trekked off to New York to choose their stock.

Kate had a sudden vision of her hand clasped tightly in Jason's. Again she felt the warmth of his skin against hers. He'd been so nice about her fear of flying. She fought a sudden, irrational fluttering of her pulse.

A shaky laugh emerged. "It was okay, I guess. I got here in one piece anyway."

"Did you come up with anything about Greg?"

"No," she answered dispiritedly. The day had been so unproductive. Maybe she'd been expecting too much, as Jason had told her after dinner. "But I think—at least I hope—that I may have borrowed a little more time. And Jason has a friend who is still an agent with the DEA. Tomorrow he's planning to see if this friend can do a little digging."

"To see if Greg is under any suspicion—"

"Yes." She cut Rita off abruptly. "And to see if they know of anywhere the kidnappers might be holding him." That Greg was involved in drug trafficking was something she hated to think about.

There was a brief pause. "Are you and Jason getting along okay?"

Something in Rita's guarded tone made her think she expected the two of them to be at each other's throats by now. She thought of Jason, alone in the next room. Alone. Just as she was.

"Everything's fine," she told the other woman. Her voice was carefully neutral.

Kate hung up the phone a few minutes later. As she sat down on the double bed, it occurred to her that she'd been hoping that talking with Rita and Toby might pull her out of her doldrums. Instead it seemed to have had the opposite effect.

She tried to sleep, but tired as she was, she was still awake at midnight. She felt suddenly restless and closed in. Sighing, she slipped out of bed. She didn't bother with the light; she managed to find her robe in the darkness, then stepped through the narrow French doors onto the balcony.

The night was alive and thriving. And, Kate thought to herself with a tiny smile, still young. Several stories below her on the sidewalk, couples walked hand-in-hand. She watched as three men emerged from the neighborhood cantina, their voices joining in rowdy, boisterous song. Judging from the way they laughed and poked each other's ribs, she was glad she didn't understand the lyrics.

A cool midnight breeze stirred her hair. She tightened the sash of her robe, absently wishing she'd brought something heavier than the thin nylon wrapper. The mild climate had been a pleasant surprise. It was the altitude, Jason had told her during one of the few times he'd chosen to converse with her at dinner.

But Jason was the last person she wanted to think about. Jason or Greg. She put them both firmly out of her mind and lifted her head to concentrate instead on the beauty of the sky. The moon was a pale circlet of silver, partially hidden by a wispy cloud. It was too dark to see the jagged silhouette of the nearby mountains, but soon the spell of the night worked its magic. It wasn't long before she felt relaxed enough to sleep.

She turned to enter her room, and it was then that she heard the sound. A faint thump, followed by a low hiss. Kate froze, her fingers on the handle of the door. Her heart thumping wildly in her chest, she peered frantically through the filmy curtains.

There was someone in her room!

CHAPTER SEVEN

JASON WAS DREAMING, but it wasn't a pleasant dream. In a state of semiconsciousness, he tossed restlessly, almost as if he were willing himself to wake up. But it was no use. His dreams carried him back in time. Back...

"DADDY'S STOPPING BY later." Kate glanced at him nervously as she set the table.

Jason tried not to look annoyed. His head hurt. His back ached. Damn! Michael Anderson was just what he needed to make a bad day a disaster.

"Fine," he muttered and started for the shower.

But he spoke too late. Kate had seen his face before he turned away. She looked ready to cry.

He tried to take her in his arms. His face tightened as she deliberately turned her back on him and moved away, as if she couldn't stand him touching her.

"I wouldn't invite him here if you would just go over there." Her thin voice was accusing.

"We're there a lot," he quietly pointed out.

She shook her head. "No, Jason. I am. You always have some excuse to stay away."

His temper began to simmer. "I have work to do, Kate. Contrary to what you and your father seem to think, I can't drop everything the minute he issues his summons."

"His summons!" She walked a thin line between anger and tears. "That's not fair of you, Jason. My father has been very generous, or at least he would be if you'd let him."

He slammed a hand against the doorframe, suddenly furious. "Are you so blind that you can't see what he's doing? He's trying to run our life, Kate, the way he's always run yours! Don't you see that?"

Her eyes were moist and glistening. "That's not true. He's my father, and he's only trying to help. He wants what's best for me—for us!" She dashed a lone tear from her cheek. "You're still angry because he asked us to live with him. I don't understand why you think that's so terrible. We wouldn't have to worry about making ends meet. And then Rosa won't have to share her room with the baby. You could sell the farm and go back to college."

This wasn't Kate talking; it was her father. He loved her, but at times like this, he felt it wasn't Kate he'd married, but Michael Anderson.

"I won't sell this farm, Kate. It meant too much to my parents—it means too much to me." There was a cold finality in his voice. "Regardless of what you and your father seem to think, I'm perfectly capable of providing for my family, without his help. And I'm just as capable of deciding what I want out of life. I sure as hell don't need *Daddy* telling me what I should or shouldn't do."

It seemed they'd had the same conversation dozens of times before. It was almost laughable that *he* had suggested selling his land and moving elsewhere less than two months later, something he'd sworn he would never do. But the situation with Kate's father was intolerable. He constantly interfered, but Kate couldn't see it. To this day, Jason felt Michael Anderson had wanted to make trouble for them so Kate would eventually leave him...and she had.

The evening ended much the same as many others. There was the usual argument with Michael. In bed that night he had listened to the muffled sounds of Kate's weeping until he could stand it no longer. He knew better than to try to console her; she would only turn away. He had finally ended up downstairs. It was pure frustration that drove him to smash a cheap vase against the wall. Even now, deep in his dreamworld, he heard the shattering of glass.

HE JERKED UPRIGHT. This was no dream. The sound he heard wasn't a figment of his imagination. There *had* been a crash.

And it came from the next room—Kate's room.

He yanked on a pair of pants and bolted into the hallway. The only light came from the far end, but he quickly saw that the door to Kate's room was ajar. It crashed against the wall as he threw it open and rushed inside.

All was dark. The only thing he could see were a few faint shadows on the wall. "Damn it, Kate!" he yelled. "Where are you?" He groped for the light switch.

"Here!" The light in the small entry clicked on. Kate stood near the dresser. She blinked as the room flared with light.

The lamp that had graced the dresser was gone. It lay scattered across the polished parquet floor, a haphazard pattern of broken ceramic. The shade lay at his feet, tilted on its side.

"Kate, what the hell...!" To say he was confused was an understatement. "How on earth did you manage to knock that thing over?"

"I didn't knock it over," she informed him crossly. "I threw it!"

Threw it! Why it must have weighed at least thirty pounds. His gaze moved from what was left of the lamp back to her face.

Her eyes looked behind him toward the hallway. "Did you see him?"

"Who?" He picked his way toward her, carefully avoiding the razor-sharp bits of ceramic.

"The man who was in here!"

"There was a man in here?"

"Of course there was!" She pointed at the dresser. "He was going through dresser drawers. Why do you think I threw the lamp at him?"

Jason reached her. For the first time he noted how pale she was. Comprehension finally set in, and he took her by the shoulders. "Someone was in here?"

"Jason!" She looked at him as if he were dim-witted. "I just told you there was a man in here!"

"Didn't you lock the door before you went to bed?"

"Of course I did! I was out on the balcony when I saw him." She frowned. "I think the hotel had better see about installing different locks. These obviously aren't burglar-proof."

Jason closed his eyes. How could she be so calm about it? "Are you sure you're okay?" His tone was urgent.

Her cheeks had regained their normal color. The eyes that looked back at him were clear and unafraid. "I'm fine," she told him.

He was already making that discovery for himself. His hands coasted down her arms and back up again. His eyes moved over her features one by one. She wore no makeup, and her hair was down and loose. It fell in full, buoyant waves well past her shoulders. She looked incredibly young and innocent. He'd been sleeping, while Kate was alone in here, alone and defenseless. When he thought of what might have happened...

"Good Lord, Kate. Why didn't you scream for help?"

"Why?" she countered crossly. "So you could come and protect me?" Her shoulders stiffened beneath his hands.

Her words earned a reluctant smile. The Kate he'd known fifteen years ago would have been frightened to death if a man had broken into her home. He had no doubt her first reaction—probably her only reaction—would have been to scream her head off.

There was a soft knock at the door. *"Señora?"* A voice identified itself as the night manager, and a small, dark-haired man stepped through the open door. His eyes widened at the mess strewn across the floor, then flashed back up to Kate's face. *"Señora!"*

Jason quickly explained about the intruder.

With two men in the room, Kate was suddenly acutely conscious of the thinness of her robe. It clung to every curve and valley. "I'll pay for the damage," she offered, anxious to be rid of them both.

The man waved his hands. "No, it is not necessary. But we can arrange another room for you, if you like."

Before Kate had a chance to speak, Jason drew the man aside. She couldn't hear the low exchange in Spanish, but it was obvious she was the subject under discussion. The manager finally nodded. He glanced at Kate with a knowing smile before he left. Jason closed the door and walked toward her.

"What was that all about?" Her eyes narrowed suspiciously.

For just a second, Jason looked uncomfortable. "I told him he didn't need to bother with another room."

"Oh? And why is that?" She knew she sounded catty, but she had the feeling there was more.

His gaze was fierce. "You should know why, especially after that phone call today."

"The kidnapper's threat was directed more at you than me," she pointed out. "It doesn't make sense for the kidnappers to try to get rid of me. Without me, there'll be no ransom for Greg. The man in here was probably just a burglar who hoped to steal a little cash."

"Whatever the case, I don't want you in here alone." Jason shoved his hands into his trouser pockets and glanced away.

She stared at him. A dull flush rose high along his cheekbones. "If I don't have another room, and you don't want me to be alone, exactly where am I supposed to sleep tonight?"

"Where else?" His voice was rough as his gaze finally swung back to hers. "With me."

"With you!" She sucked in a sharp breath. All of a sudden the bed next to her took on gigantic proportions. Her eyes darted to it in spite of herself. She shook her head fiercely. "Oh, no—"

"Oh, yes, Kate!" He mocked her. "I know what you're thinking. It's plain as the nose on your face. You think I can't wait to drag you into bed."

"I didn't say that," she denied quickly.

"You didn't have to!" His face was hard, his eyes cold as he grabbed her carry-on. He threw it on the bed and flipped it open, then stalked to the dresser.

"I'm not as hot for you as you think I am, and I haven't done a damn thing to give you that impression! But even if I did want you—which I don't—you're the last woman on earth I'd lay a hand on. I learned my lesson the hard way, and I'm sure as hell not about to give you the chance to dump me a second time!'' His laugh was bitter. "I'll keep my distance, Kate. You don't have to worry about that. This whole thing won't be over with soon enough for me.''

He looked, and sounded, absolutely furious. The broadness of his chest, and the dense mat of hair that grew there, looked both inviting and intimidating as he turned to and fro, dumping the clothes she'd unpacked earlier into her case.

He zipped it shut and dragged it from the bed. "We'll get the rest tomorrow." In light of his outburst, his voice was remarkably calm, but distant. "Coming?"

Kate felt something die inside her. Her head swam dizzily as, for a moment, she felt as if she'd stepped back in time. What choice did she have? None. None at all.

Her head held regally high, she preceded him from the room.

THE BEDSPRINGS CREAKED as she turned over. The sound seemed overly loud in the brittle silence that steeped the room. Her eyes instinctively sought the couch where Jason lay. When she detected no response from that direction, she closed her eyes and tried to relax.

If there had been any doubt in Kate's mind that she had once hurt Jason—hurt him deeply—there was none now. She could almost believe that he hated her for what she had done to him, except that he was with her now.

He had no reason to help her find Greg. Greg had certainly given him none—he'd as much as told her so. Jason might have easily refused her request, but he hadn't.

For old times' sake... It was now the only link between them, and that was a very hard cross for Kate to bear. She hated knowing that Jason was so wary of her.

That he thought her capable of hurting him again made her heart ache.

He was right. The best thing they could do for each other was to keep their distance.

Jason lay a mere five feet away. The couch was far too short for his six-foot frame. The armrest butted up against his neck, and no matter how he fidgeted, he couldn't get comfortable.

Finally he gave up. He tucked an arm behind his head and turned to peer at Kate. She was on her side, huddled below the sheet and light blanket. Her back was toward him, and he could just make out the slender outline of her body.

A sudden stab of guilt pricked him. How many times had they lain like this in the past? He grimaced as the pillow slid behind his shoulder and his neck connected with the armrest once more.

Well, perhaps not quite like this. But with both of them so tense and so aware of each other, it was like a chapter from the past.

He heaved a sigh and rolled over on his stomach. Through the darkness, he saw her turn toward him and rise up on an elbow.

"Jason?"

"What?"

"Do you want to trade places?" Her voice was tentative. "The bed would be a lot more comfortable for you than the couch."

Why the hell should she care how comfortable he was? Especially after what he'd said to her. If anyone else had spoken to her the way he had...

"I'm fine, Kate." Damn, why did he always have such a hard time talking to her? Why couldn't he just come right out and tell her what a fool he was?

Time slipped slowly by. She eased back down. They both lay silently, staring up at the muted shadows on the ceiling.

"Kate?"

"Yes?"

"I'm sorry." There, he'd said it. So why didn't he feel any better? And why didn't she say something in return?

The seconds ticked by, one by one. He sensed her eyes on him and took a deep breath. "I shouldn't have yelled at you."

"Then why did you?"

Jason blinked. The directness of the question surprised him. "I don't know," he said in a low voice. He did, only he didn't have the courage to admit it to her. She'd done nothing wrong. Nothing except look so damn beautiful he simply couldn't resist her. It wasn't Kate he'd been angry with. It was himself. But he'd taken it out on her. What a mess he'd made of things—again.

"That man could have come back." He felt compelled to explain, to rationalize his reasons for insisting she sleep in his room. "I didn't want you to be alone. There's no telling what he was after."

"I know that, Jason." She heard the faint rustle of the sheet and wished he would come closer. If not close enough to touch, then at least close enough to see.

"It could have been the money. Or it could have been..." Lord, he couldn't even complete the sentence. The thought of another man daring to lay a hand on her filled him with fury.

Her fingers clenched and unclenched on the sheet. *It doesn't matter,* Kate cried silently. None of that mattered, not now.

He moved to the edge of the bed. "I can't help the way I feel, Kate. And I feel responsible for you. But then—"

he hesitated, staring down at her "—I was certain you'd think that I was just trying to get you into bed."

"I did," she admitted guiltily. She sensed him moving toward her. The mattress dipped as he sat down. Her heart beat faster.

In the silvered darkness, their eyes met and clung. A dozen wordless messages passed between them, messages that neither seemed willing to recognize, or to deny.

"But only for a minute." Her voice accompanied the movement of her hand as it slid outward along the blanket, toward Jason. Her heart thumped wildly when her fingers crept between his. He didn't withdraw as she half-expected. "I—I trust you, Jason."

She sat up slowly, sensing that something was about to happen, but not knowing what.

Eyes like dark gold fire slid over her body. The sheet had slipped down to her hips. The moonlight was such that her body was all ivory and gold, soft hollows and muted shadows. The fine white batiste nightgown she wore was both innocent and sensual, suspended by tiny straps across her shoulders. Just enough soft flesh rose above the modestly cut bodice to send Jason into agonized longing.

"Kate," he said softly, then more urgently, "Kate!"

Exactly who made the first move, he was never certain. One moment they were apart, the next they were together, and then it didn't matter. He felt her arms slide around his back and cling. He pulled her to his chest and buried his face in the hollow of her throat. The sound that emerged from him was part triumph, part despair. "I don't want this," he moaned, even as he blindly sought her lips. "I don't..."

But he did, and they both knew it. They had been on a collision course, veering unerringly toward this moment since the first time they'd seen each other again.

His lips took hers over and over. At first hungrily, then gently, slowly, then fiercely again, as if he were starved for the taste of her. His fingers threaded through the dark silk of her hair and tilted her head to accommodate his searching mouth. She responded with a breathless little sigh and arched her neck.

Jason clamped her to him like a vise. Her breasts burned like twin peaks of fire against his chest. Her fingers clutched his shoulders, then trailed down the smooth expanse of his back. Her breath was warm and misty in his mouth. The sound of her soft panting drove him into a frenzy. He eased her back against the mattress and closed his eyes against the intense pleasure that swept through him.

Memory trailed a distant second when compared to reality. Touching Kate like this, feeling her soft body tremble against his. The sensations were indescribable, nothing at all like he remembered. It was better. *Better.*

Then suddenly he tore his mouth from hers. "God, Kate. How could you do it? How could you leave me?"

CHAPTER EIGHT

HIS TORMENTED CRY shattered the spell they were under.

Beneath him, Kate froze. With a low groan, Jason pulled away and rose to his feet. His jaw clenched tight, he fought to control his runaway emotions. His shoulders were stiff with tension.

Kate stared at him, at the blurred outline of his back. "Jason..."

He sent her a quick glance over his shoulder. Then, without a word, he moved silently back to the couch and resumed his place there.

The utter desolation Kate sensed in him made her heart ache. And he made her feel ashamed—for both of them. "Jason, please." She forced the sound past the tight constriction in her throat. "What do you want from me?"

"Not a thing. I want nothing from you, Kate."

She stared at him helplessly. "But you said—"

"Forget what I said!" The sound cracked through the air like a whip. His head snapped around at the strangled sound she made. He closed his eyes and made a conscious effort to lessen his biting tone. "It doesn't matter." He hesitated. "I'm sorry. I shouldn't have said anything."

"And what about now? Are we supposed to pretend this never happened?"

"Nothing happened," he denied flatly. "It was just a kiss. No more, no less. Let's just forget it. I'll see that it doesn't happen again." He rolled over and drew the sheet over his shoulder. "Good night, Kate."

The cold finality in his tone stunned her. Just a kiss, he said. Just as they were only words. But his words stabbed at her like the point of a knife, sharp and piercing.

Nothing had changed between them, she thought tiredly. Nothing.

KATE AWOKE SLOWLY the next morning, drowsy and lethargic. It was like wading through a dense fog, until she heard the sound of the shower running. Then her eyes swung immediately to the couch. The pillow, sheets and blankets lay in a neat pile at the far end, the only sign Jason had slept there.

Slipping out of bed, she pulled on her robe. She was a little surprised at how well she'd slept. Peering out of the window, she saw that the day was bright and sunny. A few wispy clouds dallied above the purple haze of mountains. She recalled hearing someone mention at dinner last night that it rained nearly every afternoon during the summer. Gazing at the brilliant blue sky, she found it hard to believe.

The door to the bathroom opened, then closed. In spite of the previous night, Kate had prepared herself to be civil to Jason at all costs. But the sight of him rendered her speechless. In the cold light of day, he suddenly seemed larger than life.

The towel he'd used to dry himself was draped carelessly around his neck. He hadn't yet bothered to comb his hair and it lay in damp, unruly waves across his forehead. He wore a pair of tight jeans that proclaimed his male status in a way that was far too keen for Kate's peace of mind. His thickly haired pectorals drew her gaze for an endless moment before drifting helplessly to the bronzed hardness of his arms.

With his tousled hair, bare chest and whipcord leanness, he looked raw, undisciplined, and very, very sexy.

"Sleep okay?" He tossed the towel onto the dresser.

When she finally found her voice, it was polite and formal. "Fine, thanks. And you?"

Jason grimaced. "Don't ask."

He pulled a shirt from his bag. "I got the rest of your things this morning." He nodded toward the closet. "They're in there." He shrugged into the shirt, then began to deal deftly with the buttons. "By the way, Wade's bringing some rolls up for breakfast in about half an hour."

She frowned. "Wade?"

"Wade Nelson. My buddy with the DEA. I took a look around on this floor and couldn't find a place for someone to hide without being seen. But if someone's hanging around downstairs waiting for us to show up, I think it's better that Wade not be seen with us. So I asked him to meet us here instead." His gaze was impersonal as he took in her nightgown and robe. "Think you can be ready by then?" His mild tone indicated that he didn't think she was capable of managing in twice that time.

Kate hid a triumphant smile when she emerged from the bathroom fifteen minutes later. Her hair was loose and swirled damply around her shoulders, but his surprised look was gratifying. She wore a lacy white camisole top over pleated beige slacks, dressed up by a short-sleeved cover-up.

Kate wasn't quite certain what kind of man to expect when there was a knock at the door a few minutes later, but it certainly wasn't the man that Jason greeted. She placed Wade's age at somewhere near her own. Big, tall and ruddy-cheeked, his friendly, outgoing attitude put her at ease almost immediately. At first sight she had a hard time picturing him infiltrating the drug rings that operated between Mexico and the United States. But with a change of clothes, and his face roughened by a day's growth of beard, Kate decided he would be rather intimidating. A little, she realized with an odd pang in her stomach, like Jason.

Jason did most of the talking while they lingered over a breakfast of rich, strong coffee and small pastries, elegantly flavored with almond and nuts. Still, she felt a spurt of indignation that Jason was so up-front about Greg's kidnapping and the ransom demand. But she soon discovered that Jason was deftly feeling Wade out, to see if Greg was under any suspicion by the DEA. She wondered if Wade was aware of it, too. And when a silent look passed between the two men, she was certain he was.

"There's been a number of kidnappings over the last few years," Wade said, rubbing his chin. "But most of them have been drug related." He looked straight at Kate. "This looks like another grab-the-nearest-rich-Yankee scheme. It's certainly not unusual these days."

In spite of his grim overtone, she felt some of her fears lessen. Perhaps Greg wasn't involved in anything illegal after all. Maybe they'd been too quick to jump to that conclusion.

"But I do know one thing." Wade glanced from Kate to Jason, and back again. "I wouldn't want to deal with a gang who was behind something like this. Some of them are pretty radical. And if you can't pay up..." He shook his head.

There was no need for him to elaborate. Kate got his message loud and clear. The color drained from her cheeks, leaving them almost bloodless. She didn't realize her hand had stolen into Jason's until she felt him lightly squeeze her fingers.

"We need all the help we can get." Jason looked straight at Wade. "Any suggestions?"

The other man's eyes narrowed thoughtfully. "Maybe," he said slowly. "I know of a few places you could get some information." He smiled apologetically at Kate. "No place for a lady, though. Dives—all of them."

Kate seized on his words. At this point she was ready to grasp at straws. When Wade left a short time later, she stood up and grabbed her purse from the dresser. Her chin lifted the second her eyes caught Jason's. Already she could see the warning signs on his face. "I'm going with you," she said firmly.

His mouth tightened. "There's no point," he stated firmly.

"I don't care," she announced. "I'm still going with you."

"Damn it, you heard Wade. Don't you have any idea what kind of places he meant? They're bars, Kate, and believe me, that's a hell of a nice name for these hell-holes."

"I've been in bars before."

He swore at her lofty tone. "Not like these, you haven't. Wade wasn't kidding when he said they were no place for a lady. Hell, a lot of them won't even let a woman through the door! Besides, what if the kidnapper calls?"

"He said it would be tonight, and he can hardly expect us to stay cooped up in this room every minute of the day. As for being followed, I've seen the traffic in this city. If we take a cab, then walk a few blocks and pick up another cab, we should be able to lose him.''

Jason glared at her, but he finally relented. "All right." His tone was abrupt. He didn't bother to hide his disapproval. "You can come, but don't say you weren't warned." He glanced at her disdainfully. "You'll have to change your clothes, though. Did you bring any jeans?"

She had, as he soon discovered. They were of the faded, weather-beaten variety. Jason took one look at her and wished to hell he hadn't.

Kate ran the brush through her hair one last time. Dark and shiny, it fell thick and loose around her shoulders. Behind her in the mirror, she saw Jason's mouth form a thin, straight line.

"What's the matter? Don't you like the way I look?" Her voice was innocence itself. She bent over to tie her tennis shoes.

Jason fought a losing battle with himself. His eyes feasted on the sight she presented him. He liked, all right. He liked too damn much.

"Come on," he muttered. How he managed to tear his gaze from her delectably rounded derriere, he never knew. "Let's go."

The place they were headed for was on the opposite side of the city, and Kate quickly decided that the cab driver was a madman. But as her horrified eyes witnessed too many near misses to count, she hastily revised her opinion. *All* drivers in the city appeared to have something in common—they were either in a very great hurry or they harbored a death wish.

The noon-hour traffic was, at best, a snarled mess. Nor did it help matters that many of the streets appeared to run obstacle courses around the city's numerous small squares and parks. Finally Jason lost patience as well. It was nearly one o'clock when they paid the driver and got out to walk.

A city of many faces…Kate was reminded of her first impression of Mexico City. The gloriously sunny day was almost obscene. The street was narrow and littered with rubbish. A group of children played with a ball there. A van roared around the corner, blaring its horn. The children scattered. Several men leaned idly against a crumbling brick storefront, passing a bottle between them.

"So," she murmured, just loud enough for Jason to hear. "This is the seamier side of town."

Jason glanced at her. He half-expected her to be paralyzed with fear. The Kate he'd once known would have been horrified over a place like this, maybe even a little disdainful. The eyes that briefly met his were cautious but unafraid. But this was the new Kate, he reminded himself.

And the new Kate was even more dangerous than the old. Granted, he still thought it would have been wiser if she'd stayed at the hotel, but he admitted to a certain admiration about the way she was handling this whole situation with Greg. She could have let someone else—him, for instance—call the shots, thus relieving herself of the responsibility.

She was independent and self-sufficient, without being too damned aggressive. He liked that; he especially liked it in Kate. For just a second he couldn't help but wonder what would have happened all those years ago, if she had just been a little more assertive.

But nonetheless he knew better than to get emotionally involved with her again. The kiss last night, that wonderful, impossible, soul-shattering kiss, told the story only too well. Seeing her, being with her again, close enough to touch but knowing he didn't dare…it was like salt on an open wound. She and Greg might not be married anymore, but didn't the fact that she was so determined to rescue him prove that she still cared for him?

He had no intention of beginning the slow-going process of trying to forget Kate yet a second time in his life. He had no words to describe the hellish torment he'd gone through the first time. It had taken months before he could even think of her without feeling rejected and betrayed all over again. And in spite of his loneliness and despair, he had still loved her. Once was enough, he reflected grimly. Once was more than enough.

The bar—its English translation, The Little Castle— was exactly the hole-in-the-wall Jason had expected. The door was propped open by a weathered chunk of wood. He laid a hand on Kate's arm a few feet away from the entrance.

"You sure you want to go through with this?"

She nodded.

"This isn't like any place you've ever been to, Kate."

"Consider me warned." Her slender eyebrows lifted. "Several times already."

He seemed about to say something, but suddenly he frowned. "Didn't you bring that jacket you had on this morning?"

Kate made a face at his abrupt tone. "In case you hadn't noticed, it's hot." She began to take offense at the way his eyes traveled over her bare arms and shoulders. She hadn't bothered to change the lacy little top, thinking he wanted her to look casual and offhand. But now she could see his point. "Bad move, huh?" She smiled weakly.

For once, it seemed, they were in agreement. "Just remember," he warned her, "whatever I do or say, go along with it. Okay?"

To his dismay, she propped her hands on her hips and looked at him askance. "Meaning, I suppose, that if I open my mouth, I'll put my foot in it?"

"I didn't say that." He looked even more stern than he sounded. "Damn it, Kate, why do you always have to argue."

"Oh, all right." She made a face, but couldn't resist adding smartly, "Yes, sir. Anything you say, sir."

Jason's forearm dropped heavily on her shoulder the second they entered the cantina. It didn't take long for Kate to realize the reason behind Jason's action. Every male eye was glued to her figure when they walked in. She instinctively pressed closer to Jason, her mockery extremely short-lived. Suddenly, she, too, questioned her sanity in coming to this place.

The smell of grease, stale liquor and acrid smoke assaulted her. She kept her eyes carefully glued straight ahead as they walked across the rough wooden floor toward the far corner.

The chair she sat on was wobbly, the table even worse. The wall near her shoulder had once been painted a pale beige; it was now a muddied shade of brown, the spidery surface cracked and peeling.

Jason nudged the other chair closer to hers and sat down. To someone else, it probably looked as if he wanted to be near her, but Kate knew better. This way he had an unrestricted view of the cantina.

"Well?" Again he draped his arm around the back of her chair. "What do you think of The Little Castle?"

Kate turned her head slightly. In spite of his scoffing tone, there was only a gentle resignation in his expression.

"It—it's not so bad." To her horror, her voice cracked slightly.

But the warmth that flickered in Jason's eyes soon had her on the verge of a smile. "Stay put," he told her quietly. One corner of his mouth tipped into his mustache. "Unfortunately, I'm going to have to get us something to drink."

Before she had a chance to either agree or disagree, he rose. Kate was stunned at the instantaneous transition. His face became cold and hard, void of any warmth whatsoever.

When he brought back two tall glasses of amber-colored liquid, she eyed them dubiously. Surprisingly, the glasses looked reasonably clean.

"It's beer, Kate." Again there was a flash of warmth in his eyes as he caught her look. He lowered his head to hers. "You don't have to drink it, but at least put it to your mouth once in a while so it looks like you are. I don't want anyone to get suspicious and think I'm a cop, so we'll have to sit here for a while before I can start getting too nosy."

Just then a voice rose above the rest. Jason's head snapped up, and he stared at a man sitting across from them at the bar. The man who had spoken was unshaven and thoroughly unsavory looking. He grinned nastily, glanced pointedly at Kate and wagged his eyebrows, then repeated whatever it was he'd said.

Kate's eyes slid back to Jason. His features were hard and remote, his face that of a stranger as he gave a sharp, terse reply in Spanish. The man shrugged and turned his back.

"What did he want?"

"You." Jason's tone was swift and savage. "Mexico is a country known for its bartering, and nothing is sacred, it seems."

"You mean—" She let out a gasp as his hand cupped her shoulder. She was drawn so close to him she was practically sitting on his lap.

"Don't look so surprised." His hand tucked a loose strand of hair behind her ear. He sounded rather irritated. "Why do you think I didn't want you to come?"

"What did you tell him?"

His smile didn't quite reach his eyes. "What do you think? I told him you were mine. Now we're going to have to make sure no one else gets any ideas."

Her wide green eyes met his. "You mean—"

"I do." His head lowered slowly. He nuzzled the soft skin just behind her ear. "Just pretend you're enjoying it."

A lean hand came up to tilt her face ever so slightly toward his. His touch was in direct contrast to the hardness of his voice. In spite of his warning, it took Kate by surprise, but only for a moment.

He kissed her full on the mouth. It was a long, leisurely exploration that made Kate's insides knot with a purely sensual excitement, while her limbs turned bone-meltingly limp. It was a good thing she was sitting down, she thought hazily, because surely she'd have fallen down otherwise.

She knew what Jason was up to. He was staking a claim on her, a purely male stamp of possession. While she was aware that it was strictly for someone else's benefit, Kate certainly didn't have to pretend she was enjoying anything, because she was. And she had the feeling Jason was, too, and somehow that only intensified the pleasure his seeking mouth and hands evoked. Now, if only she could forget they were the main attraction at a cheap side show...

Her breathing was soft and shallow when he finally lifted his head. "I don't suppose we could continue this later?" she murmured huskily.

The fingers that he'd slipped into her hair tightened their grip. The hand at her back slipped around to chart the narrow indentation of her waist. He rested his forehead against hers. His eyes conveyed a warning that was entirely different from the one he'd given the man sitting at the bar.

"Kate, for crying out loud, don't look at me like that," he began, then was surprised to feel a laugh coming on. She was studying his mouth in a way that was both playful and tantalizing. Before he could say more, her lashes lifted and she smiled, a slow, sweet smile that made him want to drag her into his arms and shut out the rest of the world.

But Greg was out there somewhere. He heaved a silent sigh of resignation. It wouldn't do to forget why they were here, he thought caustically, and that was exactly what he reminded Kate.

The light faded from her eyes so abruptly it was as if a candle had been snuffed out by a fierce gust of wind. One moment bright and radiant, the next dark and shadowed. The look of pain that flitted across her face left Jason in no doubt that she was feeling guilty.

He scraped the chair back roughly. "I'm going to see if I can find out anything," he said curtly.

He took a seat at the bar, far enough away that she couldn't make out his voice very well above the other noise in the room, but close enough that no one else thought he'd deserted her. One long leg was thrust out in front of him as if he hadn't a care in the world. The bartender didn't seem inclined to talk at first; Kate could tell Jason was having a difficult time drawing him out. But twenty minutes later, that wasn't the case. Several other patrons came up beside Jason, and it wasn't long before he appeared to have been accepted as another one of the boys.

Occasionally one of the men turned covetous eyes on Kate. One even started to amble toward her, but a single warning look from Jason was enough to send him back to his seat in a hurry.

Kate scarcely noticed. She remained where she was in the corner, her hands curled around her beer glass. Once again, Jason had made her feel ashamed of her feelings for him, feelings that she was finding it harder and harder to deny. The physical attraction that had always existed between them hadn't lessened over time. But Jason was fighting it tooth and nail, and she had no idea how to overcome his guard, or whether she should even try. The specter of the past still loomed before her, before both of them. They had both hurt each other so deeply. Could either one of them ever forget that?

AN HOUR LATER they left the bar.

"Find out anything?" Kate asked.

Jason shook his head. "No." He gave her a long, cold look. "Most of them were a lot more interested in looking at you than they were in talking."

"So now it's my fault?" Kate's temper sparked. "Typical, Jason Davalos—very typical!"

"You're too much of a distraction, Kate." His tone was cool. "You can't expect me to learn anything when I have to spend half my time watching out for you. That's why you're going back to the hotel while I check out the other places Wade told us about. I'll try to get back before the call comes through." He held up a hand as the telltale warning signs appeared in her face. "I don't like the idea of leaving you alone, but I think you'll be a lot safer there than with me. But for heaven's sakes, stay in the room and be careful just in case!''

Kate disliked the idea of being left behind more than being left alone, but she grudgingly conceded the logic behind his reasoning. And she had to admit to being just a little pleased by Jason's show of concern for her safety. It was worth it to be left behind, for that reason alone.

But the rest of the day dragged endlessly, while her mind raced away. Here she was, sitting in a nice, comfortable hotel room, while Greg was...where? Was he hungry? Thirsty? Broiling away in an attic somewhere, trussed up like an animal, unable to move? Unable to call for help? This was Tuesday. He'd been snatched more than four days ago.

In an effort to calm herself, Kate checked in with Rita and Toby late in the afternoon and impulsively phoned Rosa as well. Jason's sister seemed genuinely glad to hear from her; she sounded far less tense and unhappy than she had on Sunday.

Both calls provided only a brief diversion, though. By the time ten o'clock rolled around Kate was champing at the bit. The kidnappers still hadn't called yet. Every few seconds she glanced at the phone, wanting desperately to hear it ring but terrified as well.

She was also worried about Jason. Knowing that he was nosing around in places that were far from reputable made her even more anxious. Had something happened to him? He could have been robbed or assaulted. He was a stranger. Who would come to his aid? Or perhaps he'd discovered something about Greg after all, and decided to take matters into his own hands without her. Or—God forbid!—the caller last night had made good his threat.

Around and around her mind roiled. Finally, just before midnight, Jason opened the door.

"Jason!" She rushed forward. Her eyes moved frantically over his tall figure. His hair was rumpled, his shirt unbuttoned halfway to his waist, revealed a jungle of wiry dark hair. She jerked her eyes away from the disturbing sight of his naked chest. "I've been so worried about you! Are you all right?"

"I'm fine, Kate. Perfectly fine." His steps didn't waver as he advanced slowly across the room.

Kate frowned. He sounded different, as if he was very, very tired. She watched as he halted before the small table in front of the window. He kept his back to her when he reached down to pull something out of his boot. She didn't realize what it was until the light from across the room glinted off the polished surface.

A gun. Jason was carrying a gun. He appeared totally at ease, his lean hands dark and capable looking as he weighed the gun casually in his palm.

Kate stayed where she was near the doorway. She couldn't take her eyes from the small-caliber weapon. "My God," she said faintly. "Is that thing loaded?"

He laid it carefully on the table. "It wouldn't do me much good if it weren't."

Her eyes flashed accusingly up to his face. "Where did you get it? You didn't have it in your bag. You wouldn't have gotten on board the plane with it, let alone through customs!"

"I picked it up this morning."

"This morning!" She put her hands on her hips. "Where was I?" she demanded.

His half of the room now danced with shadows. Kate couldn't quite make out his expression, but she saw his mouth curve slowly upward.

"In bed," he said very softly.

His slow, seductive grin, coupled with the husky undertone of his voice, made Kate's heart turn over. He looked and sounded so much like the Jason of long ago, the Jason she had fallen wildly in love with. She stared at him, and as their eyes met for a never-ending moment, she felt they had stepped back in time.

But something wasn't quite right. "You could have told me," she said, nodding toward the weapon. She inched closer. "I might have felt a little safer this afternoon."

"I didn't want to scare you." Again he spoke in that slow, carefully concise tone. Kate eyed him suspiciously. Now that she thought about it, weren't his eyes rather bright?

She watched as he pulled off his shirt, then moved around the end of the bed to toss it on the dresser. As he did, a distinctive odor drifted her way. She stared at him. "You're drunk!"

"I probably am," he murmured agreeably. He sat down on the edge of the bed. Again that lazy grin danced across his mouth. "I couldn't very well spend the evening in one bar after another and stay sober, now, could I?"

He had her there. Kate wasn't sure whether to laugh or cry as he pulled off his boots. She ended up doing neither. "Well?" she inquired crossly. "Was it worth it?"

He heaved a long sigh. "I probably won't think so tomorrow morning."

She wasn't inclined to argue that point. "Did you find out anything?" she asked again.

His smile was as complacent as any she'd ever seen. "Wade will be dancing on his head." He looked up at her suddenly. "Don't let me forget to give him a call in the morning."

"Jason!" She couldn't hide her annoyance. "You weren't supposed to be there spying for Wade Nelson. Didn't you find out anything about Greg?"

"Greg?" He frowned at her. "It would help if I knew where the airstrip was. But no one seemed to know for sure...."

She couldn't believe it when he reached out and switched off the lamp nearest the bed.

Kate resisted the urge to stomp her foot. She could almost believe he was doing this on purpose—building her up, only to leave her dangling. She plunged forward and knocked her shin on the footboard. "Damn it, Jason, don't stop now! What about this airstrip? And what about Greg?"

A gentle snore was her only reply. Her shoulders slumped wearily. It seemed her answers would have to wait until morning, after all, for her tormentor was fast asleep.

And this time he was the one who had claimed the bed.

CHAPTER NINE

THE BOLD, BRILLIANT SUNLIGHT that streamed through the lightly woven drapes heralded the arrival of a new day. From somewhere the distant rush of water could be heard. The sound of footsteps echoed in the hallway, followed by a trilling feminine laugh.

Jason's mind was somewhat slower in responding. There was a curious lassitude in his limbs, a feeling of well-being that he hadn't felt in a long, long time.

But along with the feeling of contentment, there was also an unfamiliar warmth that spread along one whole side of his body. Swimming through the mists of semi-consciousness, he opened his eyes to examine the source of that warmth.

Kate. Her head was nested cozily in the hollow of his shoulder. Silken strands of mahogany whispered across his chest. Her breath misted warmly against his neck. She lay with her body molded lightly against his, held there by his arms. It was as if she had sought...and he had found.

A dozen strange and powerful emotions surged through him. He was immersed in the sight and scent and sound of this woman. Just being like this with Kate, with no demands, no commitments, no complications of past or future. There was only the blessed contentment of the present, the richness of being so close to her once more.

His lungs filled with air, and he closed his eyes. He would hold her like this, just a moment longer. Because then he could forget and pretend that she was his once more.

Kate awoke with the same lethargy, the same sense of rightness, of belonging. Her eyelids drifted open, and she realized she was lying next to Jason. She could see each crinkly dark hair that grew so thickly scant inches from her nose; feel the rise and fall of his chest with every breath that he took.

Her hand rested in the middle of his chest. The contrast between their skin was striking. Though she had acquired a light tan over the summer months, Jason's skin was a dark shade of teak, the wiry hair beneath her skin darker yet.

At some point in the night he must have discarded his jeans. She was suddenly very conscious of the hair-roughened length of naked thigh pressed against her own. At the same time she realized his arm was curled warmly around her shoulder. His other hand rested on the hollow below his ribs. His fingers were lean and strong.

A tingly sensation feathered through her. This was the man who knew her as no other had known her. His mouth and body had completed her journey to womanhood; his tender hands and gentle lips had eased the pain of first love.

Kate experienced a rush of tenderness so strong she felt consumed by it. She lay unmoving, and let her eyes wander up the tanned column of his neck. Beneath the thick ribbon of his mustache, the cleanly sculpted outline of his mouth was relaxed and far less harsh than usual. Again, her eyes drifted lower.

It was then that she saw it—the tiny links of a chain, the glint of silver that lay just below the hollow of his throat. Surrounded by the dense mat hair that grew there, it was almost invisible.

Her mind reeled. She had purchased the medal at an antique store in Dallas when she was fifteen. It was no larger than the pad of her thumb, small but finely crafted. An eagle was pictured on the face, wings spread wide in flight. She had only to close her eyes to envision it circling and sweeping against the deep blue reaches of the sky, searching for something...

She had added it to her charm bracelet for a time, but she felt out of place wearing it. Then she had hidden it deep in her jewelry box, though she had always found it strangely fascinating. Contrary to the predatory image depicted on the medal, Kate saw only a lonely and wild creature of the earth.

It reminded her of Jason, with his piercing yellow-gold eyes that might have belonged to an eagle, and so she had given it to him. Her bird of prey had finally found a home, a home where he truly belonged. But she had never dreamed Jason would have kept it all this time, that he would even want to.

I'll wear it forever, he had told her. *Because it's a part of you. The part you gave to me....*

Conflicting emotions bombarded her from all sides. She wanted to shout for joy. Sob in despair, for everything she had turned her back on. Cry for all the lost and lonely years without him.

So many times now, she had thought of Jason as a stranger, a cold and hostile stranger. He was always tense, as if he were on guard against her. Oddly, it was a notion that she found both distressing and pleasing. And perhaps it was unintentional on Jason's part, but every so often—on the plane, and the night before last—the tender, compassionate man she had once known slipped through. Within him, hidden deep inside, was the man she had fallen in love with.

"Kate?"

It took a moment to still the uneven beat of her heart. "Yes?" She hardly dared to breathe.

"How long have you been awake?"

There was something in his tone, something she was almost afraid to put a name to. "A while." There was only the slightest hesitation in her voice.

Was that a smile she felt against her forehead? Her heart suddenly felt as if it had taken on a pair of wings.

"About last night." He paused. "I was pretty drunk, wasn't I?"

She finally braved a glance at his face. The hint of uncertainty she detected there made her chuckle. "You weren't very coherent."

"I'm sorry I didn't make it back earlier, but it was late before I started getting any leads at all. Then I had to wait over an hour for a cab." He fingered the silk-soft strands of hair that brushed her shoulder. "I wanted to be here when the kidnappers—"

Kate bit her lip. "He didn't call," she said in a low voice. "I only hope it's not a sign that they've changed their mind about waiting for the money."

"I don't think so." Jason's tone was thoughtful. "If that was the case, they'd have told you no deal right away. If they back out now, they gain nothing."

Jason was right. Kate felt herself relax once more, feeling oddly reassured by his warmth next to her.

It was Jason who broke the comfortable silence, backtracking slightly. "Why—" he cleared his throat "— why didn't you make sure I slept on the couch?"

"You put yourself to bed," she teased lightly. "And you took my side." It was funny how she found herself remembering that so suddenly. "Now, before you ask why I didn't take the couch...I guess I'm just not as noble as you are."

It was amazing how something as small as a smile could change his whole appearance. "It's not very comfortable," he assured her.

He seemed as reluctant as she to break this gentle mood that had sprung up between them. A part of her wanted to ask so many things. Like why his eyes were filled with such distrust whenever he looked at her, and why he still wore her medal. Was it foolish to assume he did so because it still meant something to him? Or was she simply being too feminine and sentimental?

She tried not to be so achingly aware of the strong male hand that slid down her arm as she propped herself on her elbow to gaze down at him. His jaw was shadowed with a day's growth of beard. He looked dark. Rugged. Sexy.

She felt suddenly nervous. "You must have quite a hangover." Her tongue darted out to moisten her lips.

A hangover? More like a heartache, he thought, watching the path her tongue traced around the outline of her mouth. He longed to echo the movement, to taste her essence and capture it for his own.

He shook his head. "Surprisingly, no." He had to fight the urge to keep his eyes trained on hers, but even so, he saw far too much. She didn't seem to have noticed that the sheet had slipped down around her hips. Her nightgown clung to the slender shape of her body. He gritted his teeth and tried to look away, but he couldn't.

The rosy, sleep-flushed sheen of her flesh lured him. Beneath the flimsy material, the pouting thrust of dusk-hued nipples beckoned to him.

"Kate." He ignored the heat simmering in his veins, the pounding rush of desire in his belly. He purposely forced his concentration elsewhere. "Kate, we'd better get up. Last night I found out there's an abandoned airstrip somewhere in the mountains between here and Veracruz. I think it's worth checking out." He sat up and swung his legs over the bed.

Behind him, she sighed. "You still haven't told me—" Suddenly she stopped.

The sudden silence must have warned him. He swiveled around and saw Kate staring at him, her face frozen.

This was the first time she had seen his bare back up close. Above his waist, his skin was the same, smooth polished bronze she remembered. But near his left shoulder blade...Her fingers began to reach for him, but at the last second she drew back.

"Your shoulder." Her voice was shaky and faint. "My God, what happened?"

The way she looked at him, the horror on her face. The scar that zigzagged across his skin was long and jagged. He knew his shoulder wasn't a pretty sight. Shrapnel wounds never were, he thought caustically.

"Vietnam," he muttered, and reached for his shirt. "I got shot."

He would offer no more; that was very clear. But she sensed that he was hiding something, and a terrible thought abruptly seized her. "Does Greg have anything to do with this?"

Again she stretched her hand toward his shoulder, but this time Jason surged to his feet before she could make contact. He yanked on his jeans. "What makes you think that?" he asked tightly.

"The night I came to you to help me find Greg, you asked if I knew how Greg hated you. You said you didn't know it either, until you met again in Vietnam. I felt guilty because I—I knew it was because of me." A shadow slipped over her face. "But then you said that while it might have started with me, it didn't end there." Her gaze met his. "Something happened in Vietnam between you and Greg. I can feel it."

Jason said nothing.

Her eyes pleaded with him. "I have to know, Jason. What does Greg have to do with you getting shot?" Her voice caught. "Did *he* shoot you?"

He might as well have, Jason thought cuttingly. Aloud he muttered tersely, "No."

"Then what—"

He turned away. "It doesn't concern you."

"But why won't you—"

"Damn it, Kate! Just leave it alone!"

Jason didn't realize he'd shouted until he glanced back at her. She was staring at him, her eyes wide and full of hurt. The strap of her gown had slipped down over her arm, and somehow it only accentuated her look of vulnerability.

There was a hollow sensation in her chest. He was angry again, and he was closing her out. Some things never change, she thought sadly.

"Why?" Her voice trembled with the effort it took to speak. "Why do you do this to me?"

The torment on her face cut Jason to the quick. The muscles in his arms contracted. It took every ounce of willpower he possessed not to pull her into his arms. The pain of that need was almost more than he could stand. Theirs was a fatal attraction. He had no way of fighting it—and her—save one.

"I haven't done anything to you, Kate." His jaw tightened. "Commendable, under the circumstances, I'd say." His gaze slid over her meaningfully.

She detected no hint of softness there; nothing but cold contempt. She swallowed painfully. "You know what I mean."

"I'm not sure that I do." His tone was cool. Deliberately he turned his back on her.

Kate, having come this far, wasn't going to make it any easier for him. For nearly three days they had been treading lightly. But the battle between them suddenly had shifted to new ground, and this had nothing to do with Greg and Vietnam. She could see it in Jason's face each and every time that she looked at him. His bitterness. His resentment.

She knew intuitively that the strain of being together, every hour of the day and night, couldn't be borne by either of them for long. They had to confront the demons of the past. But Kate could see by his shuttered expression that Jason thought the subject was closed.

"You walked out on me fifteen years ago, Jason Davalos. I won't let you do it again—not until you hear what I have to say." Proudly she rose from the bed. Her chin lifted as she resolutely confronted him.

Jason was already halfway across the room when her warning halted him. His eyes flickered, as if her words surprised him. Then again they grew cold. "I think you've got things a little mixed up, Kate," he told her in clipped tones. "You divorced me, as I recall."

She made a vague gesture with one hand. "I was very young." There was a huge lump in her throat. "And confused."

"Confused?" His laugh was short. "You have a very convenient memory. I didn't want the divorce and you knew it. I thought we should wait—try to straighten things out between us."

Her eyes suddenly filled with tears. "Then why didn't you ever tell me?" she whispered. "You won't talk to me now. You never talked to me then."

"Talk to you! How could I? I tried, Kate, I tried. But you could never see my side, only your father's. I felt like he'd poisoned your mind against me."

Did he think she didn't know that? Every word he spoke was like a rusty knife twisting slowly inside her.

The old bitterness welled up inside him, along with the sense of betrayal that had haunted him all this time. "My God, Kate, you'd just lost the baby—*our* baby! There wasn't even time to deal with that before some fancy lawyer slapped me with a divorce suit!" His eyes burned into her. "You wanted me out of your life, Kate. So I did what you wanted. I got out. I got as far away as I possibly could."

The tension between them had never been so thick. There had been many times when she'd felt guilty over what she had done to Jason, but never more than at this moment.

She couldn't stand to see him like this. So hard and so distant. So alone. She ached inside as much as Jason. More, because she was responsible.

She didn't realize she had moved until her fingers touched his arm. At the contact, she felt his body go tense and rigid. But the emotions that churned inside her were no less tumultuous, no less sincere. Somehow she had to convince him of that.

"I never wanted to hurt you." The words were little more than a ribbon of sound. "I never wanted—"

"No. I don't suppose you did." His eyes sliced into her with the same cutting edge as his voice. "I doubt you even considered me, especially once I was out of the way. You were too busy with Greg.''

''No.'' She shook her head. ''No!''

''Yes, Kate!'' His fingers bit into her arm. ''You went straight from me to Greg!''

''It wasn't like that. I didn't marry him until nearly a year later.'' She silently beseeched that he understand, but there was no give in him, none at all. His face was chiseled and remote. She began to grow desperate. ''Jason, I can explain!''

The seconds ticked by silently. A minute passed, then another. His fingers fell away from her arm. ''It's a little late for that, isn't it?''

The gentleness in his voice was almost her undoing. She didn't realize until that moment how much she'd been hoping that they could bridge the rift between them. Her lips scarcely moved. ''What about us?'' She felt awkward and exposed. ''The other night, when you kissed me...''

There was no need to go on. She could see that he understood.

''I won't deny there's still something between us. We both know it.''

Their gazes locked. It took a supreme effort, but somehow she forced the words past the hot ache in her throat. She was perilously close to breaking down. ''Then why—why are you fighting it?''

He seemed to hesitate. Then slowly, he bent and touched his lips to hers. It was the only point of contact between them, a delicate, undemanding kiss, so poignantly sweet and full of tenderness it made her heart and her eyes finally spill over.

She was trembling when he finally lifted his mouth.

"This is why, Kate." At first she didn't fully comprehend. It wasn't until the tip of his index finger traced the salty trail of a tear down her cheek that she understood.

"It's no different now than before. We should both know to leave well enough alone." He looked at the glistening pad of his thumb and then at her. "All we do is hurt each other."

Kate couldn't look away as he turned his back on her. Oddly, the quiet resignation in his voice pierced her more than all his angry words.

THE INCIDENT scarcely made things easier for either of them. Kate was afraid, desperately afraid that she had never stopped loving Jason. Her father had stood between them before; now it was Greg. If only she knew what Greg had done, why Jason hated him so. She had never doubted his reasons for consenting to help rescue Greg; he had done it for her, which meant that he cared. It wounded her deeply to know that his feelings for her were unwilling, even unwanted. And yet he was right, so right. Hurt and pain were all that had been accomplished with their love.

Was it any wonder that her mind rebelled at the thought of loving Jason? Yet her heart knew; her heart urged otherwise. Dark as the world seemed at this moment, she just couldn't forget that Jason still wore the medal she had given him so long ago.

On Jason's part, the whole situation with Greg was getting to him, just as Kate had already gotten to him. He sprawled in the chair, waiting for Kate to emerge from the shower.

He had far too many weak spots where she was concerned, he recognized grimly. He derived no satisfaction from hurting her. Yet his bitterness, his resentment—

those he understood. She had run off with his best friend. His best friend, damn it! It didn't matter that it had happened fifteen years ago; it might have been yesterday! He hated what she had done to him. He hated what both of them had done, yet here he was, doing his damnedest to find Greg!

But what he didn't understand was this bone-melting tenderness she still managed to arouse in him. There were times he felt so out of control when he was with her. He had no idea what he was going to do or say from one minute to the next.

He couldn't be with her without wanting her, without aching to hold her close to him once more. He remembered what it was like to slide his fingers through her hair, to trace and linger over every square inch of her body, to feel the wildly sinuous motion of her hips as she moved against him in perfect harmony. He ached to lose himself in her sweet, feminine warmth in a way that bound them forever.

Only one thing could ease the ache inside him and quench the wrenching desire in his soul. Only one thing, and that was impossible. Casual sex was something he had never indulged in. And to think of doing so with Kate! It was almost laughable. There was no way on earth he could ever lay a hand on her and keep his mind and heart separate from the needs of his body.

Jason had never felt so empty. But once again, he reflected with a tight little smile, his feelings made no sense. He also felt linked to her, bound by some invisible cord that refused to be severed, no matter how hard he tried.

He tried not to look at her when she emerged from the shower, but he couldn't help it. Her hair was still damp, parted and drawn back into its usual style. He was inexplicably annoyed, yet he knew he'd have been just as annoyed if she'd worn it long and loose as she had yesterday. If she was still upset, she hid it behind a facade of cool poise. She looked remote and unapproachable as she closed the bathroom door.

Kate felt Jason's eyes on her as she crossed the room. Her steps carried her to the dresser, where she tried very hard to avoid looking at the rumpled bedclothes reflected in the mirror.

"About the airfield you mentioned earlier—the one in the mountains." She cleared her throat, then pulled a silk scarf from the drawer and began to tie it around her neck. "You said it was abandoned?"

Jason nodded.

"Surely someone knows something about it. The main airport—"

He was shaking his head. "No one was supposed to know about it. Apparently it was once a drop-off point for drug smugglers, but it hasn't been used for years."

She frowned, her fingers motionless for a second. "But I don't see what that has to do with Greg's kidnapping."

"His plane didn't just disappear into thin air. And we know it didn't crash." He cursed himself for even mentioning it when he saw Kate blanch. "I wish the kidnappers would let you know the drop-off point. Then at least we'd have some idea where to look. As it is, our hands are practically tied. Is he here in Mexico City? Or Veracruz? Or somewhere in between. We don't even know how and when Greg was taken."

Kate turned slowly, her back to the mirror. "Manuel Ortega said he was alone when he left here. It just doesn't make sense."

"It doesn't," Jason agreed. "Which means Greg must have picked up someone en route."

Someone? Kate turned around and caught his grim expression. "Whoever kidnapped him, you mean. And maybe, just maybe, it was at the airfield you mentioned."

"It makes sense, Kate." He held her gaze evenly.

She closed her eyes. "You still think he's smuggling, don't you?"

Did Greg really mean that much to her? He curbed the sharp retort that sprang to his lips at the distress in her voice. "That was Jeff's opinion," he reminded her. "And you can't deny that what Manuel Ortega said didn't put Greg in the clear."

The silence stretched out. Everything Jason said made sense, but she still hated to think that Greg was involved in something illegal. Damn Greg! How could he be so stupid? She was suddenly furious with him, but far stronger was a sickening feeling of dread. This was Wednesday; she and Jason had been here for two days already! The kidnappers wouldn't wait around forever. As soon as they realized she had lied about the ransom, it *could* be all over for Greg... Oh, God, she didn't even want to think about that!

She began to pace around the room. "Maybe we should talk to Mr. Ortega again, find out for sure if Greg planned on flying straight through to Veracruz. And the man he mentioned seeing with Greg—maybe we can find out who he is."

Jason had moved to the window and was gazing out at the traffic below. At the sound of her voice, he turned. The frantic desperation reflected on Kate's face cut into him. He longed to pull her into his arms, but he knew he didn't dare.

"And what if your friend calls about Greg?" he asked finally. "If no one's here, what then?"

"Then he'll just have to call again!" she cried, clenching her fists in frustration. "Damn it, Jason, I can't just sit here wringing my hands. We have to do something. If nothing else, I think one of us should talk to Ortega."

"It can't hurt," he agreed reluctantly. "But I have to see Wade this morning. The DEA may have some topographical maps that could help us locate the airfield. But checking the maps could take hours." He hesitated. "Although I suppose Wade could come to the room again."

"Then you'd be here in case the kidnappers call. And I can go on up to Hidalgo Field and talk to Ortega."

Jason seemed skeptical. "I don't know, Kate. I don't like the idea of you being alone for so long."

Maybe some time alone was *exactly* what they needed, she speculated silently. Kate could see by the way Jason stood stiffly on the other side of the room, his hands thrust into his pockets, that the recent exchange between them was still fresh in his mind.

"I'll be fine, Jason." Her tone was pleading. "You can see me safely into a cab headed for Hidalgo Field and ask the driver to come back for me later." She grabbed her purse from the dresser, opened it and grabbed a tiny printed book that she waved in front of her. "If worse comes to worst, I've got pencil and paper and a Spanish-English dictionary. Awkward, I'll admit, but I think I could manage to get the point across. And the exchange rate is—"

"All right, all right." Jason held up his hands. "What time do you think you'll be back?"

"As long as I'm there, I might as well have a look around and see if there's anything in Greg's office that might give us a clue." She thought quickly. "You can send the cab back for me about three."

He hesitated, then finally nodded his agreement. Kate wasted no time in grabbing the phone and calling Ortega at the airfield to let him know she was coming.

She and Jason had just entered the hallway when Kate turned to him. "Oh, I forget to tell you. I called home last night."

He closed the door behind them, then checked to make sure it was locked. "To talk to Toby?"

"Yes."

"How's he bearing up? Missing you, I'll bet."

Kate glanced at him as they moved toward the elevator, a little surprised at the familiar way Jason spoke of her son. But when she recalled his gentleness with Toby at the airport, perhaps it wasn't so surprising after all.

She smiled wistfully. "Not as much as I miss him." There was a group of people in front of the elevator. She followed as Jason bypassed them and headed for the stairs. "I called Rosa, too," she added as an afterthought.

He halted so abruptly she nearly barreled into him. She grabbed for the handrail. When he spun around on his heel, they were only a step apart, Kate above and Jason below. He stared directly into her startled eyes.

"You what?"

Kate blinked at the gritty demand, then became aware of his sudden tension. "I called Rosa," she repeated. "Is there something wrong with that?"

When he didn't answer, she straightened her spine. "I just wanted to make sure everything was okay." She matched his gaze and went on coolly, "You hadn't checked with her, had you?"

"No." A muscle in his lean cheek jerked. "I suppose Nick was there with her."

Kate was already beginning to regret telling Jason of the call. "She didn't say," she told him quickly. It wasn't an out-and-out lie, but she must have hesitated a second too long.

Jason looked away and muttered something under his breath. He turned and started down the stairs once more, leaving Kate staring at his broad back.

She had stirred up another hornet's nest, and that was exactly what she didn't need. Still, she couldn't help but feel rather protective of Jason's sister. Nick had said Jason wasn't giving him a fair shake, and seeing Jason's reaction just now, she could well believe it.

She caught up with him near the entrance to the lobby, in a small but secluded area. "Is there a reason Nick shouldn't be there with Rosa?"

Jason's mouth tightened. The slow, silent look he gave her conveyed a message she hadn't expected. Kate felt herself flush. All of a sudden she was reminded of far too many intimate encounters that had taken place in this man's arms while a small child had been tucked away in bed.

Nonetheless, she persisted. "Don't you trust her?"

Jason hesitated. He ran a hand through his black hair. Though his expression was hard, the gesture seemed oddly vulnerable. "I don't trust Nick," he said finally.

"Why? Because he's been in jail? He made a mistake. We all do. He shouldn't have to pay for the rest of his life." She looked up at him earnestly. "Besides, it's not only Nick you're hurting; you're hurting Rosa, too."

His eyes narrowed on her face. "How do you know so much about it? You only met them once. Once, Kate, and you're standing on your soapbox taking their side against me."

She flinched at the harshness in his voice. "They're old enough to know what they want," she replied quietly. "And Rosa loves him."

"He probably gives her the same song and dance." His whisper was no less than fierce. "And we both know why!"

"He wants to marry her."

"So he says. It's better that she find out now that Nick's not the right man for her." His eyes were hard as agates. "Do you think I don't know what he thinks about when he looks at her—when he touches her? Rosa's pretty; she's a sweet kid. Nick could probably talk her into anything. But I was young once, too, and I know exactly what's in his mind. I don't want to see her hurt, Kate. I don't want her to end up like us! Just because he wants to drag her into bed doesn't mean he wants to be tied down to her the rest of his life."

Hell! It didn't come out like he'd planned. He broke off as Kate's face whitened. She didn't say a word; she just stared at him. He couldn't tear his gaze away as all expression faded from her face. It was as if something inside her had just died.

That was exactly how Kate felt. The small scrap of hope she'd been half-heartedly nursing—the hope that she and Jason could somehow erase the past and start over—vanished in that instant. She scarcely noticed as he dragged his hand down his face. The low tenor of his voice seemed to come from very far away.

"Damn it, Kate I...we'll have to talk about this later. There's no time right now and I—I need to catch Wade before he leaves the office."

Numbly she let him put her in a cab. That Jason thought Nick's attraction to Rosa was purely physical was patently obvious. And all she could think was how Jason had compared Nick and Rosa with the two of them. A knifing pain slashed through her. Wasn't that how she'd thought of them right from the first?

She and Jason...and her father. Nick and Rosa...and Jason. Her eyes squeezed shut as the cab sped away from the curb. Jason was right. It was happening all over again.

Her heart ached for Rosa...almost as much as it ached for herself.

CHAPTER TEN

WITH SUCH A BEGINNING, Kate didn't think the day could get any worse. But if she had been hoping for an improvement, she soon discovered she was sadly mistaken.

Hidalgo Field consisted of a runway and two small trailers with a warehouse in between. Kate walked immediately to the one designated "McAllister." To her dismay, she found it was locked up tight as a drum. Manuel Ortega had been there less than an hour ago, she thought irritably. He had said nothing about leaving, so where was he now? She was certain she had said nothing to scare him off. Unfortunately, she had no choice but to wait until Manuel returned—and hope that he did.

An hour later she was still sitting on the single step in front of the trailer. The midday sun was hot and blazingly bright, but a thin layer of clouds had already started to gather above the mountain peaks, signaling the advent of the afternoon rain. There was a strong breeze, and she felt as if every pore in her body had been inundated by the grainy dust.

She brushed a stray hair from her cheek and glanced around the small airfield. Besides Greg's, there was one other cargo service. With a sigh, she got up and started in that direction, hoping that someone there might have a key.

Thankfully, the man inside spoke enough English to comprehend what she wanted. Whether he believed that she was part owner of Greg's business really didn't matter. He was polite, but firm; he had no key, and he knew of no one who did, except Greg and Manuel. She left empty-handed.

Her temper short, her frustration level at an all-time high, Kate slung her purse over her shoulder and marched toward Greg's trailer. This wouldn't be just another wasted effort, she vowed silently. Somehow she was going to get inside Greg's office, even if she had to break the door down.

But there was an easier way. It struck her as she rounded the corner of the trailer. She quickly backtracked to the side that faced away from the runway.

She glanced around, hoping the man she'd just talked to hadn't seen her. If he had, she had no doubt Jason would have to bail her out of a Mexico City jail. At the thought, a reluctant smile edged her mouth. At least then he would have something to be angry about.

The window was louvered. The panes of glass were simply dropped into the metal molding, much like a picture frame. One by one, she lifted them out and stacked them carefully on the ground. When all had been removed, there was just enough room for a child or a slender person to slip through the opening. Next she dragged a heavy concrete block she'd spotted nearby over to the window to use as a step. There! She was ready.

She had just stepped up on the block and placed her hands on the sill when suddenly the strangest sensation swept over her. It was as if someone were watching her...watching and waiting.

The feeling was gone before she knew it. Nonetheless, she scanned the area nervously once more. It was quiet and deserted, exactly as it had been the moment before. It took several dogged attempts, but finally Kate heaved herself up through the window and into the trailer.

Inside was a long counter, a cluttered desk, a filing cabinet and several chairs. Now what? she asked herself. Her gaze moved uncertainly around the room. If only Manuel were there. She'd been counting on him to point her in the right direction.

Some detective you'd make, she chided herself. Finally she sat down at the desk, switched on the lamp and pulled out the top drawer. Nothing unusual there. Pens, pencils, papers. The next drawer was more like it. She smiled her satisfaction and flipped open a dark green ledger.

Time passed. Kate painstakingly went over every scrap of paper—shipping statements, billing accounts—everything she could lay her hands on. There was nothing out of the ordinary; nothing that indicated Greg might be involved in any sort of wrongdoing. His cargo included everything from coffee to cotton, sugar to mining supplies. He apparently never bothered with a passenger list.

Dismayed and disappointed, she reached for the pile of invoices stacked in front of her. The top one had been billed to a mining company in San Seville.

Something clicked. She stared at the paper, her mind spinning. Greg had been carrying a shipment of silver the day he was kidnapped. San Seville wasn't far from here, three or four miles at the most. A quick glance at the map she'd found earlier confirmed it. And after what she'd spent on cab fare already, what were a few more pesos?

Her mind raced ahead. Maybe someone there could give her some leads. Certainly someone would know if the shipment was destined for Veracruz. This could be the missing link they'd been searching for.

JASON WAS GROWING more frantic by the moment. It had been nearly five when Wade had left the hotel, and Kate still hadn't arrived. That was nearly two hours ago. Where in God's name was she?

He had called the McAllister Air Express office countless times, and made a fruitless check with the cab company as well. He had even made the trip out to Hidalgo Field, only to find the place deserted. He'd then decided she was probably back at the hotel, waiting to give him hell for leaving in the first place. But she hadn't been.

He paced the room like a caged tiger. Back and forth, back and forth. Was she lost? He had been a fool to have let her go anywhere by herself. Maybe she'd been in an accident. She could be lying unconscious somewhere, alone and hurt. No one would know to contact him. They would think she was just another tourist.

Or maybe the kidnappers had gotten to her.

He was downstairs and in the lobby before he was even aware of it. Kate wouldn't like it, but he had no choice. It was time the police were informed of this nightmarish affair, and Greg McAllister be damned! He would never forgive himself if anything happened to her. He couldn't stand the thought of finding her again after all this time only to lose her.

Kate, Kate, Kate. Where are you? His mind conjured up all sorts of horrible visions, each one worse than the last. A sickening feeling of dread tightened his stomach when he pushed through the lobby doors to the street outside.

It only made his first glimpse of her all the more unbelievable. At any other time, he might even have laughed at the sight of a disheveled, sodden-looking Kate parading down the sidewalk toward the hotel entrance.

Her elegant little nose was tipped into the air as if she were entering a ballroom.

He ran to her. "Kate. My God, Kate!"

Hard hands caught her firmly by the shoulders. Jason's face flashed before her, then she found herself engulfed in a pair of warm male arms, snatched fiercely against a broad chest. The frantic throb of his heart pounded just below her ear.

She sagged against him. She was bone-tired and filthy; her clothes were torn, her face and hands were caked with dust. Her hair, half down and half up, still clung damply to her collar.

But suddenly the day didn't seem nearly as dark as it had the moment before.

"Where the hell have you been?" Jason drew back from her. His tone was a direct contrast to the gentle drift of his knuckles over her jawline. His hands resettled on her shoulders, as if reluctant to leave her.

Kate sighed and made a face. "Other than breaking into Greg's office, climbing half a mountain in San Seville, getting caught in a downpour, and then getting stuck in a horrendous traffic jam, and walking ten blocks home?" She shrugged. "Nowhere, I guess."

His hands fell away from her. "I hope you're kidding," he said slowly.

She frowned. "I left a message at the desk to let you know I'd be late. They tried ringing the room but it was busy."

"Damn!" Jason muttered. "Wade had to use the phone. It only took a few minutes, but it must have been then."

Kate's expression had turned anxious. "Did the kidnappers call about Greg?"

He shook his head.

Kate sighed, but then her eyes darkened. "You were right, after all," she said, her voice low. "Greg is—or has been—smuggling." She had scarcely finished speaking before a peculiar sensation ribboned down her spine. She glanced uneasily around, but all she saw were the same faces that had been there before. A man parking his car, a woman and her young toddler coming out of the shop next door, the street peddler selling fresh fruit and flowers on the corner.

"Let's go inside," she started to say.

Suddenly all hell broke loose. She heard the squeal of tires, the roar of an engine, shrill screams of fright. Kate had only a fleeting glimpse of a beat-up yellow Volkswagen bus as it careened wildly around the corner, veering straight toward them. Then her body was slammed sideways.

She was dimly aware that the wind was knocked out of her. There was a flash of darkness, followed by a kaleidoscope of lights spinning wildly in her brain. For a moment she stared uncomprehendingly into a pair of golden eyes that were as stunned as hers. She realized she was sprawled on the sidewalk, the hard length of Jason's body weighing her down.

"Are you all right?" he grated in her ear.

Slowly she nodded. The back of her head ached from being knocked against the sidewalk, and her lungs burned with the heavy burden of his body atop hers. But she knew instinctively that she was okay.

Jason muttered something under his breath, then quickly lifted himself from her. She watched as he took off at a dead run.

Kate struggled to a sitting position. The scene around her was chaotic. A dozen pair of legs lunged past her. The woman with the baby had snatched the child high in her arms. Tears streamed down her face. Someone was shouting, and the air was filled with a barrage of rapid-fire Spanish.

An elderly man from the swarm around her helped her to her feet. Kate didn't understand what he was saying, but the concern in his eyes was readily apparent. She smiled a shaky thank-you, and began to brush off her clothing.

Jason reappeared at her side. "I didn't get the license," he said grimly. His hard gaze scanned the crowd before returning to her face. Only then did his expression soften slightly. "You sure you're okay?"

Kate nodded. "No one—" she had to try several times before the words came out clearly "—no one else is hurt?"

"No, thank God." He glanced quickly around once more. "Come on, let's get you inside," he muttered.

Out on the street there hadn't been time to be afraid, since the incident occurred much too quickly. But once in her hotel room, the enormity of nearly being run down by a van finally penetrated, and her legs abruptly felt like wax beneath her. She sank down onto the chair, let her head fall back and closed her eyes.

"This has to be the worst day of my life," she muttered. Not quite, a tiny voice reiterated firmly. The worst day had been the one when she finally accepted that Jason was no longer a part of her life—and she had no one to blame but herself, for she had foolishly let him go.

But she didn't want to think about that now, any more than she wanted to remember the ugly scene with Jason that morning. There was so much going on right now—trying to find Greg, and trying to understand and cope with her feelings for Jason.

A shadow fell over her. Kate opened her eyes to find Jason standing above her.

"You sure you're all right?" He sat down on the bed across from her.

"I'm fine," she murmured. She lowered her lashes, then lifted them a second later to stare at him. "That van...you don't think it was—"

"Intentional?" His expression was hard.

She bit her lip, and nodded tentatively. Jason rested his wrists on his knees and tapped his fingertips together. "It's possible," he said after a long silence. "But it's also possible the driver might have been drunk. Or just crazy."

Their eyes met and held, and Kate's pulse quickened, but the moment was broken when her stomach gurgled loudly. "I'm starving," she supplied needlessly.

"You haven't eaten yet?"

She shook her head and laughed shakily. "I was too busy—"

"I know. Breaking into Greg's office and climbing mountains." His dry tone was accompanied by a slight smile.

Kate's heart fluttered. He smiled so little, she suddenly realized. Not that there had been much reason to these past few days, but she sensed a feeling of sadness in him. Perhaps he was lonely, as lonely as she was. Or were her musings simply the whimsical fancies of a woman in love?

The thought shook Kate to her very core. For the second time that day, she had thought of herself as being in love with Jason. And it wasn't a gentle kind of love, simple and uncomplicated. It was a fiery, consuming emotion that overpowered the senses and stormed the heart...the kind they'd had before.

But time could never mend the hurt they had inflicted upon each other; if nothing else, Jason's actions this morning had convinced her of that.

As soon as Greg was safe and sound, she and Jason would go their separate ways once more. Jason would be out of her life forever. There would be no reason for their paths to cross again.

She would do well to remember that.

"I haven't eaten, either," she heard him say. "Do you want to shower while I get something from room service?"

She forced herself to gaze directly into his eyes. They reflected only concern. Concern and something she didn't dare put a name to. For once she wished he would look at her with his usual wariness and distrust. The way he gazed at her now made it far too tempting to pull down walls rather than build them.

She stood. "That'll be fine," she said briefly, averting her eyes.

When she closed the bathroom door behind her, she couldn't shake the feeling that she was running. It was even stranger that she didn't know if she was running to Jason or from him.

KATE FELT REVIVED after a long, hot shower and a change of clothes.

Over dinner, Jason told her about his day spent poring over topographical maps. It had been a fruitless one. There were a thousand and one places where an airstrip could be hidden away in the mountains.

Kate relayed what she had discovered in Greg's office and in San Seville. She shuddered as she spoke of her impulsive side trip to the village. The cab driver had been a little too eager to deposit her there, and far less inclined to return as she'd requested. Nor had she counted on hiking up a narrow dirt track in order to find the boarded-up ruins of a mining company that had closed its doors half a century ago.

"So," Jason spoke thoughtfully. "The mining company doesn't exist."

Kate toyed with the flan Jason had ordered for their dessert. It was creamy and light, but she suddenly had lost her appetite. "Greg must have been using the mining company as some kind of cover—transporting silver on paper, but in reality, carrying something else entirely. Something illegal."

It was a moment before Jason agreed. "Sure looks like it."

Kate turned her attention to her coffee. Spoken or unspoken, if Jason conveyed an I-told-you-so, she didn't think she could bear it. But when he said nothing, she risked a peek at him.

"Do you think Manuel Ortega knows what's going on?" she asked quickly. "Maybe that's why he left before I got there."

Jason seemed skeptical of the idea. "He didn't strike me as being the most diligent person I've ever met. He probably just decided to head home early." He shrugged. "With Greg gone, I'm surprised he was even there at all."

Kate hesitated. She wondered if she was grasping at straws, but she had this feeling...

"Do you think his cargo had anything to do with the reason for his kidnapping? I know Wade said he wasn't under suspicion by the DEA and that it was probably a get-rich-quick scheme, but what if that's not it? What if Greg was smuggling drugs or guns, and that's what the kidnappers were really after?"

Jason had never discounted that assumption, but he didn't say so. The past two days had netted them no substantial leads whatsoever. If they didn't find Greg soon, there was no telling what the kidnappers might do to him when the ransom wasn't paid.

Yet Kate had coped with this entire situation far better than he'd ever anticipated. He felt a surge of self-loathing. He'd done nothing to make this any easier for her. He was on such shaky ground, torn by warring emotions. But he couldn't deny he'd been far too busy feeling sorry for himself, as well as being jealous of Greg, to give much thought to how Kate was taking this whole thing.

But instilling false hope in her would do more harm than good. "It's possible," he admitted. "Maybe someone else found out about it and decided to get in on the action. Either one—guns or drugs—would be easy to unload with a few well-placed questions."

Her eyes grew wide. "Then why keep him? Why the ransom demand?"

"I don't know, Kate. Unless…" He hesitated, not certain if he should go on.

But she had already drawn the same conclusion. "Unless they want to milk him for everything he's worth, or everything they think he's worth. After all, he's right where they want him."

"There's no point in speculating. We won't know anything for sure until we find him."

If they found him, Kate thought despairingly. Even then, what condition would he be in?

"Did you say you brought along some of the invoices Greg made out to the mining company?"

Kate was only too glad to show them to Jason. It offered a momentary diversion and the chance to shut down her disturbing train of thought.

"They don't say much, other than listing a shipping fee," she told him as she rose to find her purse. "They're obviously just dummied up to verify the flights, in case someone gets suspicious."

But to her surprise, her purse was nowhere to be found. "I know I had it with me when I left the trailer," she muttered, checking the closet again. "And I couldn't have forgotten it in the cab, either."

He watched as she perched her hands on her hips and cast an exasperated glance around the hotel room. "You're sure?"

"Positive. I paid the driver through the window when I got out to walk the rest of the way." She crossed to the dresser and started to rifle through the drawers for the third time, muttering to herself all the while. "It bugs me that I don't know where I put it. You know how it is when you're looking for your keys and you can't find them? And you know they're probably right in the front of you."

"Maybe not, Kate." He paused. "With all the commotion, someone probably grabbed your purse when that car almost ran us down."

She straightened up and stared at him, torn between anger and frustration. "I'll bet that's what happened. There was so much confusion and—" Suddenly she stopped.

"Don't worry about spending money," he told her. "I've got enough to last us through the middle of next week, if necessary. And you paid the hotel bill in advance." He was a little puzzled by the odd expression on her face. "If you're worried about your credit cards, you can report them missing now so you won't be liable."

"It's not that."

"What then?" He moved a step closer. "Tell me, Kate."

She drew a deep breath. "When I left the cab, I was right across from the bank. I wanted to make sure I'd have no trouble withdrawing the ransom money. Maybe they thought I had it so they decided to steal it. That's all they want, Jason. Maybe they don't intend to release Greg at all!" Her mind continued to race long after she'd stopped speaking. Just because Greg was alive when the photo was taken—and she had no guarantee that he was—didn't mean that was true now. He could have tried to escape...

Jason's eyes sharpened. "The kidnappers?" When she nodded, he knew what was on her mind. Farfetched as it seemed, he couldn't discount the possibility, either. He hesitated only a second before he spoke. "Kate. The next time they call, I think you should say you have the ransom."

Her mouth dropped open. "All of it?"

"Yes."

She shook her head wildly. Her stomach began to churn. "No! It's too risky. If they suspect we're trying to double-cross them—"

"Kate!" His voice was sharp. "The longer this goes on, the less chance there is of finding Greg, dead or alive. If we can get them to give us the drop-off point, I think there's at least a chance of getting him back. Then we'll have some idea where to look. They want us to come to them, not the other way around. But the way things stand now..." He shook his head.

He was right. Deep in her heart, Kate knew it. But she was so desperately afraid for Greg.

At precisely that moment the phone began to ring. And ring...

It was Jason who finally picked it up. He muttered a terse, "Hello," then held the receiver toward Kate.

"It's him."

She didn't need to ask who he meant. She stumbled toward Jason. He pressed the phone into her icy fingers.

Kate couldn't look away from him. There was a warning in his eyes, a warning and a reassurance that gave her the strength to put the receiver to her ear.

"Yes?" Her voice was low but very clear.

"*Señora!* I am glad to see you have recovered from your little—" a hoarse chuckle came over the line "—accident."

A fiery wave of anger shot through her. "It was you, wasn't it?" she demanded.

He neither confirmed nor denied it. "A warning, *señora*. Perhaps now you and your friend will do as you are told."

"But we have!" she started to protest.

"You have not!" The man's voice was low and guttural. "I saw you leave the hotel today. I saw you return. You were gone a long, long time. Me, I do not mind so much, but my friends... They will not like it when I tell them. They may even take it out on—"

"No! I have the ransom," she cried. "All of it!"

"Do you? I am beginning to wonder."

Nerveless fingers clutched the phone. "Why? Why don't you believe me? Of course I'm not stupid enough to carry that much cash, but I brought it with me, I swear!"

His chuckle made the hair on the back of her neck stand up. "I know, *señora*. But I have reason to believe it was not nearly as much as you told me earlier."

There was only one way he could possibly know that. He had snatched her purse. Why, she couldn't even begin to guess, but she had no doubt that he'd seen the receipt the bank had given her on Monday. Her knees buckled. There was no hope for Greg, she thought despairingly. No hope at all.

But then a strong male hand slid around her waist. Jason still stood next to her. Reassured by his presence, she took a deep breath. "I told you before, I had to sell some investments. If you're really watching me, you'll know I stopped at the bank near the hotel today. I found out that the rest of the money will be available tomorrow. So if you want it, you'd better tell me where you want it delivered." Kate bit her lip and began to pray.

Minutes seemed to drag by before she finally heard his voice again. "I will need to talk with my friends first. And I want to make certain you haven't contacted the *policía*." He laughed harshly. "I will call you tomorrow. In the meantime, we must trust each other, *sí*?"

The line went dead. Kate was left listening to the dull buzz of the dial tone.

"Damn!" she cried. She flung the receiver back into its cradle. "Damn it, Jason, he didn't believe me. Oh, I told you it wouldn't work!"

"It will, Kate." He laid a hand on her shoulder. "It's only a matter of time before they—"

"Time!" She wrenched away from him, both furious and frustrated at his calm. "How much time do we have left? How much time does Greg have left?"

But suddenly she went pale. "Oh, God," she whispered. She sank down weakly on the mattress.

The look on her face was more than mere alarm; more than the stress and strain of the last five days. Jason saw panic reflected there. Pure, unadulterated panic.

He was beside her in an instant. "What is it?"

She had to struggle to force her voice past the strangled knot in her throat. "Toby," she finally choked out. "They have my purse. They know I only brought five thousand dollars with me...and they have my driver's license...my address. They know where Toby is...."

He understood her fear immediately. "That won't happen." He tried to reassure her.

She resisted his attempt to draw her into his arms. "We don't know that. And we can't stop them from taking him, either. Not from here."

He deliberately spoke very calmly. "They already have Greg. I don't think there's any reason for them to even think of taking Toby."

Fire blazed in her eyes. She snatched her hand away when he touched it. "Maybe they think I need a little more incentive."

"We don't know—"

"That's the whole problem! We don't know *anything*. Maybe there's only one man behind this. Maybe there's ten or twenty."

"Kate," he began. Again he tried to pull her into his arms.

"Damn you, Jason, I won't take any chances where Toby is concerned!"

The voice of hysteria? Maybe. Then again, maybe not. But he did know that she was terrified of losing her son.

She fought against him once more and managed to wedge her arms between them, but this time he refused to let her go. He closed his arms around her taut, trembling body. For a long moment she remained stiff and unyielding, but then all the fight seemed to drain from her. Her head dropped forward.

"I know you think I'm making too much of it," she whispered into his shoulder. "But Toby's all I have."

"It'll be okay, Kate. You'll see." Her muscles were stiff with tension. Over and over, he stroked the slender lines of her back, soothing her as if she were a child.

Her fingers slowly unclenched against his chest. "If I lose Toby, I lose everything. I'm scared, Jason."

"I know," he said gently. He pressed his cheek against the fragrant silk of her hair. "We won't let anything happen to Toby. Maybe it would be best if he stayed at the ranch until this is over. I doubt he could be traced there. They know I came with you to Mexico, but they don't know who I am."

He was right. She had purchased the airline tickets, and the registration at the hotel was in her name as well. Still, he had done so much for her already.

He must have sensed what she was thinking. He slid his fingers into her hair and tipped her face up to his. "I don't mind, Kate, and I'm sure Rosa won't, either. There's room for Rita, too. In fact, it might be wise to have someone with Toby whom he knows. As young as he is, it's probably hard on him with you away." His hands dropped to her shoulders. "We can call now, if you like. It's not that late. Then they'll be able to head out there first thing in the morning."

"But it's so far for Rita to drive to the shop." She withdrew from the shelter of his arms almost reluctantly.

"Not that far. Forty-five minutes if the traffic is really heavy. Besides, if we're lucky, this will be over by Monday. She shouldn't have to bother for more than two or three days. And we've got a little pinto Toby can ride. It'll probably be like a vacation to him.''

Half an hour later, everything was settled. Kate tried not to listen while Jason spoke to Rosa, but if there was any friction between brother and sister, she couldn't detect it. Neither Rosa nor Rita objected under the circumstances, and certainly Toby didn't. Jason heard his whoop and holler clear across the room when Kate mentioned the pony.

She was silent for a moment when she replaced the phone in the cradle. Jason stood at the window, his hands tucked into his pockets as he gazed out at the stark blackness of the night.

Kate hesitated, then moved slowly across the room to stand a few feet behind him. "Thank you," she said very quietly. "For everything."

He turned at the sound of her voice. "There's no need to thank me, Kate."

"There is," she affirmed quickly. "You could have refused to help find Greg, but you didn't. I know how difficult that decision must have been for you. I also realize that my being here with you hasn't made things any easier." She had to fight to keep her eyes from straying to the bed. "I guess I thought you might resent Toby," she added very quickly. "Because he's Greg's son. Greg's and—and mine."

Jason's eyes narrowed. "Do you think so little of me, Kate?" His voice sounded taut and strained. "Whatever happened in the past—do you honestly think I would hold it against him? Toby is just a little boy, an innocent little boy."

Her gaze dipped to the tanned column of his neck. She found herself suddenly unable to look at him. "With you, I—I don't know what to think."

Jason winced inwardly. He'd given her no reason *not* to believe that his bitterness and resentment had survived all this time. In fact, he'd seldom wasted an opportunity to remind himself—and Kate—of that fact.

When she had reentered his life four days ago, she had called up so many memories that he'd spent years trying to forget. He resented her for still having such power over his emotions. He had been cruel and taunting; there were times when he actually *wanted* to hurt her.

He'd succeeded this morning. Kate had never been able to hide what was in her heart. Yet every time he thought of the utter desolation in her eyes when he'd put her in the cab, a knifing pain ripped through him. And then tonight, when she hadn't returned on time...

He'd lied to his heart once. He could do so no longer.

But this was so damn hard! His mouth was dry, and he realized he'd never been more scared in his life. For years now he had guarded his feelings closely, held them deep inside to shield against further pain. To love was to lose. It was a lesson he'd learned very early in life. First his parents, then Kate. Even Rosa was drifting further and further away from him.

He'd never felt so alone or so desperate, so lacking or so needing. He'd never felt so lost....

His glance flickered toward the window. He stared sightlessly at the twinkling lights of the city, seeing nothing but her face. "Kate?" His voice sounded hoarse and unnatural, even to his own ears.

"Yes?" Hers was a mere breath of air. When he finally glanced back at her, she looked as frightened, as vulnerable, as he felt inside. He could sense her uncertainty, see it in the faint tremor of her hands as she clasped them together in front of her.

He made a vague gesture with one hand. "Kate, I—I've made a lot of mistakes in my life where you're concerned. Some I can change, and some I can't." He hesitated. "That day on the plane, when you told me about your father. It just occurred to me that I never said I was sorry."

It wasn't what she expected. He could see it in the sudden widening of her eyes. Then they dulled and became totally lifeless.

"You don't have to say that," she said in a very low voice. "I know how you felt about him."

He frowned. "I don't think you do. We may have disagreed over a lot of things—"

"No," she whispered, and there was a world of torment in her voice. "Only me, Jason. Only me."

The silence was nearly unbearable. Kate felt completely defenseless.

Uncertainty gnawed at Jason. "Maybe you were right this morning," he said finally. "Maybe we do need to get everything out in the open, clear the air once and for all. Then when it's done," he took a deep breath. "We'll say no more about it...ever."

Kate stared at him. This was what she'd wanted, wasn't it? But now that the moment was actually upon her, she wasn't certain this was right after all. Somehow she had always thought that Jason had at least cared *something* for her during their marriage. Yet this morning he had shattered that conviction with such taunting clarity. Somehow he always managed to strike a blow where it hurt the most.

But he had put out a hand, perhaps not in friendship or love, and she couldn't just thrust it aside. She laid a hand on top of the dresser, feeling direly in need of a little support. "Is that what you want?" she asked very quietly.

His gaze held hers. "Right now, it's what I want more than anything in the world." He moved a step closer. "You asked me about Toby. I'll tell you, Kate. Do you know what entered my mind when I first saw him?" His tone grew fierce. "All I could think was that he should have been ours. *Ours*, Kate. And suddenly I knew how much I'd lost when you left me."

Her lips parted. "But that doesn't change the fact that Greg is his father."

"And you are his mother. You, Kate... No one else."

For a moment she didn't comprehend, and then she was almost afraid to. Her lips scarcely moved. "That makes a difference?"

There was a heartbeat of silence. "All the difference in the world."

CHAPTER ELEVEN

THE QUIET INTENSITY in his voice made her mind reel. She stared at him, and, unbelievably, detected no sign of the self-protective barriers so much in evidence these last few days. The words he spoke were straight from the heart.

But Jason had the power to hurt her as no one else, and the realization made her more vulnerable than ever. From somewhere deep inside, there came a show of strength she hadn't known she possessed.

"I'm not sure what you want from me," she told him very quietly. "You can be a very caring, sensitive man, Jason. It's one of the things I loved most about you. But now, one minute you're so sweet and gentle, and the next..." She swallowed. "You look at me as if—as if you hated me." The last words emerged with difficulty. "I don't understand you. I don't understand what you're trying to say."

Jason was silent for a long moment. "I can't deny what seeing you again did to me. Everything I'd tried so hard to forget came rushing back. A part of me wanted to hate you, but another part couldn't stop remembering what you once meant to me. It's been like a nightmare, Kate. I despised myself for still wanting you, yet every time I held you and touched you—" his voice dropped to a husky pitch "—it was like a dream come true. I didn't know how to deal with it."

This time it was Kate who couldn't hide her bitterness. "After this morning, I can't believe it really matters." Deliberately she turned her back on him. "You only married me because I was pregnant. I've always known that, and yet I thought you cared, just a little."

"More than just a little, Kate. Much more." He came up behind her. Their eyes met in the mirror.

Kate's were faintly accusing. "That's not what you said."

"I was talking about Rosa and Nick," he emphasized. "Not us."

"You said you didn't want them to end up like we did. And you said you knew exactly what was in Nick's mind." The pain that twisted through her was excruciating. How she went on, she never knew. "You said you knew that marriage was the last thing he wanted."

"Forget what I said. That's not what I meant and you know it!" He capped the lid on his temper. Time dragged while he took several calm, restorative breaths.

"It was different with us," he continued in a low voice. "I'll admit maybe the timing wasn't right. You were so young, not much more than a kid yourself. God knows you probably weren't ready to take on a husband, a baby, and another kid as well." His gaze softened as it rested on her. "No one forced me to marry you. I did it because it was what I wanted."

If he was trying to break her down, he was doing a very good job of it. The feeble barrier she'd erected against him tumbled a notch, then crumpled altogether.

Kate had never regretted their parting as much as she did at this moment. Slowly she turned. "I've often thought things might have worked out differently if I hadn't let my father push me around," she murmured.

Jason's eyes darkened. "Don't blame yourself, Kate," he told her gently. "You were all he had. He didn't want to lose you. It's taken me a long time, but I think I can understand the way he felt."

They stood a mere breath apart. He had to fight to keep his hands at his sides when he saw her lips tremble. "Where you were concerned, I was just as possessive as your father."

"I didn't realize until much, much later how intolerable the whole situation really was." It cost her a slight pang of betrayal, but she made the admission nonetheless. "I think Daddy was jealous of you."

"And I was jealous of him." His lashes briefly shadowed his eyes. "I asked too much of you. I know that now. It wasn't fair that you had to choose between us, but I was too proud and stubborn, too hotheaded and headstrong." His eyes came back up to snare hers. "I never gave you a chance, Kate."

Her shaky smile held a touch of wistfulness. "I never gave you a chance. And you certainly didn't get any bargain. One imperfect and childish woman was all you got."

His response was very quiet. "I never wanted the perfect woman. All I wanted was you."

She tried not to think of what they had each gone through to come to this point. It was years too late, perhaps, but at least Jason was sharing a part of himself with her—the tender, compassionate side he so seldom revealed.

She turned pleading eyes to his face. "Will you let me explain about Greg?" Her voice caught raggedly. "Please?"

He started to stiffen, but even then his mind telegraphed the message that if he refused to listen, he might never have a second chance. And perhaps that's what this was all about. He let out a deep breath and slowly nodded his head.

As low as Kate's voice was, there was a slight tremor in it as she began to speak.

"You were always after me to make my own decisions. I've often reflected how ironic it was that when I finally did, my decision wasn't the right one. Even then, I still hadn't learned. It was too late when I realized I'd been secretly hoping you'd come back to me and we could start all over. But by then, you'd joined the army. For all I knew, you had no intention of ever returning to Bradley."

At that point in his life, he hadn't. But this he kept to himself and remained silent.

"I'd never felt so alone. I felt both you and Daddy had betrayed me. I was miserable, but at least Greg was there. No, don't turn away! Let me say this, just this once!" she cried out when he averted his head. Without realizing she had even moved, she latched onto his hand and drew him to the side of the bed.

Sitting beside him, she focused her eyes on her hands. It was cowardly, she knew, but she couldn't maintain eye-to-eye contact while she said this. "I'm not sure what would have happened to me if it hadn't been for Greg. I felt comfortable with him. I thought I could depend on him. He made me laugh, and after a while, it didn't hurt so much to think about you. When Greg asked me to marry him, it seemed the right thing to do."

Jason's throat was raw with the effort it took to speak. "Did you love him?"

Her breath caught, as if the question had taken her by surprise. "We've hurt each other so much, Jason." She shook her head. "Please, ask me anything but that."

"I have to know." His voice was hoarse. "Did you love Greg the same way you loved me?"

"No one could ever take your place in my heart, not Greg or any other man," she said very quietly. "But he helped me through the worst period in my life, and for that I'll always be grateful. I won't lie and say I never loved him, because I did. And for a long, long time I let myself believe we could make it."

The room was steeped in silence. Kate was afraid, desperately afraid, that with her declaration, she had unraveled what little they had gained.

Yet she needn't have feared. Jason knew what price her honesty exacted; his own was no less costly. But painful as the truth was, he knew that they suffered together.

And it was just as he had told her. It made all the difference in the world.

When Kate finally raised her head to gaze at him, her delicate features were filled with torment. If there had been any anger left in him, it would have vanished in that instant. As it was, he had to struggle not to pull her into his arms to ease her guilt and pain. But he sensed that what Kate was undergoing was a kind of purge, a cleansing of the soul.

And he needed to prove that he could listen . . . listen and understand as he had never done all those years ago.

His hand found hers. She clung to it blindly, as if she sought to bind herself to him forever.

"Why did you stay with him?" he asked very gently.

"I'd already failed miserably at one marriage," she confided hesitantly. "I was determined to make this one work, with or without Greg's help."

"And which was it? With or without?"

Her eyes evaded his. It was the only answer Jason needed, but he listened as she tried to explain.

"Greg and I wanted different things. I wanted a home and a family, while Greg…" She was silent for a moment. "Flying was his first love. I came to accept that, and because of it, I learned to stand on my own. I'd like to think that I'm a survivor."

Jason tightened his grip on her hand. "You are, Kate. You're strong and independent. It was one of the first things I noticed."

Kate glanced down in surprise. Their fingers were twined closely together, and rested lightly on her thigh. She dimly recalled him reaching for her. At the realization, her throat tightened oddly. It seemed a small thing, insignificant perhaps, but to Kate it meant more than she could say.

"Kate, are you sure—absolutely sure—Greg means nothing to you?"

Her eyes were drawn to his face. For a moment she simply stared at him; at the deep grooves beside his mouth, at the guarded hopefulness in his eyes. She had the strangest sensation that her future, and possibly her life, rested on her answer.

She chose her words carefully. "I care what happens to him, yes. But Greg's life no longer includes me. That was my choice, and it's the only way I would have it." She touched his face. "Please try to understand. When I married Greg, I wasn't trying to get back at you. The last thing I wanted was to hurt you. I just needed someone to hold me, someone to love me."

Slowly, slowly, his hand came up to cover hers where it rested on his lean cheek. "What about me, Kate?" His intense gaze never wavered from hers. "Did you need me, too?"

His craggy features suddenly swam before her. "I've always needed you," she whispered tremulously. "I think I always will."

Everything she felt was reflected in the diamond-bright glitter of her eyes: her uncertainty, the loneliness and pain she had suffered, the vivid remembrances of the love they had shared, the yearning to reclaim all that had been lost to them, the anxious hope she didn't bother to hide.

Jason was gripped by a rush of emotion so intense he felt dizzy. Speech was impossible. Overpowered by the need to touch her, his fingers explored the delicate contours of her face, over and over again. He felt as if a veil had just been lifted from the world. Everything was brighter, the colors more intense than ever before, and the air was sweet and pure.

"I've never forgotten how it was with you." His breath emerged as a long sigh. "We had something so special."

"I was a fool to let you go, Jason."

His thumb traced the outline of her trembling lips. "Do you believe in fate? In second chances?"

"Yes. Oh, yes..." But the eyes that searched his face were almost fearful.

His voice dropped to a low and husky pitch. "I never thought about it before, but it stands to reason that those who love the most, hurt the most." His eyes delved deeply into hers. "Do we dare, Kate? Do we dare try again?"

For one brief second the world around her tipped. "I can't answer for you," she told him, the words wrenched from deep inside her, "but I don't have any choice!"

Jason reached out blindly at the same instant she flung herself into his arms. He buried his head in the curve of her shoulder; she buried her face against the solid warmth of his chest. They clung to each other with a desperate, almost bruising strength.

His body trembled with the force of his emotions. Jason was so relieved he felt weak, yet his heart was so full he thought it would burst. He squeezed his eyes shut and savored the sweet fulfillment of being able to hold her again, her body soft and warm against his. She was in his arms, where she belonged, and for the first time in fifteen years, he no longer felt empty.

His hand traveled the length of her back with long, soothing strokes. Kate responded by nuzzling her cheek against his chest. He smiled as her lashes brushed the hollow of his throat. But his heart contracted when the trickling warmth of a tear followed.

"Don't, Kate." His tone was very gentle as he drew back slightly, then framed her face with his hands.

"I won't," she promised.

"It tears me up inside when you cry." His touch was infinitely tender as he wiped away the moisture. The action was barely completed before another crystalline droplet splashed his hand.

She smiled mistily up at him. "I know."

"The time for tears is past."

But the tears only flowed faster, harder.

Jason groaned softly. He closed his arms around her and gently brushed his lips upon her temple. At the feel of her trembling against him, the storm of emotion in his heart broke free. He threaded his fingers through her hair and tilted her head back once more. "We'll start all over. It will be different this time—better—I promise."

It was too much to ask for, too much to hope for. One last tear slipped from beneath her lids as she uttered a soft cry of joy. The sound echoed in his mouth as he kissed her. It was a gentle kiss, a healing, tender caress, a kiss filled with gentle promise. But oddly, it was the moist and salty warmth of Kate's tears, trapped and sealed between their lips, that bespoke a far deeper bond.

But one kiss was not enough. Their need was too great to be restrained. They were both starved for the taste of each other, hungry and aching to fill the dark, empty void created by the passage of time.

Their lips met again and again. He explored and enticed, advanced and retreated. She taunted and teased and met his every demand with one of her own until they were both gasping.

"Oh, Kate." He rested his forehead against hers and closed his eyes. His heart was beating like a trip hammer. His eyes flicked open and he stared directly into hers.

They were warm, those strange golden eyes, warm and clear as whiskey and just as potent. Kate's heart executed what felt like a triple somersault.

"I want you," he whispered. "I want to touch you. I want to hold you. I want to love you the way I used to." His hands slid down to cradle her hips. "I need you, Kate."

The aching intensity in his voice made her want to cry and shout at the same time. Held against the thrusting hardness of his body, she was almost painfully aware of that need. Deep in the pit of her stomach, a fluttering sensation of heavy warmth unfolded.

Her fingers slipped into the thick hair that grew low on his neck. She could sense the hunger in his body, feel the tense yearning in the arms that held her, see the lines of strain etched in the jagged planes of his face. There was no reason to hold back any longer, nor did Kate want him to.

"We have all night," she murmured.

An incredible feeling of tenderness washed through him at the faint shyness he heard in her voice. He was near to bursting with the need to love her. He wanted nothing more than to crush her to him; to respond to the fierce rush of desire that swamped his veins. Instead he simply held her, relishing the beauty of the moment, the peaceful contentment that came with the knowledge that she was his once more.

He took her face between her hands. "Are you sure?" he asked quietly. "I didn't come prepared...."

Nor had Kate, but she was touched at his concern. Her mind groped fuzzily for a date just past, then she pressed her lips to his. "It's okay," she said huskily, kissing him deeply.

"I'm shaking," he whispered when his hand finally slipped around to the front of her blouse.

Her hands closed around his forearms as she leaned back to allow him better access. Fireworks exploded inside her when her fingers lightly gauged the shape and texture of him, the rock-hard muscles beneath the dense layer of crisp dark hair.

"So am I," she confided breathlessly.

Jason's mouth found the tender spot between her shoulder and her neck. "Remember the first time?"

The second button on her blouse slipped free; another followed. Anticipation spilled through her like warm, sweet wine. She could almost feel the callused touch of his hands on her bare skin. "How could I forget?"

He smiled at her breathlessness. "Were you as scared as I was?"

"You were scared? Why?" There was a cool rush of air as he drew her blouse over her shoulders. He fumbled a little with the front clasp of her bra. Then it joined her blouse on the floor.

"I was terrified that I'd hurt you." His voice deepened. "I didn't want to lose you, Kate." His arms came around her in a viselike grip. "I love you, Kate. I don't think I ever stopped." He clutched her fiercely. "I couldn't stand it if I lost you again."

He sounded so tortured, so tormented, that Kate felt something come apart inside her. There were no half-measures for a man like Jason. He was too intense, a man capable of a sweeping range of emotions. When he hated, it was with all that he possessed. And when he loved, he loved with all of his heart.

For the space of a heartbeat, she was too full of emotion to speak. Then she whispered brokenly, "You'll never lose me. And the only thing that would ever hurt me is if you stopped loving me." She tangled her fingers in his thick, black hair and drew his head back so she could look at him. "I love you, Jason. I love you...."

All the anguish, the fears and uncertainties that had once driven them apart, scattered to the winds of time. Only their deep, driving need for each other remained. With a hand on either side of his face, she sought his mouth, reveling in the sandpaper roughness of his cheeks. She kissed him tenderly, gently. Wispy exchanges of breath and tongue soon became bolder, swirling far and deep in a breath-stealing encounter that parodied the act of love.

Her slacks and underwear joined the growing pile at their feet. She watched as Jason began to rid himself of his own clothes. She heard the whisper of his jeans as they slid to the floor.

He was such a beautiful man, so utterly male. His body was lean and muscled and rough with hair. She ached for him, longed to mold her softness against his hardness.

Behind him, Kate could see the bronzed expanse of his back. His muscles rippled beneath his skin with each movement that he made. Unable to hold back, she stretched out her hand when he turned to slide onto the bed.

But suddenly he froze, an arm stretched out to support the weight of his upper body, one foot still poised on the floor, when her fingers encountered the network of scars. He started to make an instinctive movement of protest, but she pressed both hands on his shoulders. "Don't!" she cried softly. "I love you—all of you."

Her touch was immeasurably tender as she traced the jagged outline. His eyes closed when her mouth replaced the soothing touch of her fingers. It was as if she sought to heal his wounds, absorb his pain and suffering and take them unto herself.

It was an act of unselfishness, an act of giving. Jason's throat tightened, but he remained perfectly still. He knew she would be hurt if he resisted.

At last she slid her arms around his waist. With a breathless little sigh, he turned so that her nipples settled into the dark forest on his chest. The feel of her naked breasts cushioned against his bare skin was electrifying.

With gentle possessiveness, he eased her back upon the mattress. Eyes like dark gold fire roamed her nakedness, searing her with their heated intensity. It was a look that sent a slow surge of anticipation through Kate's body, like tiny, ever-widening ripples on a pond. Her nipples tightened and deep in her belly, a spiraling heat began to uncurl.

She waited impatiently for his touch. When it came, his rough palm closing reverently over the fullness of her breast, it was almost like a benediction. Her sigh of relief became a gasp of pleasure when his thumb stroked the dark center to a straining peak.

Heaven was only a prayer away. Jason's head dipped down, his target the same breast. His mustache was like a brush of finest sable as he placed his lips over the curving mound. Then very gently he drew the aching bud into his mouth and initiated a slow, mind-spinning tugging rhythm that sent her pulses clamoring. His tongue was an instrument of torture and delight as he shifted to the other breast, but this time his hand stole down her stomach to the treasure that lay below. She gasped at his intimate touch. His strong fingers tempted, parted, teased and probed. He aroused her to a fevered pitch of excitement, but never lingered long enough to fulfill the throbbing emptiness that cried out to him.

She felt bereft when his fingers left her, but the next instant she released a bubbly sigh of relief when his body molded to hers. By slow degrees, he eased down to her compelling softness.

It was an exquisite torture to feel the entire sweet length of her burning into him, yet Jason yearned to prolong the pleasure, unwilling to let it end too soon. He wanted to burn the memory of this night into his soul, to carry it with him through all eternity.

"Oh, Kate." Both tenderness and a fierce desire rained down on her as he raised his head. His lips discovered the downy softness of her cheek, the corner of her mouth. His voice was almost unbearably gentle in comparison with the coiled tension in his body. "You make me crazy...you're so beautiful...I want to make up for all the lost time...I want to make it last forever...."

"Jason, please." She breathed his name pleadingly. Her emerald eyes were so clear and pure he felt he could lose himself in them forever. "I need you," she whispered. "I need you...." Beneath him, as if to lend credence to the words, her legs angled invitingly.

He gasped when the heated strength of his maleness touched the warm cove of her femininity. Whatever intentions he might have harbored disintegrated.

Her arching hips were captured and held in strong male hands. For a heart-stopping moment, they stared long and deep into each other's eyes. Then he settled between her thighs and claimed full, hot possession of her body.

Jason closed his eyes at the unbelievable sensations that swept over him. She was so warm, so smooth. "Oh, Lord," he muttered thickly. "This feels so..."

"I know," she whispered, and smiled at him through love-misted eyes.

His fingers slid into her hair. Their lips met over and over again, their arms enfolded and entwined. They moved in an ancient ritual of desire that required no words, no sounds, only touch. The yawning emptiness since they'd last been together only intensified their need. Each throbbing caress, each parting and rich melding of their bodies took them higher, further than ever before, soaring beyond the sky and into the heavens. Release came in a blinding crescendo of white-hot sparks and blazing fire.

She sobbed out his name.

He whispered hers.

JASON WAS THE FIRST to awaken the next morning. Sunlight winked through the drapes, bathing the room with a hazy shade of gold. The memory of the night just past penetrated his consciousness, and he turned his attention to the woman at his side.

His eyes were tender as he gazed at Kate. As he did so, the sunlight caught in her hair, weaving through the loose waves. It rippled like silken threads of dark copper when he lifted it from her cheek. He sifted through the strands, marveling at the texture.

One of her hands was nestled beneath her cheek. He smiled at the air of childlike innocence she projected. She looked very delicate as she lay there slumbering peacefully, a slight flush tinting her cheeks. His attention wandered to the curve of her bare shoulder. Drawn by the need to touch her, he reached out and splayed his fingers against her flesh. His lean fingers were dark against the fairness of her skin, the contrast striking. He continued to gaze at her, entranced by the sensuous sight.

Lord, but he loved her. He loved her so much he ached with it. The battle had not been an easy one, but he was a man who had accepted and learned to deal with his loneliness...or so he thought.

But last night had taught him another of life's lessons. He had no idea how he'd survived all these years without her; he hadn't been aware of just how empty he was.

Kate was a part of him, the other half of himself. He needed her in much the same way that he needed air to go on living.

Her slender body was outlined beneath the thin sheet, and his eyes were soft as they swept once more down the sweet length of her. He'd once thought he'd never seen anyone quite as lovely as the innocent and tempting child-woman she'd once been. But the mature Kate was far more beautiful.

She was awake when his gaze eventually returned to her face.

"Couldn't sleep?" she asked softly.

He shook his head. "You're on my side of the bed." He took immense pleasure in reminding her.

She laughed, a pure, sweet sound that made his heart turn over. Propping herself on an elbow, she extended a lone forefinger toward him. "Why didn't you wake me up?" She twisted idle curls in the dark mat on his chest.

"I thought I did," he commented dryly. "Several times, in fact."

She frowned playfully. "Are you complaining already?"

His eyes grew tender. "No," he said huskily. "No complaints at all."

And he proceeded to prove his point beyond the shadow of a doubt, pulling them both into the raging center of a whirlwind that left them both weak and breathless.

Much later, when the storm had passed, the winds of passion blew quiet and gentle. No words were necessary as Jason eased his weight from her and drew Kate's trembling body into his arms. Her labored breathing slowed to a trickle, warm and sweet against his skin. Soon they were wrapped in the same tranquil serenity.

Slowly he stroked the slope of her shoulder. These past days of having Kate so close at hand, wanting desperately to touch her but knowing he didn't dare, had strained Jason's control to the limit. Yet even now, with his body sated and content, he knew it would take only a single caress, a mere look, to send the dormant spark of desire into flames once more.

But there was more to it than just sex. He wanted her for more than just the moment. He wanted her tomorrow. The next year and the next. He wanted to wake up beside her for the rest of his life. He wanted to plant his seed in her; watch her grow round and plump with the fruit of their love. He wanted to see her smile, hear her laughter, feel her hand in his while they traveled life's journey together.

"We should get up." Kate broke the long, easy silence.

"Mmm." He had no desire to interrupt such blissful imaginings.

Since neither one seemed inclined to leave the bed, she half-turned in order to look at him.

Feeling her gaze on him, Jason shifted his eyes to her face. "See something you like?" he asked lazily.

Her lips curved. "Mmm." Her fingers explored lightly, as if she were memorizing his features by touch instead of sound. Lovingly she traced the network of fine lines extending outward from his eyes, investigated the flat hollow beneath his cheekbones, stroked the faint grooves etched beside his mouth. She stopped only when she reached the luxuriant band of his mustache.

"How long have you had this?"

He shrugged. "Four or five years, I guess."

Her eyebrows lifted. "That's a long time."

"I'll shave it off if you want." He kissed the forefinger that dimpled his lower lip.

"Don't you dare!"

He laughed at her vehemence.

"I like it," she confessed. Her eyes dipped inevitably to the small silver medal hidden in the wiry curls at the base of his throat. She felt suddenly shy. "I'm glad you never got rid of my medal," she murmured.

The expression on his face grew incredibly tender. "I couldn't," he told her, his voice husky. "But it's mine now, remember? The part of you—" he slipped his hand beneath the fall of her hair and gently urged her forward "—you gave to me."

This last was whispered against her mouth. Kate wasn't prepared for the heart-wrenching surge of emotion the words evoked. Her lips trembled like the wings of a butterfly when he kissed her with lingering sweetness.

When they finally drew apart, Jason groaned at the betraying moistness in her eyes. "Kate," he began, then sighed.

"I'm sorry." She smiled at him tremulously. "It's just that I'm so happy."

At that precise moment the telephone rang. Since Jason was closest, he reached for the receiver and spoke a hello into the mouthpiece.

The next second he said harshly into the phone. "She's busy. If you want to talk, talk to me."

Kate's heart began to thud fearfully. She sat up in bed and pulled the sheet over her breasts, her ears straining. She pulled frantically on Jason's arm as soon as he hung up the phone.

"What?" The grim look on his face scared her. "What is it?"

Jason had left the bed and was pulling on his pants. "They want to make the exchange. Tomorrow at three o'clock, which means we only have a little over a day to see if we can find Greg."

Tomorrow! Exactly one week after she'd learned Greg had been kidnapped. Suddenly she was torn between joy and pain. A nameless ache spread through her limbs.

But tomorrow suddenly seemed eons away. Where was Greg now? This very minute? It hurt to think of him, but his face flashed before her, battered and bruised as it had been in the photo. She winced as she thought of the beating he must have taken. Perhaps it had been only the first of many. Her heart lurched. Was he even alive?

No. She couldn't think that way; she couldn't give in to the nameless fear that clutched at her. Nonetheless, she cringed inside. Greg was out there somewhere, hurt and alone and probably frightened to death.

And she had just spent the night in Jason's arms, with absolutely no thought of Greg.

There were no guarantees that they would find Greg, she thought bleakly. No guarantees at all that if they did, he would even be alive. And when the kidnappers discovered she had only five thousand dollars...

Even where Jason was concerned, there were no guarantees. His bitterness over her marriage to Greg had festered for years. In spite of what he'd told her—that they would say no more about it—could he erase those feelings easily? And what would happen once they were back in Texas? Would this entire affair just be one more chapter from the past?

She was caught in a tangled web from which there was no escape. Trapped between her loyalty to Greg and her love for Jason. A soundless sob broke from her lips and she covered her face with her hands.

The mattress dipped. "Kate, don't do this to yourself." Jason's hands closed around hers, gently pulling them away from her face. She could sense his penetrating gaze boring into her but couldn't find the strength to look at him.

Eyes downcast, she wrapped her arms around her knees. "What do you expect me to do?" She raised her head, uncaring if he saw her pain. "Don't you realize what we did last night?" Her voice rose sharply. "My God, Greg was the last thing on my mind!"

Jason's face shut down all expression. She knew the minute the words were out she'd made a terrible mistake. She could feel him retreating into his self-protective shell.

"Regrets already?"

She flinched at the coldness in his voice. "Jason, please try to understand. It's not that I regret it." She struggled to find the words and came up empty. She forged ahead anyway. "I just feel so...so guilty, I guess."

"Guilty? Not ashamed?" There was mockery mingled with the skepticism in his voice.

Kate's jaw fell open in disbelief, but the next second her temper was off and running. "You haven't changed, have you," she flung back hotly. "You're just as blind and stubborn as ever. You think you know all about bias, don't you? Well, I'm beginning to think you wrote the book on it! Exactly who are you trying to punish anyway? Me? Or yourself? Or maybe all of us, including Greg?" Incensed, she threw off the blankets, yanked on a robe and stamped around the end of the bed.

"Kate, wait." He caught her arm and spun her around. The air was fraught with tension as he silently struggled with himself.

"I'm sorry," he said finally. "I had no right to jump down your throat like that. It's just that last night—" he shoved his fingers through his hair and glanced away. When his gaze swung back to her, she thought she detected a silent plea there.

Unconsciously she moved closer. They now stood only a breath apart. "Yes?" she encouraged.

"Last night was special. Just the two of us together." He hesitated. "I hated for anything to spoil it."

She sensed that the confession cost him a great deal. Suddenly she could see the same doubts, the same fears that had plagued her only moments before, reflected in his dark gold eyes.

Her expression was wistful. "We had to come down from the clouds sometime. I'm sorry it had to be so soon, but for Greg's sake I suppose it's best."

Jason hesitated. "You haven't deserted him, Kate."

Her eyes grew pensive. "I know." She paused. "The place the kidnappers want the ransom delivered, where is it?"

"It's a little village in the mountains, about fifty miles west of Veracruz. Probably a four hour drive from here, if we're lucky."

Lucky? Kate wasn't sure she liked the sound of that, but she held her tongue.

"You sure you're up to this?"

Kate lifted her chin proudly. "I'm not staying here."

"The terrain isn't what you're used to. The heat is—"

"I know, I know." She held up both hands in a conciliatory gesture. "The heat is intense, the humidity unbelievable. No roads, no hotels." There was a faint light in her eyes. "Didn't we have this conversation just a few days ago?"

"And I can see you're going to be just as stubborn about it." The gentleness in his expression took the sting out of his annoyance. "You left out one thing, though."

"What's that?"

"It's the rainy season." He held out his hand to her.

She bypassed his hand and stepped straight into his arms. "I'll take an umbrella."

A laugh rose unbidden in his throat. He suspected Kate was going to be in for a rather rude awakening. He sighed and rested his chin on her shining hair. "I worry about you," he murmured over her head. "I don't want anything to happen to you."

"I don't want anything to happen to you, either." Her arms tightened around his lean waist.

"So you want to come along to protect me?" He couldn't quite keep the thread of amusement from his voice.

She lifted her head and smiled at him, aware that her heart was in her eyes. "Something like that."

His lips brushed gently over hers, but when he urged her head back down to his chest once more, there was almost a frantic urgency in the way they clung to each other. It was as if they both feared that precious moments like this were measured.

And Father Time was counting the hours...with relentless persistence.

CHAPTER TWELVE

WHILE KATE TOOK CARE of packing their belongings, Jason went in search of a car to rent. She had just finished snapping her suitcase shut when the phone rang again.

A feeling of dread welled inside her, and she froze for a split second. Had the kidnappers changed their minds already? After five rings, she reluctantly dragged the receiver to her ear. "Hello?"

"*Señora*? Señora McAllister?"

The accented voice belonged to a man, but it was loud and booming. She relaxed instinctively.

"This is Manuel. Manuel Ortega. You remember me, *sí*?"

Sí, she echoed silently. After the way he'd stood her up yesterday, how could she forget? "Of course." Her tone was deliberately cool. "Is there something I can do for you?"

"I want to tell you how sorry I am that I could not meet you yesterday."

Kate twirled the cord around her finger and sat down on the bed. "It's a little late," she said stiffly. "Especially after I made the trip for nothing."

"I'm sorry," he said again. "But my son Roberto was sick and we had to take him to the doctor *inmediatamente*. He is okay now, but—" a sigh came over the line

"—you have a little boy, *sí*? You know how it is when he is sick."

Hmm, she thought silently. He sounded genuinely contrite, but how much of his excuse was fact or fiction, she wasn't certain. More than likely, it was just as Jason said. With Greg away, Manuel will play.

"I can meet you at Hidalgo Field in half an hour, if you still wish it, *señora*."

"I'm afraid I can't," she said absently. "We're leaving Mexico City this morning."

"So you have found Señor McAllister?"

That made her stop and think. "We've got just about everything taken care of," she hedged.

"Bueno, bueno!" The little man sounded quite happy. "I am so glad for you. I will see Señor McAllister soon, *sí*?"

"Very soon, I expect." Kate frowned. She was certain she made a terrible liar, but she didn't give the call a second thought after she'd hung up a minute later.

Jason was gone a little longer than she'd expected, but they checked out of the hotel as soon as he arrived back with the Jeep he'd rented. Their first step was to withdraw money from the bank where Kate had deposited the draft on Monday. She purposely requested small bills, hoping that if worse came to worst, she would be able to bluff the kidnappers into believing she'd brought the full amount.

She tried not to watch as Jason locked the small pouch of money in the glove compartment. They had just emerged from the bank and carrying so much cash made her nervous. Conversely, it seemed an inordinately meager amount compared to the fifty thousand the kidnappers had demanded. It made her even more nervous to wonder if it would be enough to buy Greg's freedom. In spite of what Jason seemed to think, she was beginning to suspect that their chances of rescuing Greg were practically nonexistent.

In an effort to rid her mind of such disturbing thoughts, her eyes moved to the back of the Jeep, which was cluttered with various articles. "Looks like we're planning to stay for a week instead of just a night," she commented.

The firm contours of his mouth curved. "We're not headed for a pleasant stroll in the neighborhood park, Kate. We needed a few essentials, like food and water and something to sleep on."

"Don't tell me." She was unable to take exception to his gentle chiding. "We get to sleep under the stars. Roughing it, right?"

"Roughing it." His slow-growing smile deepened.

"One sleeping bag or two?"

"It's too hot for sleeping bags. The further east we go, the warmer it gets." A hint of unwilling amusement edged his voice. "We're stuck with a couple of blankets."

"Too bad," she murmured with a sigh. "I was hoping we could generate a little body heat."

Jason wanted desperately to laugh, but at the same time he experienced a wave of fierce protectiveness. He suspected Kate wasn't inclined to take his warnings at all seriously, but traipsing around in the mountains would cure her of that, as well as the faintly provocative gleam in her eyes. He had no doubt that making love would be the last thing on her mind.

IT TOOK NEARLY AN HOUR to escape the snarled traffic and urban sprawl of the city. Once they were out on the open highway, Kate had expected the road to be narrow, winding and full of potholes. Instead it climbed fast and steep and smooth toward verdant forests of pine, offering a splendid view of snow-decked volcanoes framed by the deep bowl of blue sky.

They passed numerous small shrines built into the roadside and tiny open-air stands with fresh fruit piled into elaborate pyramids. Absorbed as she was by the sights and sounds, a faint pang of dread gripped Kate's heart as she thought of Greg. Her smile was half-sad, half-wistful as she spied a busload of *turistas* swarming the steps of an enormous church topped by a brightly painted dome of gold and blue.

Jason seemed to sense her feelings. "It's almost over," he said very quietly. His fingers swallowed hers as he pulled her hand across the seat and laid it familiarly against his denim-sheathed thigh.

"Is it?" She couldn't quite control the tremor of fear in her voice. "I wonder."

She lapsed into silence. She fought against it, but suddenly she was seized by a feeling of near panic. The night they had spent in each other's arms was precious beyond words, but everything was still so new between them, so tentative and fragile. With such a shaky foundation, it was easily destroyed.

The thought was far from comforting. The love she and Jason shared had never been simple and uncomplicated. When they were together, it was too easy to shut out everything but themselves. But facing the outside world was a fact of life. What would happen once they were home again?

Kate had no desire to find herself hurtled back in time, caught between Greg and Jason as she had once been caught between Jason and her father. There had been so much against them all those years ago. Was it really any different now? Did they dare brave such odds once more?

Her grip on his hand was almost frantic. "Jason?"

"What, babe?"

She'd never heard such tenderness, such caring in his voice. She was immediately ashamed for harboring such foolish doubts. A galvanizing rush of emotion, sweet and pure like a wild mountain stream, poured through her. The answers she sought so desperately were before her very eyes.

Right next to her, to be precise. She leaned across to brush her lips against the hardness of Jason's cheek. *I love you,* she whispered silently.

Without taking his eyes from the winding road, he turned his head at the last second so that their lips met instead. In the fraction of a second allotted them, he communicated and she received a soundless echo of the voice in her heart.

It was enough, for now. It was more than enough.

"DAMN!"

Kate didn't even hear Jason's muttered curse, nor did she realize she had fallen asleep until she felt the Jeep grind to a halt. She stretched in the seat and saw that the sky had turned the color of lead. Just in time for the afternoon rains, she thought gloomily. Glancing at her watch, she saw that they had been traveling for nearly three hours.

She turned to Jason with a startled murmur. "Are we there already? I thought—"

Something was wrong. She could see it in the thrust of his jaw, the coiled alertness in his big body as he yanked the keys from the ignition, his eyes focused over his shoulder.

"What is it?" The hard look on his dark face frightened her.

When he said nothing, Kate followed the direction of his eyes. Behind them, the unpaved, one-lane road was steep and twisting, an endless series of loops and hairpin turns that snaked up the mountainside.

She was suddenly very glad she'd been asleep during the treacherous ascent. "Where are we?"

"We turned off the main road about half an hour ago." Jason shoved the door open and whipped around to the front fender. Kate's stomach dropped when she saw that he had pulled off onto a narrow ledge. Only a few inches of gravel and a crumbling stone wall no more than a foot high stopped them from plunging into a deep chasm gouged between the mountains.

She watched as he paused only long enough to release the catch on the hood and lift it high.

"Jason!" Kate sputtered when he yanked her door open. Unlocking the glove compartment, he grabbed the leather pouch containing the ransom money and shoved it inside his shirt. "What are you doing?"

He grabbed her hand and pulled her from the Jeep, his face grim. "I want him to think we had engine trouble and we've walked ahead to the next village."

His jerky mutter made no sense. "Who?"

"Whoever is following us!"

"We're being followed?" Her gasp was cut short as he ran across the road, towing her behind him like a puppet on a string.

"Yes, damn it! I noticed a pickup tailing us about an hour ago." Kate barely caught the words before he shoved her behind the trunk of an enormous tree. High above, the gnarled branches flared like huge gray-black shadowed wings.

Frantically she twisted her head to try to see Jason, but he had crouched down behind her. "Who? Who is following us?"

"That's what I want to find out! And for God's sake, keep your voice down!" Jason's whisper was rough and urgent.

Her pulse skittered alarmingly. Who would want to keep tabs on them? A shiver rippled along her spine. Behind her, she could feel the heat of Jason's chest trapped against her back, the strength of his hands anchored firmly to her shoulders. His warmth and his touch were comforting, but she could also feel the rigid tension of his body. His senses were straining as he restlessly scanned the roadway, watching and waiting, silent and alert.

The minutes dragged by. Five. Maybe ten. Kate was beginning to think he had only imagined someone was following them.

"Jason," she began. His hands bit into her shoulders, silencing her as effectively as a hand clamped over her mouth. She turned her head and glared up at him, but he pressed a finger to his lips then pointed toward the Jeep once more.

Kate was ready to scream. Her legs had gone numb and much to her disgust, a faint drizzle began to fall. And still they waited.

Her patience had just about reached its limit when the sound of a laboring engine reached her ears. Her eyes widened, glued to the Jeep as a battered-looking pickup lumbered to a halt behind it.

The engine was cut abruptly, but several minutes passed before a man got out. Kate heaved a silent sigh. The fine drizzle that showered from the sky was like a thin filmy curtain, obscuring her vision. To make matters worse, the man had jammed a hat down low over his forehead.

Her breathing quickened as he rammed a hand in his pocket. His other hand fingered his jaw as he leaned back against the door. The pose was one of casual nonchalance, as if he had all the time in the world, but she wasn't fooled. Her breath quickened. She felt every muscle in Jason's body tighten at exactly the same moment.

The man glanced covertly in all directions, then ambled toward the Jeep. There was only an instant's hesitation before he boldly opened the door and slipped inside.

Jason lowered his mouth to her ear. "I'll go find out who our friend is."

Kate nodded.

He started to move away, then abruptly checked himself. "You stay here!" he added fiercely. "And don't you dare move until I come back for you. You're a little too headstrong sometimes, but this time I really do know best!"

An unwilling smile edged her lips. Too headstrong? This was a change, indeed. "Anything you say," she murmured. She resisted the urge to salute smartly.

He briefly searched her eyes. Then, apparently satisfied with what he found, he pressed a hard kiss on her lips. When he slipped away, he was careful to stay low and behind the intruder's line of vision. Kate knew he was completely capable of taking care of himself, but a tiny frisson of fear inched down her spine when she saw him draw the pistol from his belt. He crept stealthily alongside the Jeep, then yanked the door open and lunged inside.

There was a moment of breathless panic until she saw Jason drag the other man out by his collar. The man's hat came off in the process, and then all Kate could do was stare in furious recognition.

CHAPTER THIRTEEN

"LOOKING FOR SOMETHING?"

For all its mildness, it was the type of voice to send chills up a man's spine. Neither the lethal undertone nor the ominous glitter in Jason's eyes went unnoticed by his audience.

Without another word, he hauled Manuel Ortega from the front seat and shoved him against the side of the Jeep. The flurry of movement scarcely caused a break in his breathing, but beads of sweat popped out on Ortega's forehead, mingling with the fine mist of rain. His dark skin turned a mottled red. His black eyes flitted to and fro before fastening on a point just past his shoulder.

Somehow Jason wasn't surprised to find Kate at his side.

"Why, you little runt!" She planted her fists on her hips and glared at Ortega indignantly.

Jason raised his eyebrows. Not precisely the words he would have chosen, but they did manage to convey the general idea.

"Why are you following us?" she demanded hotly.

Ortega's eyes darted to Jason. He still held Ortega pinned to the Jeep with one strong hand, the other casually held the pistol at his side. "Let's hold off with the questions for a minute," he said softly, "and see if our friend here has anything he'd like to show us first."

It didn't occur to Kate that he was talking about weapons until he pressed the pistol into her hand and asked her to kindly keep it pointed away from him and on their guest instead. Even then, she silently scoffed. She admitted that Ortega following them was rather suspicious. But with his drooping mustache, snapping black eyes and eagerness to please, he seemed perfectly harmless.

Scant seconds later, she passed the gun back to Jason, too stunned to say anything. Ortega had been armed with a small derringer, a switchblade and a vicious looking stiletto. Jason's face was hard as he tossed all three down the mountainside, as well as a crumpled pack of cigarettes.

"Now," he said in an unexpectedly pleasant tone. "Shall we take up where we left off? I believe the lady asked why you were following us. And I would like to know exactly what you hoped to find in our Jeep."

The fat man's Adam's apple bobbed, but he said nothing. At his silence, Jason shoved him back against the Jeep. His fingers tightened around the man's pudgy throat, then he slowly brought the nose of the pistol level with Ortega's chest.

This time all traces of pleasantry had vanished from Jason's voice. "Talk. Now," he demanded.

The two words were all that was necessary. Sweat began to pour down Ortega's face. "The money." He gulped. "I was after the money."

"The ransom money? For Greg's return?"

"*Sí. Sí!*" Ortega's head bobbed vehemently.

Jason's eyes narrowed. "How do you know about it?" he demanded harshly. "We only told you that Greg had been kidnapped. The ransom was never mentioned. Was it, Kate?"

Kate had been looking on with a kind of dazed numbness. At the sound of her name, she glanced up at Jason, desperately trying to gather her scattered wits. "I never said a word to him. I'm positive!"

He stared at Ortega, and suddenly the pieces of the puzzle began to fit. "You're in on it," he muttered, almost to himself. Then he jabbed the gun in Ortega's ribs. "Damn it, you're in on it!"

Ortega erupted into a spiel of Spanish. Kate's eyes darted between the two men. Ortega seemed genuinely terrified. Watching Jason's expression harden further with every word that poured out of the other man's mouth, Kate was glad she wasn't in Ortega's shoes. Every so often Jason interrupted with a clipped demand.

Finally Ortega lapsed into silence. Kate wasted no time in turning to Jason. "What?" she asked urgently. "What is it? Is he the one who kidnapped Greg?"

He nodded. "One of them," he said curtly. "The other two are holding Greg. He stayed in Mexico City to keep an eye on us."

"So he's the one who's been calling?"

"Yes." There was a barely restrained savagery to Jason's voice. "But he decided he didn't like the idea of splitting the ransom with his buddies."

Kate gasped. "That first night. The man in my room."

"It was him. He didn't show up at Greg's office yesterday just in case you happened to recognize his voice."

"And the van that swerved toward us yesterday? He was behind that, too?"

"No, or so he says." Jason's eyes never wavered from the other man's face. "Either way, he's certainly a man to make the most of his chances. He saw you stop at the bank on your way back to the hotel, and took advantage of all the commotion to snatch your purse, hoping the ransom was in it.''

"So he really believed me when I told him I'd managed to get my hands on the rest of the money?''

"Exactly. He really thought we'd played right into his hands. He set up the drop for tomorrow, knowing you'd have the money. He followed us, hoping to be able to steal it before then. But even if he couldn't, he still figured he'd have his share of a three-way split.''

Kate went pale. "So if we showed up minus the ransom, his buddies would have thought we'd decided to renege on the deal.'' And there was no telling what might have happened to Greg.

Jason nodded, his mouth tight with self-disgust. How could he have been so blind? He had brushed Ortega aside with scarcely a thought, passed him off as being lazy, eager to make a buck the easiest way possible. Well, he was right there.

"There's more,'' he told Kate, then glanced up at the threatening sky. "But it'll have to wait until later. If we wait any longer, it'll be too dark to find a place to spend the night.''

"What about him?'' She gestured to Ortega. "Is he coming with us?''

Jason's gaze swung to Ortega. "He certainly is,'' he said very softly. "He's going to lead us to Greg. He may even come in handy as a bargaining tool, although I can't imagine anyone wanting him that badly.''

Ortega blanched visibly at his nasty smile, and went paler yet when Jason whipped his belt off. He spun him around and pulled his arms behind his back, then proceeded to wrap the leather belt tightly around his wrists and through Ortega's belt loops so he couldn't move his hands. If the circumstances hadn't been quite so grim,

Kate might have laughed at the sight of Ortega's belly and nose mashed against the side of the Jeep. But as it was, she was very very glad Jason was with her. She shivered every time she thought of the weapons Ortega had been hiding.

Jason nudged Ortega toward the battered pickup. Without releasing his hold on him, Jason tossed the keys to Kate. She reflexively caught them. "Can you get our stuff from the Jeep and put it in the truck?"

Her jaw sagged. "We're taking that?"

"Uh-huh." At her incredulous expression, a faintly teasing light appeared in his eyes.

Kate wasn't amused. "Why can't we take the Jeep?"

"Because I don't want to take the chance that one of Ortega's buddies will wander down this way and recognize his pickup. If they see it's been abandoned, they might suspect something."

While she begrudged the wisdom of his patient explanation, he dropped the next bomb. "You get to drive, Kate, so I can keep an eye on our guest."

Her? Drive this dangerous gravel road that threatened to drop off the ends of the earth with every bend they approached? And in the rain yet! She hated heights nearly as much as she hated to fly.

"I don't know if I can." She sounded shaky and breathless, exactly the way she felt inside. Her horror must have been mirrored on her face, because Jason stared at her for a long moment.

"You can do it," he told her softly. "All you have to do is take it slow and easy, and keep your eyes straight ahead on the road." He paused. "You'll do fine, Kate."

Would she? It seemed she had no choice, though. She nodded jerkily and went to collect the luggage, backpacks and blankets.

By the time she'd finished stowing everything beneath a tarp she had found in the back of the pickup, the drizzle had stopped. That, combined with Jason's words, managed to instill in her at least a small measure of confidence, which was certainly more than she'd had a few minutes before. She caught a glimpse of Ortega's extremely apprehensive expression when she climbed up beside him, and she derived a grim satisfaction at his wariness. Her spine stiffened automatically. He didn't like women drivers? Then let this be a lesson to his Latin machismo.

The only hitch in the next half hour came when Kate encountered a bus coming up the mountainside in the opposite direction. She was forced to find a niche to back into so the bus could pass. By the time she started the descent into a valley rich with flowers and greenery, she was feeling rather proud of herself.

She heard Ortega say something to Jason, then he said sharply, "Here, Kate. Turn to the right."

The road was no more than a dirt path, full of potholes and ruts, with an overgrowth of weeds separating the tire tracks. Kate clung to the wheel, grateful for something to hang onto as they bounced along. The whine of the engine told her they were heading uphill again, and branches slapped against the top of the cab and the windows as they headed into a dark tunnel of trees. She breathed a silent sigh of relief when Jason instructed her to veer off to the side. "End of the line," he said with a faint smile.

Kate opened the door and jumped down from the driver's seat. She studied the thickly wooded area with a mixture of curiosity and caution. "Greg is near here?"

Jason shot a hard look at Ortega, who stood docilely several feet away, his hands still tied behind his back. "A couple of miles to the north, or so he says. We don't have much choice but to trust him. We'll find a place to sleep, then I'll have him show me where Greg's being held.''

Kate said nothing. Instead her eyes traveled assessingly around their surroundings once more. The air was warm but dense and heavy. With the passing of the afternoon rain, the last remaining rays of daylight had brightened the valley floor. But here the light was dim and muted. In their struggle to seek sunlight, various plant life climbed high on the tree branches.

She had to admit the rain forest had a wild, unrestrained beauty. The soft ground underfoot was a furious tangle of dark shrubs and creeping vines, while lushly colored flowers blossomed high in the treetops, blending with the first faint embers of twilight. Light and dark. So bright and beautiful it might have been Eden.

''Now?'' She moistened her lips. ''You're going now?''

He heard the faint note of dismay in her voice. ''Just to have a look around, so I know what we're up against. That way I'll have at least tonight to figure out the safest way in and the best way to get Greg out tomorrow.'' He hesitated. ''It'll be okay, Kate.''

He was right, Kate told herself as they collected the gear from the pickup. Jason could hardly plunge in blindly and expect to be able to rescue Greg. The chance of something going wrong or someone getting hurt would be far too great.

She sensed that he was in a hurry to leave before it turned dark. He cleared a small area and set up the nylon tent and built a fire. He then freed Ortega's wrists, a concession to the uneven terrain, she supposed. When he turned to Kate, he smiled a little at her woebegone look.

He settled his hands on her shoulders and gently squeezed. ''You'll be fine, Kate. The smoke shouldn't come to anyone's attention.'' He glanced from the fire to the thick foliage overhead. ''Besides, I don't think there's anyone around for miles. Just stay near the fire or in the tent.''

''It's not me I'm worried about.'' Her eyes were dark with concern. ''Can't I come with you?''

''No,'' he said firmly. ''Just in case something goes wrong, I want you here where it's safe. If you have to, you can take Ortega's pickup and go on to the nearest village.''

She stiffened. ''I thought you were just going to scout the area.''

Jason sighed. ''I am.''

''You aren't going to try to nab Greg out from under their noses tonight?''

''Then come back here after you?'' A frown appeared between his dark brows. ''I'm not Superman, Kate. And I wouldn't put you in a situation where I had to choose between you and Greg.''

Because for Jason there would be no choice at all. She winced inwardly and wished she hadn't mentioned it. Glancing at the dense green barrier that surrounded them, she muttered, ''You sure you can find your way back here?''

''I'll leave a trail of bread crumbs,'' he said lightly. His arms were fiercely tender though as he drew her to him for a painfully brief but thoroughly passionate kiss. When he pulled away, he smiled directly into her eyes. ''If I'm not here by midnight, take the money and run.'' He withdrew the pouch from his shirt and pressed it into her hands, keeping his back to Ortega so the other man was unable to see what he'd done.

Take the money and run. I'll leave a trail of bread crumbs. More than likely it would be cracker crumbs, she decided dourly, eyeing the remains of the meal of cheese, crackers and beef jerky she'd just eaten. Manuel Ortega hadn't looked especially pleased with the rations he had been given. Or perhaps he had disliked the idea of eating on the run. Either way, Kate hadn't felt sorry for the man.

The mosquitoes and the darkness finally drove her into the tent. She was too tense and keyed up to sleep, but she wrapped a blanket around herself and lay down anyway. What if Manuel had lied about Greg's whereabouts? What if he led Jason straight into a trap? Though Jason certainly seemed to have put the fear of God into him, the thoughts didn't make her feel any more at ease. She sighed, absently wishing the ground weren't so hard.

Kate wasn't the type of person to fall apart at the seams at the first sign of danger, but she was afraid. Not only for herself and Jason, but for Greg. She envied Jason's calm and control. But, she reminded herself, between Vietnam and his stint in the DEA, Jason had undoubtedly been trained to encounter the unexpected, to adapt to any situation.

There it was again. Vietnam. And Greg. She rolled onto her side. The eerie silhouette of the fire could be seen through the thin wall of the tent. She stared at the dancing shadows, but pictured in her mind were the ragged boundaries of the scars on Jason's shoulder.

She remembered the night he had told her Greg hated him, that the enmity between them had started because of her, but hadn't ended there. She thought of the scars he still carried that didn't show. Some dark, obscure secret still lay between the two men. What had Greg done to Jason that haunted him to this day? Certainly Greg had never seen fit to tell her. If Jason hadn't already denied it, she could have easily believed that he had provided Greg with more than a verbal target.

It was still on her mind when Jason returned a long time later. Kate scrambled to her knees when the flap parted. A beam of light preceded Ortega, who huffed and puffed as he crawled through the opening.

Jason ducked through next, holding a flashlight. Just the sight of him brought a wealth of turbulent emotions to her chest. He looked strong and very intent, but for an instant she felt she was facing a stranger. She could read nothing—whether he had met with success or defeat— from the totally inscrutable expression on his face. It was only when his gaze cut across to hers that she felt herself relax.

"You okay?" he asked softly.

She nodded. Her eyes clung to his, fraught with unspoken messages.

Jason turned his attention to Ortega. The tent was perhaps eight-by-eight, and the other man had moved to the opposite corner. "Let me have your shoes," he said curtly.

Kate's eyebrows shot up but she said nothing. She didn't really know what was in Jason's mind until he asked her for the keys to Ortega's pickup and disappeared outside once more, the other man's shoes tucked under his arm. No one but a fool would trek across the rain forest barefoot. The terrain was far too rough.

Kate hugged her knees to her chest and glanced at Ortega, who seemed none the worse for his journey. The man grinned at her, but she didn't smile back. He was far from being the teddy-bear type in her eyes, especially considering the weapons he'd been carrying.

Jason retied Ortega's wrists when he returned, then dropped a blanket on his squat shoulders. The man promptly laid down and turned his back on them.

"Am I next?" She teased him a little, thrusting her booted feet out before her.

Jason planted a hand near her hip and dropped down beside her. With his other hand, he adjusted the glow of the flashlight toward the side so that it illuminated only a small section of the tent.

"I couldn't stop with just your boots." His eyes were soft with an oddly tender light that warmed Kate clear to her soul. "Come to think of it, if you weren't here, I probably wouldn't have quit with his shoes, either." He nodded toward Ortega.

It took a moment before she gleaned his meaning. "That's a rather unorthodox way of discouraging someone's escape."

"Unorthodox," he agreed. "But effective." He caught her hand. "Let's go outside and I'll tell you the rest," he said quietly.

He grabbed the blankets and pulled her to her feet. The darkness outside was so absolute it seemed as if a thick black quilt had been draped over her head and pulled tight. But even if Jason hadn't flicked on the flashlight, the guiding warmth of his rough palm sliding against hers was reassuring. He spread one of the blankets, then tugged her down once more.

She drew her legs up to her chest and glanced at him. "Did Ortega give you any trouble?"

"No." He seemed to hesitate. "He was a lot more cooperative than I thought he'd be."

"So you know where they're holding Greg!" She scrambled to her knees and clutched Jason's arm, torn between hope and fear. "Did you see him? Is he all right? Can you get him out okay?"

The muscles of his forearm stiffened beneath her touch. He met her gaze, but in the fraction of a second before he jerked his eyes away, she saw the silent battle he fought with himself. A muscle twitched in his cheek as he stared straight ahead.

Kate realized too late how Jason might interpret her eagerness. She was concerned only for Greg's safety, but it was not the loving concern of a wife for her husband. She choked back a small cry of distress. It stung her deeply to know that after all they had shared—and just last night—that Jason could doubt her already. But it also pained her to admit that she understood his uncertainty, for she was responsible for it.

She drew a deep, shaky breath. "I'm sorry—" she started to say, but he cut her off.

"Don't be," he said tautly. "You've done nothing wrong, Kate."

No? Kate wasn't so certain. She had dredged up old ghosts, called back haunting memories he had tried so desperately to forget. It had been no less an ordeal for her, but... She sighed. They had found each other again, but they couldn't erase the past. The pain they had inflicted on each other was far too deep. Only time would heal the wounds. Time, patience and a great deal of love.

She breathed a silent sigh of relief when he stretched out and pulled her down next to him. Kate waited expectantly, listening to the steady drumbeat of his heart beneath her ear.

It was a moment before he spoke.

"Freeing Greg shouldn't be as difficult as I thought," he said finally. "They're holding him at an abandoned coffee plantation a few miles from here. Ortega says there are only two other men guarding him, and from what I could tell, he isn't lying.''

"What about the plane?''

"It's in a field near the house, thank God. There's an old dirt road that leads up to the plantation, but we'd have to head back the way we came to pick it up again. I think we'd be better off leaving before dawn and sneaking in through the jungle.''

"The way you just came from?''

He nodded. "We can grab Greg at first light and make a run for it. If necessary, I'll have to create some kind of distraction.''

Simple in theory, Kate thought to herself. Probably not so simple to execute, but she intended to keep her fingers crossed. "A coffee plantation,'' she murmured. "That's where he's been all along?''

"Apparently.'' Jason sounded grim. "Greg wasn't alone when he left for Veracruz, after all. Ortega was the one who was with Greg when he left Mexico City. He forced him to land at the plantation, where his two buddies were waiting.'' He paused. "They planned to hijack a shipment of silver.''

Kate blinked. Her mind backtracked to the mine that had closed years ago. "But there isn't any...or is there?''

"No. Ortega only knew what Greg wanted him to know—what showed on the books. And the books showed that he was transporting silver. These guys got Greg down on the ground expecting to make off with a mint in silver bars. The last thing they expected were pre-Hispanic Indian artifacts.''

"Artifacts! That's what he's smuggling?''

"That's it. Ortega showed me.''

She frowned. "But where would he come by something like that?''

"Who knows? There's always a dig going on somewhere in Mexico. He could be hooked up with a crooked
archaeologist, someone who's pilfering pieces and selling them on the black market in the States. Or maybe
Greg's doing it on his own."

It made sense, she thought with a sigh. She'd known
almost from the start that Greg was involved in something shady, but she couldn't help feeling a pinprick of
hurt.

"Kate, you won't believe this, but Ortega and his
buddies thought—they still think—those artifacts are just
a bunch of junk. They've got cartons and cartons of
pottery and jewelry and jade figurines just sitting in an
old shack behind the house. 'Useless pieces of clay' is
what Ortega called them."

Jason was right. She didn't believe it. "Don't tell me,"
she said slowly. "They thought it wasn't worth much, but
since they already had Greg, they came up with the ransom scheme instead."

He nodded. "Greg apparently did a lot of talking
about you and the shop. And your father, too," he admitted. "Ortega got the impression you were from a
wealthy family. And he said Greg always carried a lot of
money around."

"His fee, I suppose, for smuggling the artifacts." Her
tone was blistering. It made her furious to know that
Greg had been stupid enough to involve himself in
something so underhanded. "He must have known what
he was doing was illegal. I don't think he can plead innocence, since it's his business to know."

True, Jason confirmed silently. Not only was it illegal
to remove national treasures from Mexico, but it was just
as illegal to bring then into the United States.

"Kate." He hesitated. He knew the timing couldn't have been poorer, but there was something he had to get off his chest. "Kate, if we get Greg out of this, don't expect too much of me." The pitch of his voice was not precisely ominous, but very low.

"What do you mean?" She raised herself slightly and gazed down at him.

Jason shook his head. "Where Greg and I are concerned...I don't think it's possible for me to ever forget what happened between us."

"You're saying that you and Greg can never be friends again?"

His laugh was short and harsh. "I seriously doubt it."

Kate's heart skipped a beat. "Because of me?"

"That's one of the reasons." He didn't look at her.

She stared at him. Her heart resumed with thick, almost fearful strokes. "And the other?"

There was no answer.

Her earlier thoughts came back in full force. Did she dare broach the subject of Vietnam? She felt her way very carefully. "The other has to do with the war, doesn't it."

It wasn't a question. It was a quiet statement of fact.

Again Jason didn't answer. A deathly silence vibrated between them. His withdrawal was almost tangible. Kate felt as if she could see him slipping further and further into himself, and the realization was like a knife to the heart. Had they come so far only to slide back into the same old niche?

Slowly she eased forward, so that she lay just above him. Her arm rested on the broad landscape of his chest. "Tell me what happened," she urged softly.

He was as tense as a thin metal wire about to snap. She could feel the rigidity of his body against hers, see the lines of strain etched beside his mouth. His eyes were open as he stared into the stark blackness of the night, but he seemed so far away. Back in another time, another place.

She bent her head and pressed her lips to the hair-roughened hollow beneath his throat. "Please, Jason," she whispered. "Tell me how you got shot."

After the smallest of hesitations, both his arms slid around her. She allowed him to tuck her head under his chin. There was a world of emotion reflected in the deep sigh he gave. He sounded so tired, almost defeated. His voice was very low when he finally spoke.

"I had about a month left in my tour there. I guess I thought I was practically home free. We'd started withdrawing troops, and the fighting had finally dropped off a little. But then it started all over again. A Viet Cong outpost and supply point had been located, and the assault teams were going at it with everything they had.

"I don't know how many missions we flew that day—so many I lost count. We set down late in the afternoon near a village in the jungle. The first thing I saw was a chopper that had been shot down. There were holes ripped in the fuselage big enough to put my fist through, but for the first time that day, the gunfire wasn't close enough to make my ears ring."

He paused, and his arm tightened around her. "I remember thinking it was almost too quiet. The casualties were heavy. We'd just been advised there was dense fog moving in and we didn't want to end up stranded. We needed every available hand, including the pilot's."

Kate's heart began to pound dully. A heavy knot of dread formed in the pit of her stomach. Greg. He was talking about Greg.

"There was no one around. We thought the Vietnamese had deserted the village before the shelling even

started. And it was so damn hard to figure out if someone was Viet Cong. They'd grab a hat and a hoe and
you'd think they were just another farmer.''

Jason stopped for a moment, and took a deep, not
quite steady breath before continuing. ''We'd barely even
started to load the wounded when all hell broke loose. A
grenade went off. A man and a woman charged out of
one of huts—both carrying machine guns. Our gunner
dropped the woman right away, but the man nailed him
just as fast. In the blink of an eye, Greg and I were the
only ones left. I'd been hit but I was still standing. He
thought he had us both. I was maybe a hundred yards
from the chopper. Greg wasn't more than a few feet
away. But he pointed the gun at Greg and kept moving
closer, so I grabbed an M-16....''

There was no need for him to go on. Kate understood,
but she instinctively knew the story wasn't finished.

''There were so many hard feelings between the two of
us. Greg couldn't hide it and neither could I. But I
thought the fact that we were once friends counted for
something.''

The silence dragged on endlessly before she heard Jason's voice again. His tone was carefully controlled, void
of any emotion at all. ''He left me there, Kate. Greg left
me there. I hadn't taken more than three steps before he
was in the chopper. I've gone over it in my mind a thousand times, trying to come up with an excuse for him.
That maybe he was scared, or just not thinking clearly.
But I'll never forget the way he looked at me, just before
he lifted off. As if—as if he just didn't give a damn.''

Kate's breath came jerkily. It was the only way she felt
she could breathe. Greg had left Jason alone, among the
dying and the dead. ''My God,'' she choked. ''How
long—''

"The fog rolled in later that night. It didn't lift for three days." His answer was almost deathly quiet. "There was no way any other units could get in or out. After the salvage crew found me, I spent the next few weeks in the hospital before I was shipped home. I never saw Greg again."

Kate closed her eyes. She felt cold and empty, yet she was filled with a burning rage at Greg. She knew, better than anyone perhaps, how cold and inconsiderate he could be. But to know that he was capable of such deliberate callousness... She shuddered.

Jason had a right to be bitter and disillusioned. He had been betrayed by the man who was once his best friend. If only she were able to soothe Jason's hurt, take away the pain and anguish he had suffered. Regret poured through her for reopening such a raw wound.

Her eyes flicked open. Slowly she raised her head and gazed down at him. His face was haggard and drawn; it made her throat ache.

"I'm sorry, Jason. I'm so sorry." The words were as shaky as she felt inside. "If I'd known, I would never have asked you to come with me."

In a lightning movement, he turned on his side. His arms bound her tightly against him, and he held her shaking form against him until he felt the tremors subside.

"You see why I didn't want to tell you?" His fingers tenderly smoothed the hair away from her temple. "It's not your fault, Kate."

Her expression was bleak. The anguish in her eyes cut him to the quick before she dropped her gaze. She gave a tiny shake of her head. "That night at your ranch, do you remember what I said? For old times' sake..." Her breath caught raggedly. "I knew you wouldn't refuse if I asked you to do it for me. I—I used you—"

"No." He hooked his fingers under her chin until she was forced to meet his eyes. "It was my choice, Kate. I'm the first to admit I didn't do this for Greg. I came because of you. *For* you. But now—" the expression in his eyes grew incredibly soft "—now I'm doing it for us."

Jason kissed her then, and it was more than a melding of mouths, a merging of souls. He conveyed every nuance of emotion that filled his heart, from the aching tenderness she roused in him to the fierce desire that stormed his senses whenever he touched her.

She clung to him tightly when it was over. "I'll be so glad when this is over and we're home again."

Home. He eased onto his back and resettled Kate's body against his. His hands idly stroked her back as he waited for the familiar sense of peace to fill his mind.

It didn't happen.

He couldn't explain his sudden edginess. He had the strangest sensation that a dark shadow loomed before him...before both of them. A shadow with the name of Greg McAllister.

CHAPTER FOURTEEN

BY KATE'S STANDARDS, it was still night when Jason woke her early the next morning. Above the forest ceiling, the sky was an inky stretch of black velvet.

"What time is it?" she mumbled. She yawned sleepily, her body protesting the early awakening. She had to struggle to keep her eyes open or she would have fallen back to sleep.

"Four-thirty."

Low as his voice was, there was a no-nonsense ring to it that she couldn't ignore. She scrambled to her feet while Jason disappeared into the tent after Ortega.

Ortega stumbled out, clumsy and bleary-eyed. Kate scarcely had time to run her brush through her hair before Jason had the tent dismantled and the wad of blankets piled into the back of Ortega's pickup.

Kate bit her lip. "I thought you didn't want to drive there."

"I don't. Someone might hear the engine." He walked back to untie Ortega's hands, then glanced up in time to see her face brighten. "But don't get your hopes up," he added with a chuckle. "The way we're going is just as rough."

"Through the forest? Like you did last night?"

He nodded.

"Anything's an improvement over that rickety old crate, especially if I don't have to drive it." She slipped her shoulder bag over her arm. "Is he going with us?" She nodded at Ortega.

Jason's gaze swung to the other man. He paused as if considering, his eyes hard. "After all the trouble he's caused us, I ought to leave him here." A slow smile spread across his face when Ortega's eyes filled with relief. "Even if we kept his keys, though, he'd probably know how to hot-wire the engine—"

"No! No, *señor*!" Ortega shook his head frantically. "I know nothing of such things. Nothing!"

The smile was wiped from Jason's face. "I'll bet," he said coolly. "No, I'm afraid you're going to have to come with us. That way we can leave your friends a little calling card." He shrugged. "I wonder what they'll think when they find out you planned to steal the ransom. And it shouldn't take them long to figure exactly who put us onto them in the first place."

Ortega's shoulders sagged defeatedly when Jason turned him around, but Kate wasn't feeling particularly charitable toward him. As they trudged out of the makeshift camp, she decided that wily as he was, the shifty little man would undoubtedly find some way of convincing his accomplices he was completely innocent.

It was slow-going in the darkness. Even following the beam of light from the flashlight, Kate lost her footing more than once hurrying over moss-covered tree roots that rose from the ground like giant claws. She had no idea how either Ortega or Jason knew where they were going; they were surrounded by a confused jumble of dark green.

Jason finally caught her hand and pulled her along beside him. It was easier after that, but along with the concern in his eyes, there was also a hint of urgency. She knew how important it was that they arrive at the plantation while the outside world still slept. Not wanting to be any more of a burden, she quickened her pace and pushed herself harder.

She was breathless and gasping when a faint glimmer of gray finally sifted through the seemingly impenetrable canopy of trees. Droplets of moisture, glittering like tiny diamonds, bathed the surface of broad, leafy foliage. Finally, they broke free from the forest and stood at its edge.

"Keep your head down!"

Kate obeyed Jason's low command instinctively. A yard ahead of her, Ortega dropped where he stood. She stifled a weak grin when he hit the ground with a grunt and a thud. Her lungs ached from lack of air, but the fat man seemed half-dead.

She scarcely had time to draw even a single breath before she saw Jason crawl up behind him. His hands snaked out and he stretched a large handkerchief across Ortega's mouth, then tied it at the back of his head.

"Sorry, pal," he muttered. "But I can't take the chance you'll blow the horn on us." He dealt just as efficiently with the man's hands and feet. In seconds, Ortega had been neatly trussed up and secured to a misshapen tree stump.

Jason silently beckoned to Kate. She stayed low to the ground and edged up beside him, near the top of a gentle rise. When she was crouched next to him, she peered cautiously over the hill.

Below lay a small, natural clearing. The first thing she spotted was Greg's twin-engine Cessna, no more than three hundred yards away at the end of the clearing. Beyond was a cluster of ramshackle buildings, the largest of which was a long, adobe structure. The large fountain in front of the house was crumbling and eroded. Many of the roof tiles were cracked or missing; the same was true for the windows. But it had once been a grand old plantation. A dented-up van was parked near the house.

"Look. There!" Jason pointed to the side of the house where a brightly colored blanket hung from the window-frame. "That's the room Greg is supposed to be in."

"What now?" She gazed almost desperately at the eastern sky. Misty fingerlings of dawn—pink, mauve and pale gold—streaked the horizon.

"I want you inside the plane, that's what. You'll be safe there." They were already halfway down the hillside, scrambling toward the Cessna. Kate felt as if her arm had been yanked out of its socket. Before she was even aware of it, Jason had jerked open one of the double doors behind the wing and thrust her inside. Her shoulder bag landed on top of her. "Stay here!" he ordered roughly. "I mean it, Kate! Get down on the floor, keep your head away from the windows and stay inside the plane, no matter what!"

She was left staring at the dull metal casing of the opposite wall. Jason's stinging warning still rang in her ear, so she forced herself to lie still on the floor. But the suspense soon became too much. She had to know what was going on.

She pulled herself onto one of the passenger seats, then eased back as far as she could so she wouldn't be seen. Her eyes homed in on the house, and for a split second, her heart lurched. Where was Jason? Then, as if on cue, she saw a shadow shift against the wall and move stealthily toward the blanketed window.

He was inside! Jason was inside! Her nails dug into her palms as she watched and waited...watched and waited. The seconds became an eternity. Had he found Greg? Or had he, too, been caught? Would they harm him? Hold him for ransom, as well? It wasn't likely. Both men, she realized, would be able to identify...

No. No! She drew in a deep, shuddering breath. She wouldn't let herself give in to the feeling of blind panic.

At precisely that moment a man ambled through the front door. Damn! Greg's captors weren't asleep after all, at least this one wasn't. Dark and bearded, obviously of Latin descent, he stretched, yawned and rubbed his chest, then idly picked up a rifle at his side.

He disappeared into the house once more. He obviously didn't know Jason was inside—his attitude had been too casual. But there were two men guarding Greg. And what if Jason was discovered?

Her blood ran cold as she thought of the rifle.

Stay here, Kate! Stay inside the plane, no matter what! But she couldn't. She just couldn't! What was it Jason had said last night? *If necessary, I'll create some kind of distraction.* But Jason was already inside the house. It was too late for that. Or was it?

There was no time to debate. Kate jumped to the ground before she had time to think better of it. Her frenzied gaze swept the area—the ramshackle buildings, the clumps of trees and bushes, the small dented van parked in front of the house...the van!

Her thoughts were a mad jumble of hope and fear. But suddenly something Jeff had said—was it only last week?—flitted into her mind. *Short of hiring a commando team to blast him the hell out of there...*Granted, this wasn't quite the same thing. Would it even work? She didn't know; she only knew that she had to try.

Rags—she needed rags. Her eyes eyes lit on her shoulder bag, and she dropped to the ground and yanked a blouse from it. Another followed, and she tied them together. But then she realized she had no matches. Her heart sank like a stone. She couldn't start a fire without matches...no, wait! A cigarette lighter. Matches. Either one would do!

The world spun crazily as she tore back up the hillside, heedless of the scrub and branches whipping her legs and hands.

"Matches!" She dropped to her knees before Ortega. "Do you have any? You had cigarettes yesterday. Damn it, don't you have any?"

Ortega shrank back. His eyes above the gag telegraphed a message loud and clear: he thought this redhaired *norteamericana* was loco. Kate gave a hopeless little moan and began to rummage through his pockets.

"You've got one! Oh, thank God!" She clutched the small chrome lighter as if it were a gift from heaven.

Her heart was pounding furiously when she reached the plane. Her gaze swept frantically toward the house, but there was still no sign of either Jason or Greg. With scarcely a pause, she ducked down and ran toward the rear of the building. Her destination was the dented old van parked on the far side.

She uttered another fervent thank-you when she located the gas tank. The tires shielded her from the sight of anyone who might happen to come out of the house, and she was so close to the side of the building, she could slip around to the rear, then back to the plane unnoticed. She flipped open the tank and unscrewed the cap, then stuffed one end of the blouse down into the opening, praying there was gas in the van. It took several attempts to light the cigarette lighter, and her fingers were shaking so much she was half-afraid she would burn herself. But finally the edges of her blouse began to smolder. She waited until the flame started to lick up the thin cotton material, then she made a mad dash in the other direction.

She was panting by the time she ducked around the tail section of the plane. Her lungs burned and her thighs ached from trying to run while maintaining a half-crouch. She peered toward the house just in time to see Jason and Greg being pushed through the front door, their hands raised high in the air. Two men followed, each with a rifle trained straight ahead. The hefty, bearded one appeared dirty and unsavory, but the other man, tall and muscular, had a look of cruelty about him.

Kate began to pray.

One of the men barked out something in Spanish. Jason appeared to hesitate, then slowly he withdrew the pistol at his belt. He tossed it on the ground. A puffy cloud of dust whirled in the air when one of the men kicked it away.

Fear clutched at her insides. Every muscle in her body seemed frozen as she watched helplessly. Had she gone through all this only to see both Greg and Jason die before her very eyes? At the thought, panic swelled in her chest until she could scarcely breathe. If only there was something she could do...

Suddenly, without warning, the van burst into flames with an explosion that pierced her ears and sent scraps of metal rocketing in every direction.

It worked perfectly. Their captors turned instinctively toward the ball of fire. Jason moved first, intent on the tall one nearest him. His foot sliced up beneath the barrel of the rifle. It sailed end over end through the air and landed in a clump of weeds. Jason was on him with a flying tackle. His fist crashed into his jaw and the man was out like a light.

From the corner of her eye, she saw Greg and the bearded man rolling wildly in the dirt. Where the other rifle was, she had no idea. Her heart in her throat, she watched as Greg jumped to his feet. The man charged, head down, arms raised like a raging bull. Greg neatly sidestepped and the man rammed headfirst into the side of the house. A second later he sprawled face-down in the dirt.

Jason and Greg began to race for the plane.

She spied a faint movement behind them. The man Greg had taken down raised up on his elbows. He was shaking his head, as if he were dazed.

Her head snapped up and she surged to her feet. "He's awake!" she cried, waving her arms. Greg was falling further and further behind Jason. The man behind them staggered to his feet. "Hurry...hurry!" The hoarse scream sounded thin and far away. It took a moment to realize it was her own.

"Damn it, Kate, I told you to stay inside! Instead you're out running around behind my back!" Jason's lungs were on fire, his knuckles scraped and bleeding, and she was standing outside like a sitting duck, waving her arms! Still on the run, he caught her around the waist and half-dragged, half-carried her toward the hatch.

"Behind your back!" Her breath caught furiously. She twisted her head around to try to see him. "Why, if it weren't for me, you'd still be back there—"

His hands pulled her around for a brief hard kiss. "I know, and thank you. Remind me later to ask you how the hell you blew up that van."

Kate was thrust bodily into the plane. She had barely scrambled to all fours when she heard a loud popping sound. At first she couldn't identify the source, or perhaps her mind wouldn't accept it.

Gunfire.

She went numb. "Jason, he's shooting..."

But Jason was already gone. Kate dragged herself to the window in time to see an orange flash of fire spurt from a rifle held by the man who had regained consciousness. Greg wasn't more than fifteen feet away from the plane. But he was winded, exhausted.

She clapped her hand to her mouth as she cried out. Greg dropped to the ground, clutching his left arm. He was hit! Kate's heart lodged in her throat. Greg lurched to his knees, then fell back down. Another burst of gunfire came. Her heart throbbed fearfully. Oh, God, where was Jason?

Suddenly he zoomed into her line of vision. For the split second he bent over Greg she pictured another scene entirely. Jason and Greg running, not toward a plane, but a helicopter. Jason hit by a bullet, and left behind to die....

He slung Greg's arm over his shoulder and hauled him to his feet. Together they began to struggle forward. Again there was a burst of gunfire. It all happened in a matter of seconds, but to Kate it was like watching a horror movie in slow motion.

Greg's head popped through the doorway, followed by Jason's. The door slammed shut, but Kate hardly spared a glance for either man. The sudden quiet was ominous. Her eyes widened when she peered out the window again.

"He's running this way. He's loading the gun again!"

Jason swore and dropped the other man into the pilot's seat. "Can you get us out of here?"

"No problem." Greg's gasp was weak, but even as he spoke the engines gave a low whine.

Kate still hadn't taken her eyes from the bearded man. He was so close she imagined she could see the angry red flush of his skin. "Hurry!" she cried. "He's almost here!" As if the words needed more credence, a bullet pinged against the metal exterior.

A hand with a fearsome grip dragged her down to the floor. She heard a furious curse in her ear a fraction before a hard body landed atop hers, knocking the breath from her. Below her, the plane's wheels began to bump and roll over the rocky field. It seemed an eternity before they finally started to gain speed, and then the wheels left the ground.

She'd never have dreamed it possible, but they lifted smoothly into the air. Kate heaved a heartfelt sigh of relief.

MOMENTS LATER, it was a different story.

"Damn. I wish we were home." The low mutter came from Greg. His eyelids drooped shut, and his head lolled back like a wilted flower.

"Oh, God!" Kate cried, panic-stricken. "Jason—"

At the sound, Greg opened his eyes. "Don't get shook, Kate. It's on autopilot." He smiled weakly. "Besides, anybody could fly this baby, even you."

But it was Jason who dropped into the co-pilot's seat and who received a crash course in flying.

Kate tried not to think about it. Greg's face was smudged with grime, his lips almost colorless. Rivulets of sweat traced muddy tracks down his forehead and temples. Through the dirt and the stubbled growth of a week's worth of beard, his face was gaunt, the skin over his cheekbones stretched tightly. He'd lost weight since she had seen him last.

He turned slightly, wincing as he did so, and it was then that she noticed his shirt sleeve was crimson. She was out of her seat in a flash, the first-aid kit in her hands seconds later.

"Let me look at your arm," she said urgently. She held his arm tightly while he staggered into the passenger seat.

His shirt sleeve was so wet and bloodied, she decided it would be easiest all the way around if she simply cut it away. She peeled the material from his skin slowly and thrust it aside, but her breath caught at the sight of so much blood. For a second her stomach churned sickeningly, but she swallowed the feeling and forced herself to concentrate on Greg. She took a wide strip of gauze from the kit and began to clean his arm with painstaking care.

From behind her, she heard Jason's voice. "How's it look?"

"It's still bleeding," she said with a frown. On closer inspection, she saw where the bullet had penetrated the back of his arm. The hole was small, almost neat, but where it emerged on the fleshy part of his arm, the skin was jagged and torn.

"It looks like the bullet went completely through." She hesitated. "About all I can do for now is bandage it up until we can get him to a hospital."

This time it was Greg who gasped when she pressed a pad to the underside of his arm and clamped her fingers around it to apply pressure. "You're trying to get even with me for all my past sins, aren't you?"

Kate smiled slightly, but she said nothing. It took a few minutes to staunch the flow of blood, then she bandaged his arm as best she could. Greg pressed his lips together when she cleaned his face with a moistened towelette, but by the time she had finished some of the color had begun to seep back into his cheeks.

It was an unforgettable flight—and one Kate cared never to repeat—with Jason at the controls and Greg weakly calling the shots beside him. Kate wanted to land just across the border in Brownsville, but Greg insisted they go on to Dallas.

Kate noted with a mixture of fear and anxiety that Greg's hand wasn't quite steady when he radioed the control tower they were coming in. He seemed to rally, though, when Jeff came on the air with a whoop and a holler a moment later. Kate closed her eyes during the bumpy landing, and it wasn't until they had coasted to a stop that she realized Greg had once again taken over the controls. Jason was haggard and drawn, white-faced with strain.

The cargo door was flung open. Jeff was inside, grinning from ear to ear. "Hey, Greg, you planning to retire this bird early? Another landing like that one and you won't have any choice."

Greg struggled to his feet. He turned toward Jeff and as he did so, his knees buckled beneath him. Jason's arm shot out and gripped him around the waist. It was only his quick reaction that kept Greg from falling to the floor.

Kate, too, was beside Greg in an instant. She looked up into his weary eyes and pleaded shakily, "*Now* can we get you to a hospital?"

CHAPTER FIFTEEN

JASON WAS IN TROUBLE. He'd been waging an inner battle ever since this morning. He felt angry. He felt hurt. He felt used.

He didn't know why Kate had insisted he accompany her and Greg to the hospital. She had paced nervously while Greg was examined in Emergency, scarcely saying a word to him. She'd held Greg's hand only minutes ago when he was wheeled upstairs, smoothed his blond hair from his forehead with a soft and gentle hand. He felt like a fifth wheel.

He got up and slapped the magazine he'd been trying to read back onto the table. He jammed his hands into his pockets and strode to the narrow window. Several stories below, vibrantly colored flowers spilled over the sides of huge stone planters. At the center of a small fountain, the evening sun glinted off clear, bubbling water that cascaded into a rippling pond. The hospital courtyard looked cool and serene, a stark contrast to the raw emotion roiling away inside the man who watched.

He loved Kate, and during the spellbinding night they had spent together in Mexico City, she had whispered her love for him over and over, with each slow, sensuous arching of her hips beneath his. But that seemed a lifetime ago. Was it possible that she had simply needed someone, in much the same way she had needed Greg so long ago? Only this time he was there instead of Greg. He recoiled at the thought. She certainly had no need of a crutch. She was strong, stronger perhaps than she realized, and Jason certainly didn't begrudge her that. Yet everything had happened so quickly, perhaps too quickly. Once she had time to think things out, would she regret their stolen idyll?

It galled him to see her with Greg. He was filled with a burning resentment he couldn't suppress. Kate's attentiveness, her gentle concern for the man who had once been his friend—and her husband—burned into his soul like acid. He fought against giving in to his jealousy, but he was losing the battle more and more as the day wore on.

He suddenly sensed he was being watched. He turned to find Kate standing in the doorway of the waiting room, her eyes fixed widely on his profile. She reminded Jason of a lost little soldier determined to keep up a brave front no matter what. At his look, she summoned a weak smile. His heart twisted at the sight.

"Well?" He hesitated only an instant before taking her hand and pulling her down onto a small bench against the wall. "How is he?"

His thumb stroked a soothing, absent pattern on the inside of her wrist. Her hand was swallowed up in both of his larger ones, and Kate felt safe and secure for the first time that day.

"They want to keep him for a few days. He's dehydrated and he lost a lot of blood. The kidnappers roughed him up quite a bit, too. Several ribs are cracked." Her eyes fell. "He wants to see you."

"Now?" Jason's voice was sharper than he intended.

Kate nodded. The grip on her hand tightened to an almost painful intensity. She stole a sidelong glance at him.

He looked rough and dangerous, his jaw dark and unshaven, his features carved in stone.

"He's been through a lot, Jason."

"I know that." There was no give in his voice.

She hesitated. "No one is asking the impossible of you."

No? Jason's lips compressed into a thin line. They hadn't even been back one full day and already things looked impossible. He and Kate...and Greg. Just like old times, he thought bitterly.

Kate moistened her lips, her eyes large and pleading. "Just listen to what he has to say...please?"

There was a charged silence. She could almost feel the tension that had invaded his body. Finally he nodded. He started to rise, but Kate stopped him with a hand on his chest.

"I love you, you know." The declaration was quiet but intense.

An expression she couldn't fathom flitted over his face. "Do you?" He posed the question almost whimsically.

She looked both hurt and surprised that he had asked. "Of course I do. You *know* I do."

He sighed, and brought her hand up to his lips. "I'm sorry," he muttered. "It's been a long day, I guess."

"It has." She leaned over and kissed him lightly. "We'll go home after this. I promise."

Greg was lying very still when they entered his room. His left arm was swathed in bandages and rested in a sling. Bottles and tubing hung from the bar suspended near his head. His eyes flickered open when Kate gently pushed the door open.

He smiled slightly when he saw Jason looming behind her. "Seems like I owe you two, doesn't it?"

Kate held her breath. She took the chair at the bedside, and saw that Greg was looking at Jason, standing at the foot of the bed.

"You don't owe us anything," Jason said briefly. The response wasn't as cold as Kate had expected.

"I do," Greg insisted. "If you two hadn't shown up when you did, I don't know what would have happened to me. I knew Kate couldn't get her hands on the kind of money those guys wanted."

Kate glanced uneasily between the two men. Jason's lips had thinned to an ominous line. "If you're up to it, I think we could both use an explanation," she suggested.

Greg's brow furrowed, as if in puzzlement. Kate recognized the telltale warning signs before he could open his mouth. She knew he was about to plead innocent.

"You were smuggling, Greg. Don't bother to deny it." Her voice was quiet but firm.

He was silent for a long moment. "You know?"

She nodded. "The kidnappers hid the artifacts in an old building where you were being held. Manuel Ortega showed them to Jason last night."

Greg rolled his eyes. "Those idiots thought I was carrying silver!"

She raised her eyebrows. "Small wonder." She didn't bother to hide her sarcasm.

He stared at her. "You saw the books?"

"I did. I also paid a little visit to the mining company."

"I suppose that's what tipped you off." He grimaced.

Kate shook her head. "We suspected long before that. Jeff even suspected. That's why we didn't bring the police in."

Jason watched the exchange intently.

Greg looked away. "Guess I wasn't so smart after all," he muttered.

"No. In fact, it was pretty stupid to take such a chance in the first place. If you'd been caught by the Mexican government, there's no telling how long you'd have been shut away in prison." She folded her arms. "About the only thing we don't know is who you were smuggling for, and why. Or was it a solo venture?" she finished mockingly.

Greg had the grace to look guilty. "It wasn't my idea," he muttered.

Kate raised her eyebrows.

"It wasn't!" Seeing the silent demand in her eyes, he continued. "A guy approached me a couple of months ago. His name is Luis Valasquez. He's a curator for a museum in Mexico City—*Nacional* something or other. Some of the pieces he's been taking have been in storage for years. He figured they'd never be missed. Other ones have come in from various archaeological digs."

"And you've been smuggling them into the States."

"Valasquez has a contact in Dallas—some kind of broker who sells them to private collectors and other museums."

"So all along you knew what was going on."

"The money was too good to pass up." He stopped her protest with a hand. "I know, I know," he said wearily. "That's no excuse. But at least I wasn't doing something where people could get hurt."

"I'm not sure Kate would agree. *I* certainly don't."

Jason's voice was razor sharp. Greg flinched from the silent accusation in his eyes. "I'm sorry." He glanced uncertainly at Jason and then at Kate. "You won't turn me in to customs, will you?"

Kate's eyes clouded. "What you did was illegal, Greg. Can you live with your conscience the rest of your life?" She folded her hands in her lap. "I'm not sure that I could," she added very quietly.

"You think I should turn myself in?" He sounded incredulous.

She hesitated. "It's the right thing to do."

Greg made an impatient sound and turned his head away, but they both looked up at the sound of Jason's voice.

His eyes were fixed on Greg. "The broker you mentioned. Do you know who he is?"

"His name is Mike. That's all I know." Greg's tone was guarded.

"Then how do you usually get the artifacts to him?"

"He calls me and makes arrangements to pick them up at my warehouse."

"And the shipment you were carrying when you were kidnapped?"

"He's supposed to come by sometime next week."

"Then maybe it would be wise to tip off someone from customs now."

"Set a trap for him, you mean?" Greg's expression hardened. "I'd be cutting my own throat in the bargain, but then you'd like to see that happen."

"No!" Kate jumped up, and glanced nervously between the two men. She took a deep breath, then turned to Greg. "He's right, Greg. If you let customs know what's been going on, they'll have a case against this broker. The Mexican police should be able to arrest Valasquez, too, and they're the real culprits. If you work with the authorities instead of against them, I think that would be taken into consideration. This way at least some of the artifacts could be recovered."

"I suppose you're right," he conceded after a moment. "Just don't tell Toby about it until I find out what's gonna happen to me. Okay?"

Kate reached out and touched his hand. "I won't," she promised softly.

He squeezed her fingers, but then an uncomfortable expression flitted across Greg's face. He glanced at Jason and opened his mouth, but whatever he was about to say never materialized. A nurse came in at that moment, so Kate took advantage of her timely appearance. She didn't like the dark look on Jason's face. There had been enough said between the two men. Any more and she was afraid she'd have been prying Jason's fingers from Greg's throat.

Jason was silent and remote on the walk through the parking lot to a dark blue Blazer. Jeff had arranged to retrieve the car from the Dallas-Fort Worth airport while Kate and Jason took Greg to the hospital.

"Where to?" he asked briefly when she pulled the door shut.

A pale pink haze spread its shadowy light on the horizon. Soon it would be dark. Kate absorbed the sight for a second before answering. "Home," she said with a fervent sigh. "When I talked to Rita earlier, she said she'd go out to the ranch to pick up Toby and bring him home. They're waiting for us there."

A terse nod was all she received in response. He said nothing after she gave him the address. They were nearly at her house before Jason finally spoke. When he did, it was with an abruptness that startled her.

"He doesn't know, does he?"

Something in his tone put her on guard. "Who?"

"Greg." His gaze was riveted to the ribbon of road ahead. "He doesn't know about us, does he?"

Kate experienced an unwarranted feeling of guilt. The hardness in his voice was in perfect accord with the grim slash of his mouth. His knuckles showed white where he gripped the steering wheel. He looked ready to explode.

Greg meant nothing to her, not in the way Jason seemed to think. How could he possibly believe otherwise?

She took a deep breath, prepared to choose her words carefully. "No," she began, "but that doesn't mean—"

She got no further. "Why not, Kate?" The Blazer had no more than rolled to a stop in the drive than Jason lashed out at her furiously. "Are you afraid he'll disapprove, like your father? Or are you going to string both of us along this time?"

Her mouth dropped open in disbelief, but anger quickly followed. "My father has nothing to do with this," she said tightly. "And I don't think I like what you're saying. Furthermore, you're forgetting one very important thing. The divorce was my idea, not Greg's. I was tired of coming in second in his life, tired of being an afterthought. But with you the problem seems to be exactly the opposite! You make me feel as if you'd like to put a leash around my neck!"

Put that way, he could see her point. Hell! No doubt Kate thought he was acting like a crazy man. At this moment, with his heart and mind so torn in two, he felt like one.

His head dropped back in a gesture of utter weariness. His breath expelled in a rush of air. He spoke in a very low voice. "I'm sorry. I had no right to jump down your throat like that." His voice dropped further. "But I need to know you're not still in love with him."

Hadn't he listened to anything she'd just said? She resisted the impulse to screech at him. As he turned his head to look at her, a night breeze whispered through the open window. It stirred the black strands of hair on his forehead and made him look rather uncertain. He was fiery-tempered and impassioned, but he was also the most sensitive, caring man she had ever known. And he was also so very, very vulnerable.

Kate felt something melt inside her. Oh, yes, Jason had been listening…with his heart and not his head.

She reached out to trace the blunted outline of his jaw, loving the sandpaper roughness of his skin. "Don't doubt my feelings for you," she told him huskily. "What we have is very, very precious. The years we've been apart have taught me that, if nothing else. I would never do anything to hurt you. Please believe me."

It was a quiet, intense moment. The seconds ticked by while he stared at her, as if he were trying to gaze clear through to her soul. Then he pulled her into his arms with a low groan.

"Kate. Oh, Kate." He gathered her more tightly to his chest and buried his face in the soft curve of her neck. "I'm still having trouble believing this isn't a dream. I'm afraid I'll wake up and you'll be gone." He wound his fingers in her hair and tipped her head back so he could look at her.

Kate gazed back at him, aware that everything she had ever felt for him was reflected in her eyes. "I'll never leave you again," she vowed softly.

Touched by the depth of emotion she made no effort to hide, he lowered his head and tenderly kissed her.

"Aren't you two a little old to be sitting outside necking in the car?"

The cheery voice broke them apart. Kate opened her eyes to find Rita standing next to the car, arms akimbo and grinning ear-to-ear. At precisely that moment she heard the screen door slam. Toby tore across the front lawn to the driveway.

Kate leaped from the car to greet him. "Toby. Oh, Toby!" She caught him and swept him into her arms.

"You won't stay away again so long, will you, Mom? I missed you!" Anxious green eyes looked into hers.

She clutched him fiercely. "I missed you, too, sweetheart. And I won't leave you—ever again!" She hugged him tightly, then hugged Rita as well.

"Aw, come on, it wasn't that bad, was it?" Rita chided the little boy who still clung tightly to his mother. "Especially with Pete to keep you company."

"Pete? Who's Pete?" Kate set Toby on his feet, her eyebrows lifted curiously.

It was Jason who answered. "Pete's the little pinto I told you about." He ruffled Toby's blond curls. "He's a pretty nice fella, isn't he?"

Toby beamed. "Rosa told me I could ride 'im any time I wanted, and Nick showed me how," he announced proudly.

Rosa and Nick. Uh-oh, Kate thought. Her gaze flitted uneasily to Jason, but Toby's remark didn't seem to have bothered him. He was smiling slightly, his eyes still on Toby. "I hope staying at Jason's didn't put you to too much trouble," she murmured to Rita. "At the time, we thought it was best."

"I didn't mind." Rita shrugged. "And Toby loved it. He spent most of the time around the corral, watching the horses."

"'Cept when I was ridin' Pete." Toby's tone was self-important.

They all laughed, then Rita glanced at Jason. "Your sister is really sweet. And so is her Nick."

Her Nick? This time Jason's smile seemed a bit forced. Kate decided this was as good a time as any to change the subject. "Why don't we go in the house?" she suggested. Her hand stole into Jason's. "You'll stay, won't you?"

He hesitated a fraction of a second, then nodded. Time had been at a premium when Kate had spoken to Rita earlier. The other woman was anxious to hear the events of the past week, but much of what had transpired was too intense for Toby's tender ears. He clung to his mother's side, but it wasn't long before he drifted off to sleep in her arms.

She tucked him into bed, and then the three adults gathered around the kitchen table, quietly talking. It was nearly eleven o'clock when Rita finally rose, but Kate suddenly felt as if it were 3:00 a.m.

She walked with Rita to the front door. "Thanks for staying with Toby." She hugged her once more. "I don't know how I'd have managed if you hadn't."

"It was nothing," her friend insisted. "Toby was an angel, or as close to it as a six-year-old boy can get!"

They both laughed. "I'm just glad everything worked out okay—on all counts." Her eyes slid meaningfully toward the kitchen where Jason still sat. "By the way, when I picked up Toby and told Rosa that you were back, I mentioned I wouldn't be surprised if Jason stayed the night in Dallas."

Kate stared at her. "You did?"

Rita's blue eyes were sparkling. "Don't get shook. I explained about Greg being in the hospital, so I don't think she'll think it's all that unusual. Besides, she and Nick would probably like some time alone together."

"But how did you know that Jason and I.." The smile Kate had been trying to hold back suddenly materialized. "Well, you know what I mean."

The other woman chuckled as Kate's cheeks bloomed with color. "You sounded different when I talked to you this afternoon. Tired and worried about Greg, but there was something else. It didn't take long to figure out what." She picked up her bag and opened the door. "Don't worry about coming into the shop tomorrow. I'll handle things."

Kate stood smiling at the door for a few seconds. Rita must have read her mind. She'd been hoping Jason might spend the night. The spark of love that reignited in Mexico wouldn't end now that they were home. *We'll start all over,* Jason had said. And they would. She had no intention of letting happiness slip through her fingers once again.

Only moments ago she'd been exhausted, but now she seemed to have gotten a second wind.

Jason's hands were curled around his coffee cup when she went back into the kitchen. She moved silently across the floor. Coming up behind him, she laid her hands on his shoulders. "Alone at last," she breathed against his raspy cheek.

He turned slightly. One of his hands caught at hers and he brought her around to the front of him. With a gentle tug, he pulled her down to sit on his lap.

"Rita's gone?"

She nodded. Her eyes traced lovingly over his rugged features.

"She's nice," he said after a moment. "I like her."

Kate raised her eyebrows. "Not too much, I hope."

He laughed. The sound tugged on her heartstrings, and she realized how long it had been since she'd heard him laugh.

She frowned teasingly. "You're supposed to say 'I only have eyes for you.'"

His hand slipped under her blouse to caress her bare skin. There was a soft glow in his eyes. "I do," he said with a warm smile.

"It might be nice if you said so!"

"I just did."

Kate shook her head. "Listen very carefully." She fixed him with a stern glare that somehow lost its effect because of the teasing glint in her eyes. "You're supposed to say—"

"I only have eyes for you." The soft murmur wafted into her ear. He kissed the baby-soft spot just behind it.

She smiled. "That's better. Now, when I ask if you want to spend the night, you say..."

Before she could utter another word, a firm hand captured her chin and brought her mouth down on his. The kiss started out as a gentle acceptance, but quickly escalated to a feverish intensity.

"You don't have to ask twice." He dragged his lips away only to sear a heated path down the tender cord of her neck. "Although I hope you don't intend for me to sleep on the couch this time."

"I wouldn't dream of it." Her voice was husky as she told him how Rita had told Rosa not to worry if he didn't come home.

"A wise woman," he murmured warmly.

"A very perceptive woman." She laughed shakily, quiveringly aware of the bold swell of his desire beneath her. He held her still for another breath-stealing kiss, then slid her gently off his lap.

Kate's bedroom wasn't frilly or feminine. She'd chosen the modern oak furniture with an eye for practicality. She found the pale blue and gray color scheme attractive as well as soothing.

There was an appreciative glint in Jason's eyes as he looked around. It deepened when it finally came to rest on Kate. "I almost hate to say this—" his smile was rueful "—but I think we could both use a shower."

Kate wrinkled her nose at him, though the idea of a shower appealed mightily. After the night in the jungle, she felt as though every pore had been scoured with dirt. "Just what I always wanted," she said tartly. "A man who has his priorities straight."

He gave her a playful swat on the bottom. "You go first. I need to get my things out of the car anyway."

Kate opted for a bath instead. The steamy warmth relieved the ache in her tired muscles, and she was sorry when the water cooled and she had to climb out. She slipped on a thin robe and stepped back into the bedroom.

Jason was sprawled in the chair by the window. "Took you long enough," he complained, but he was smiling.

She wanted to look especially appealing to him, so while he took his turn in the bathroom, she sat on the edge of the bed and contemplated what nightgown to wear. The pink baby-doll shortie she dismissed as too girlish, the cool cotton jersey not feminine enough. She thought wistfully of all the wispy, silky lingerie they carried in the shop. But her nightwear, too, was something she'd chosen for service and practicality.

The bathroom door opened. Kate looked over her shoulder instinctively. At another time, perhaps, the sight of Jason, so dark and wholly masculine, with a bright pink towel knotted loosely around his waist, might have made her chuckle.

As it was, just looking at him gave her goose bumps. He had shaved, she noted at once. The droplets of water sprinkled in the dense mat of hair on his chest picked up the light from the bedside lamp. He was a superbly fashioned man, from the roped muscles of his arms and shoulders to his trim, well-shaped calves.

The mattress sagged beside her. "What are you thinking about?"

She turned to smile at him. "I was just wondering what nightgown to wear."

He laid back on the bed and pulled her along with him. When he was reclining fully, her upper body was nestled against the rock-hard wall of his chest. "Don't wear any," he told her softly. "I don't plan to."

"I certainly hope not!" Her eyes were filled with an equal measure of tenderness and laughter. "You aren't planning on falling asleep on me again, are you?"

He grinned beguilingly, his teeth very white beneath his mustache. "Have I ever?"

She traced the outline of his mouth. "Yes—just a few days ago." When his heavy brows lifted doubtfully, she added, "The night you went to all those bars. Although I wanted you awake for a very different reason that night...."

"A pity. I'll have to make up for it then."

"You do that," she invited. The towel had fallen from around his hips. She was quiveringly aware of the lean length of his body under her own.

The slow smile that spread across his mouth made her catch her breath. Kate knew instinctively there would be no fierce, torrid session of lovemaking tonight, no heated rush to completion. They were both too tired. But to Kate their exhaustion was a blessing. She wanted to take the time to memorize each word and caress, cherish the wonder of sharing the greatest of intimacies with him once more.

Jason eased her to her side, then leaned over to switch off the bedside lamp. Even in the shadows he could see the brilliant glow of her eyes, soft and beckoning.

His mouth took hers with tender temperance, while his hand moved to the knot at her waist. Kate drew in a sharp breath when the backs of his fingers brushed her bare skin. He smiled against her lips, then raised his head.

Slowly he parted the folds of her robe, slipping it gently from her shoulders. Time seemed suspended as he gazed at the pouting fullness of her breasts, the sleek limbs now completely bared to him. She was stunning, clad only in gossamer beams of moonlight.

Her skin was pale compared to his hands. He spread his fingers across the concave hollow of her belly, seemingly entranced by the sight. The naked bounty of her breasts was a temptation he couldn't ignore. His hand molded her swelling fullness; his thumb brushed an evocative rhythm across the tender summit and then his mouth teased it to a straining peak. All the while he stroked and caressed, cherished and promised.

Kate felt as if she were on fire. Her breath quickened. Her skin burned with an aching sensitivity that both tortured and delighted. The heated strokes of his tongue swirled wetly around her nipple. Then Jason lavished the other breast with the same exquisite care.

A throbbing void deep inside her began to build. She nearly cried out when his hand pursued a relentless path down her belly. He paused for a long heart-stopping moment at the juncture of her thighs. She nearly cried out in relief when his fingers at last slid through the soft down. His touch was tantalizing and sure as he sought out the moist secrets of her femininity. She bore the tender forage until she could stand it no longer.

Consumed by the need to touch him as he was touching her, she pushed gently at his shoulders with the heel of her hand. He understood immediately and drew back to allow her access to his body.

Her palms stroked the warm satin of his back. Her fingers gauged the well-honed muscles of his shoulders and arms.

Jason's pulse went wild as she began to work her spell. She combed through the mat of hair on his chest. His stomach muscles clenched when she brushed slowly across his abdomen. Her fingers whispered over his skin, danced daintily around the heart of him.

His eyes flicked open to stare directly into hers. They seared her with their golden flame. "Touch me." His whispered plea was hoarse and urgent. Their breath mingled. Their lips almost touched. "I want you so much, Kate. Touch me..."

Her fingers were first timid, then bold. She initiated a stroking caress that inflamed his senses and rendered him nearly mindless. Coherent thought was impossible. All he could do was feel—and he felt as if she were turning him inside out.

She renewed her intimate knowledge of his body, marveling silently at his heated strength, the satin-and-steel texture of him. She experienced a purely feminine satisfaction in knowing how deeply she aroused him, and it heightened the throbbing ache inside her. Jason was like the other half of herself. Without him, she was so alone. Only with him was she complete.

"Jason.." She tried to speak. She wanted him to know how much he meant to her. But he cupped her head in his hands and sealed his mouth to hers in a hot, consuming kiss. And then she found a better way to communicate the depth of her feelings.

He was still lying on his back, their legs intimately tangled. Kate had only to shift her weight and execute a single, sinuous movement....

Jason groaned when she took him slowly into her, melting him with the silken heat of her desire. Her wildly exciting claiming of him left him in no doubt that she now possessed a part of him forever. He celebrated his joy, his hands on her hips binding them together as one, as they spun away into a realm where no one else existed.

When it was over, she collapsed against him, weak and spent. She buried her head against his shoulder and sighed, a sound of supreme satisfaction. Jason kissed her temple and smoothed her hair away from her love-flushed cheeks. Reluctantly he moved her to his side, then wrapped his arms around her. They fell into a sleep more peaceful than any they had ever known.

CHAPTER SIXTEEN

THE MORNING LIGHT painted the room with a rosy glow. Kate opened her eyes slowly, a delicious lethargy weighting her limbs. She had awoken earlier to the pleasant sensation of firm lips brushing her cheek, a hand tracing the shape of her breast. Still deep in the world of dreams, she had swatted the hand away as if it were a bothersome fly. She vaguely recalled a warm masculine chuckle before she rolled over and promptly fell back to sleep.

It had been a perfect night. The pleasure she had derived from Jason's slightest touch had been unlike anything she had ever known. She had never experienced such closeness with another human being. It had seemed almost too good to be true.

But Kate had only to spy the dented plumpness of the pillow beside her to realize that it was true. She smiled, and her eyes moved to the clock. It was nearly ten now and Jason was gone, but she heard the distant rattle of a pan, and assumed he was in the kitchen. She stretched languorously, then slid out of bed. She showered quickly and dressed in lightweight tan slacks and a striped pullover.

She found Jason in the kitchen, sitting at the table with a cup of coffee in his hands. He wore jeans and a light blue denim shirt. He had rolled the sleeves up to his elbows, revealing bronzed hairy forearms. He was smiling slightly as he watched Toby stuff his mouth full of scrambled eggs.

"Hi, Mom!" Toby waved his fork at her and went back to his food.

Kate smiled, shook her head and poured herself some coffee. Things were back to normal, she decided. She took a seat at the table and glanced at Jason through the screen of her lashes. "Good morning," she murmured.

"Morning." His slow easy smile warmed her heart. He, too, was freshly showered.

Toby finished his breakfast and hopped off his chair. "Can I go over to Ronnie's and play for a while? His mom said I could."

Ronnie was the same age as Toby, and he lived across the street. The two boys were nearly inseparable.

She glanced at Jason. "He was here already?"

His eyes crinkled at the corners. "Scrawny redhead with a cowlick? Looks like Dennis the Menace?"

And acts like him, too, she thought, though not without a helping hand from Toby. "That's him," she confirmed. She gave a go-ahead nod to her son, and Toby raced out the back door.

"He was here, all right." Jason's tone was dry. "Didn't you hear the doorbell at eight o'clock?" He chuckled when she shook her head. "No, I suppose not. You were deep in never-never land."

She wrinkled her nose at him. "You always were a light sleeper," she accused without heat.

Jason smiled and shrugged, then laid his hand over hers where it rested on the table. "You look very happy this morning," he said softly.

The horrors of the past few days were gone. Greg was home and soon he would be completely well; she and Jason were together again. Oh, yes, life was good.

"I am," she said gently. Somehow she couldn't seem to stop smiling.

He squeezed her fingers and leaned over to kiss her lightly on the mouth. "What's on the agenda for to-day?" he asked when he drew back. "I heard Rita tell you not to bother coming into the shop today."

Kate blew on the steaming surface of her coffee, her expression thoughtful. "I think I will anyway, at least so she can have the afternoon off. I know this past week couldn't have been easy for her, what with watching Toby and handling everything at the shop."

"Do you have anyone else working for you?"

"No. We've talked about hiring someone part-time, but we've never gotten around to it. It would give us both some more time off, though." She paused. "I thought I'd drop by the hospital to see Greg later, too. I'm sure Toby would like to see him."

Jason had moved to the sink to rinse his cup. Kate caught at his hand when he turned back. "Do you mind?" she asked quietly.

He shook his head. She looked so relieved that Jason was glad he'd managed to curb the pinprick of jealousy he felt. He squeezed her fingers. "I need to head home anyway," he said with a lopsided smile, "and see if the place is still standing."

The front doorbell chimed just then. Kate got up to answer it. "I wonder who that is," she murmured.

Her eyes widened when she saw the two people standing on her doorstep. "Rosa. Nick!" she exclaimed, then opened the door wide. "What a surprise. Come in, both of you."

There was just a hint of uncertainty on their faces when they stepped inside. Kate hugged Rosa warmly and smiled at Nick. He smiled back, then glanced beyond her.

Kate turned slightly and saw that Jason had followed her. He stood in the wide doorway between the living room and dining room, but moved toward them when he caught her look.

Rosa rushed forward. "You're all right!" She threw her arms around her brother's lean waist.

Jason hesitated, then closed his arms around his sister. "I'm fine, hon." He brushed a kiss on her forehead.

Rosa gazed up at him, her dark eyes suspiciously bright. "I've been so worried about you." She extended a hand toward Kate. "And you, too."

"I've been holding her back all morning." Nick smiled slightly.

Rosa returned to Nick's side. "Rita said you were both okay." She sounded apologetic as she held her brother's gaze. "But I had to see for myself." Her eyes moved to Kate. "How's Greg?"

"He has to spend the next few days in the hospital, but after that, he'll be as good as new." Kate inclined her head toward the living room. "Why don't we go in there?" she suggested.

"Oh, we can't stay. I just wanted to make sure everyone was okay." Rosa's eyes met Nick's. An unspoken message passed between them. Nick pulled her to his side and let his hand rest on her waist.

Something was up. Something was most definitely up. Kate sensed Jason's prickly awareness as well.

"Nick and I have some news, too." Rosa was smiling, but her gaze didn't quite meet Jason's.

"Oh?"

Kate felt Jason's body tense. She knew by his tone that his eyebrows were raised imperiously.

Rosa nodded. Her smile slipped a notch, but her voice rang out clear as a bell. "We were married Wednesday.

See?'' She held out her left hand. The light glinted off a shiny gold wedding band.

Kate didn't dare look at Jason. The silence that followed was overwhelming. She'd have sworn it lasted an eternity, though she knew it couldn't have been more than a few seconds.

Rosa's eyes finally settled on her brother's face. Her mouth trembled slightly. She was crying out silently for acceptance, pleading for forgiveness. Watching Rosa was like watching a mirror image of herself fifteen years earlier, standing before her father. Kate's heart ached for her.

Jason said nothing. He simply stood there, as silent and motionless as a statue.

Kate moved without thinking. "Congratulations, both of you." She hugged and kissed Nick on the cheek, then did the same to Rosa. She lifted the other girl's hand and exclaimed over her ring. "Oh, it's beautiful, Rosa. I'm so happy for you!" And she was, even while a part of her was breaking up inside. She gave Rosa one more impulsive hug, then braced herself to face Jason.

His expression was everything she had feared. His lips were a thin, contemptuous line. His eyes blazed yellow fire. Kate had never seen him so angry, yet the very fact that he controlled it so well made it even more overwhelming.

His gaze moved slowly from Nick to Rosa, then rested on Kate. He didn't relieve her of that accusing stare for the longest time, then finally he spoke to Nick.

"You're fired," he said harshly. "I'll mail you your paycheck." His eyes traveled to his sister. "You better pick up your things today. If anything's left tomorrow, I'll throw it out."

Nick glanced at Rosa. He muttered what sounded like "I told you so," but Kate scarcely heard. She stared at Jason numbly. She knew how much he loved his sister.

"Jason, you can't be serious," she began. She couldn't believe he could be so cruel and so blatantly insensitive.

But the proof was right before her eyes. "Oh, but I am." His voice was cold. He jerked his head toward the door, a parody of a smile on his lips when he looked at Rosa and Nick. "You weren't staying, remember?"

Kate gasped. He might as well have told Rosa and Nick to get the hell out. A fiery anger shot through her at his insolence. "They're welcome to stay if they want," she informed him stiffly.

"The hell they are!" His jaw jutted out. "Stay out of it, Kate. This doesn't concern you."

"No?" Her chin lifted. "It does when it happens in my house, something *you* seem to be forgetting—"

Rosa clutched at her arm. "Kate, don't," she said in a low voice. "We'll go. I don't want to make trouble."

She hesitated. She hated to see them leave on such a sour note, but considering Jason's reaction, perhaps it was best. Jason stood in the living room doorway and watched while Kate saw the couple to the front door.

"He just needs some time to get used to the idea." She squeezed Rosa's hand reassuringly. "He'll come around."

"I wouldn't count on it." Nick's expression was as fierce and angry as Jason's.

"It'll work out soon. Please, try not to worry about it. Don't cheat yourselves of the happiness you deserve." Kate wished she felt as bright and promising as she sounded. "I'll come and see you after I've had a chance to talk with him. Where will you be?"

Rosa bit her lip. She glanced at Nick, and he gave a tiny nod. "We'll have to stay with Nick's parents for now."

"In Bradley?"

She nodded.

Behind her, Jason's voice rang out sharply. "Rosa!"

Rosa didn't say anything. She gazed at him expectantly, but Kate could see she was miserable and trying very hard not to show it.

"Don't come crawling home ready to cry on my shoulder when he decides to dump you." Jason's eyes were brooding. "I told you a long time ago not to expect too much from him."

Nick's hands balled into fists. "Damn you!" he said hoarsely. "I love her! Why can't you see that!" He took a step toward Jason, but Rosa stepped in front of him. In a fraction of a second her expression changed from dark and troubled to proud and haughty.

Her small chin lifted. "You don't need to worry," she told Jason evenly. "I wouldn't give you the satisfaction." She turned on her heel and walked out. Nick stood his ground for a moment, then followed behind her.

Jason muttered something under his breath, pivoted and strode into the living room. Kate's shoulders sagged as she quietly closed the front door.

Could the three of them have talked it out? Compromised, perhaps? Kate felt as if she had just witnessed a declaration of war. She strongly suspected that Nick, like Jason, possessed a volatile nature and a lightning-quick temper. They were probably far more alike than they realized. As for Rosa, Kate knew Jason's reaction had hurt her deeply, but at least the couple had harbored no illusions about Jason. Kate was secretly glad that Jason's furious disapproval hadn't defeated Rosa's fiery spirit.

But when she came upon Jason, sprawled on the sofa, she felt anger and resentment. "I hope you're proud of yourself. Not only did you manage to drive Rosa away, you practically shoved her out the door!" She sat down in the armchair across from him, crossed her arms and glared at him.

His eyes narrowed. "Damn it, Kate, she did exactly what I told her not to do!"

Kate's jaw sagged. Of all the egotistical, chauvinistic... "It's too bad you didn't send her to obedience school," she shot back hotly.

Jason's mouth tightened. "You know what I mean. The minute my back was turned, she ran off and married that no-good—"

"Hold it right there! My, how things have changed." She sweetly mocked him. "Nick deserves a fair shake, and you're not giving it to him. My father had a few choice names for you, too, but you seem to have turned out all right." Although it seemed a debatable point at the moment, she thought grimly.

"This isn't the same thing."

It was, but he was just too blind to see it. Or perhaps just too stubborn. If she had thought it would do any good, she wouldn't have hesitated to try to shake some sense into him. She watched bleakly as he got up and paced the room. When he finally stopped, he slammed a hand against the doorframe.

"Hell!" he muttered. "If I hadn't gone to Mexico, this wouldn't have happened."

Her eyes widened. "You blame me?" she asked incredulously. "Because I asked you to go with me?"

He didn't answer, but his unyielding expression didn't alter, either.

The spurt of doubt Kate felt was quickly swamped by a surge of resentment. She didn't flinch from his brittle stare. "Damn you, Jason Davalos!" she cried. "That's not fair."

"I don't blame you," he said, but there was still a cutting edge to his voice. A hint of mockery entered his eyes. "Besides, you know what they say. It takes two to tango. Rosa's at fault just as much as Nick."

"At fault? Two people in love—and they're at fault?" Kate couldn't believe what he was saying. "You're just angry because they got married without your consent."

"I never would have given it, at least not now. Rosa knew that."

"And that's exactly why they did it! My God, Jason, if anyone is to blame, it's you. What did you expect Rosa to do? You pulled the reins too tight and she reacted like anyone else would have! She rebelled!"

"Like anyone else?" He rolled his eyes. "Like a child, you mean."

"And that's exactly how you treat her!"

His eyes darkened. "You don't know what you're talking about, Kate."

"So you keep telling me." She jumped to her feet and planted her hands on her hips. "Maybe I don't know what I'm talking about, but I sure as hell know what I see. And when I look at Rosa, I see a woman in love. Nick makes her happy, Jason."

He snorted. "Happy? She didn't look happy when she left here."

"Really?" Her voice dripped with sarcasm. "I wonder who she has to thank for that. Certainly not her husband."

Jason said nothing for the longest time. Yet Kate didn't bother to deceive herself. She knew he wasn't feeling even the least bit guilty, as he soon proved.

"I don't see why you were so damned eager to take their side against me in the first place. How do you think I felt while you tried to soothe their ruffled feathers? After everything we've been through, you turn around and practically stab me in the back!"

It was getting harder and harder to curb her temper. "So now I'm supposed to agree with everything you do and say? Thank you very much, but I do have a mind of my own!"

He made an impatient gesture. "You're deliberately trying to misunderstand me."

"Am I? I wonder."

"Come on, Kate. Don't lay this all on my doorstep. They should never have gotten married in the first place. They'll be lucky if they last six months before they find themselves in a divorce court."

Such trust. Such faith. He couldn't even give Rosa and Nick the benefit of the doubt. She was beginning to wonder if she even knew Jason—if she had *ever* known him. The man before her was a stranger.

She shook her head. Her shoulders sagged limply. "There's no talking to you." She suddenly looked as bone weary as she sounded. "You're no different now than you ever were, Jason. You just don't listen. You're too busy feeling sorry for yourself."

"Sorry for myself! Coming from a poor little rich girl, that's quite a statement. But I get the hint, Kate, and you know what? It's true that things get easier the second time around. And at least I've learned something. This time I know when I'm not wanted."

The harshness of his voice was like a knife twisting in her heart. She watched numbly as he surged toward the doorway. She stared at him, unable—or perhaps unwilling—to comprehend. "Jason, I never said that!" To her horror, her voice cracked. She stumbled after him. A feeling of déjà vu swept over her. Dear God, it was happening all over again. "You can't leave, not like this!"

"Can't I?" He yanked the front door open. "As you just reminded me, this is *your* house. You want me out— I'll get out."

The door slammed so hard the windows shook. She heard the roar of an engine, and the squeal of tires a second later. He was gone.

Kate felt as if she'd just had the wind knocked out of her. Her chest was like a vast, empty drum. She couldn't breathe. She couldn't even see for the tears that blurred her vision.

The cold hollowness inside her grew until she thought she couldn't stand it. Her thoughts were wild and disjointed. She wanted to tell herself that everything was okay, but the words wouldn't come. Yet somehow, one thought came through above all others, and it caused hot, scalding tears to slip unheeded down her cheeks. Last night had seemed too good to be true...and it was.

DO YOU BELIEVE in fate? In second chances?

Yes. Oh, yes.

Do we dare, Kate? Do we dare try again?

I can't answer for you, but I don't have any choice.

We'll start all over. It will be different this time—better—I promise....

Whispers in the dark. Promises in the night. Kate found herself haunted by both. She cried herself to sleep night after night.

A week later there were no more tears left.

She'd thought Jason would be back. If not that same night, then the next day...or the next. She didn't want to believe that when he had walked out the door—out of her house—that he had walked out of her life as well.

Greg was free, alive and well. His kidnapping was no longer a dark, threatening cloud overhead. With that behind them, with their past differences out in the open and dealt with once and for all, she had hoped that she and Jason could look to the future, a future they would share together. She had thought that the hurt and pain was behind them once and for all.

She couldn't have been more wrong. Jason wouldn't be back. Past experience told her so. But regardless of her feelings, the tiny ember of hope that burned in her heart refused to die out. And Rita fanned the flame a little higher.

Kate couldn't quite forget Rita's parting remark when they closed the shop on Saturday. "You know what they say—" she raised finely arched blond brows "—if Muhammad won't come to the mountain..."

Her meaning was clear. She thought Kate should go to Jason. And maybe—just maybe—she was right. Jason was a strong, proud man. Admitting he was wrong wouldn't be easy. Perhaps all he needed was a little encouragement.

Toby, too, was all for a trip to Bradley on Sunday. Kate kept her promise and showed him the sprawling white house she'd grown up in. They walked around the small brick elementary school and played for a while on the playground. She took him to the candy store and they splurged on peanut butter fudge. It wasn't until they left that he grinned impishly and told her Rosa had already taken him there.

She was glad she'd brought Toby along. He provided the distraction she needed to keep her mind from dwelling on Jason. She also decided to take advantage of the trip to see how Nick and Rosa were faring.

A slight frown marred her brow when she pulled up before a narrow two-story house just off the main street of town. Half a dozen tricycles and a variety of toys littered the cracked driveway.

"Why'd we come here, Mom?" Toby glanced at the house curiously.

"To see Rosa and Nick." She opened the car door. "Come on, let's see if they're here."

Toby obligingly climbed out of the car. "How come they're not at home?"

Kate bit her lip. She knew he meant the ranch. "They just got married," she told him quickly. "They're staying here with Nick's parents until they find a place of their own."

Thank heaven he was satisfied with her answer. They moved up the sidewalk, and she smiled at the two toddlers—twins from the look of them—playing on the porch. One of them tottered to his feet and ran inside. A second later the screen door slammed. A wide-eyed girl of about ten peered at Kate, then rushed back in. Another little boy stared at her and Toby curiously as they mounted the steps.

"Is someone at the door, Maria?"

The voice came from inside the house. Kate had just raised her hand to knock when Rosa suddenly appeared in the doorway.

"Kate!" she exclaimed. "What on earth are you doing here?"

Kate glanced at Toby, who was giving his attention to a small puppy that had wandered up the steps along with them. "I was worried about you and Nick," she said in a low voice. "How are you?"

"Fine. Just fine!"

Rosa's voice was just a little too bright. Kate studied her intently. "Really?"

This time Rosa hesitated. "Things could be better," she finally admitted. She held the door open. "Why don't you come in?"

Kate called Toby and the three of them went inside. Nick's mother was a big, buxom woman with snapping black eyes and an infectious laugh. Kate liked her on sight, but she discreetly withdrew when Rosa led her into the kitchen. She explained that the children were Nick's younger brothers and sisters—all six of them. Toby returned to the porch with the puppy and the little girl called Maria.

"So." Kate paused while Rosa filled two glasses with iced tea. She asked the question that she knew was on both their minds. "Have you seen Jason since last Saturday?"

Rosa sat down across from her. "No," she said very quietly. She carefully stirred a spoonful of sugar into her tea, then she glanced up. "Have you?"

Kate shook her head.

Rosa frowned. "But I thought you and Jason had finally straightened things out—" She broke off at the flash of pain in Kate's eyes.

"We did." How she managed to sound so calm, Kate didn't know.

"And?" Rosa's look was questioning.

"And it obviously isn't going to work out after all." Kate's attempt at a smile fell flat.

Comprehension dawned on Rosa's face. "It's because of me, isn't it? Oh, Kate, I'm so sorry," she began.

"No." Kate shook her head firmly. "It's not your fault, Rosa. And it's not Nick's, either."

Rosa wore a guilty expression. "But if Nick and I hadn't gotten married—"

"You and Nick love each other, and that's all that matters. You couldn't let Jason push you around, any more than you could stand by and let him drive a wedge between you and Nick." She hesitated momentarily. "If you had let him, he would have done the same thing to you that my father did to us all those years ago. I'm glad you were strong enough to stand up to him, to do what you felt you had to do." She smiled sadly. "I wasn't, at least not then."

Rosa's eyes were swimming. "I love him, Kate, but I love Nick, too. We didn't want to get married the way we did, but he left us no choice. Jason has a blind spot where Nick is concerned, and I don't think that's ever going to change!"

Kate's heart ached for her. "I know how you feel," she said gently, then paused. "Remember the night you told me he wasn't the tyrant he seemed?"

She nodded slowly.

"You're probably right, you know." Kate attempted to reassure her. "Maybe all he needs is some time to cool off."

Rosa didn't look convinced, and to tell the truth, Kate wasn't so sure, either. The young woman seemed so troubled, she wished there was something she could do to help. Short of drumming some sense into Jason's head, Kate didn't know what. And Jason was so stubborn, she didn't think it would help anyway.

"Has Nick found another job yet?" she asked presently.

"He's pumping gas at a service station." Rosa's voice was low. "It doesn't pay half what Jason did, but I suppose it's better than nothing. I've been looking, too, but so far I haven't had any luck." She grimaced. "There just aren't that many jobs available in a town the size of Bradley."

Kate silently agreed. Bradley was largely a farming and ranching community. Rosa would probably have to go into one of the larger towns around Bradley to find a job, or maybe even Dallas itself.

She was suddenly seized by an inspiration. "Wait a minute," she said slowly. She reached out and squeezed Rosa's hand where it lay listlessly on the tabletop. "How would you like to come to work for Rita and I?"

Rosa looked startled. "At your shop?"

"Yes! Unless you think Nick would mind."

"No. No, of course he won't!" Her voice gained enthusiasm. "He knows how much I love working with clothes. And we're hardly in a position where we can turn down the extra money."

Kate glanced around once more. The house was neat and well-ordered, but it was also very small. The children's clothes were spotlessly clean but just a little worn. On the way into the kitchen, Rosa had mentioned that Nick's father worked as a gardener in a nearby town. Kate didn't think it presumptuous to conclude that the addition of a couple more mouths to feed might soon constitute a hardship. Plus there was the fact that such a cramped household was really no place for newlyweds.

"You and Nick could probably find a place of your own then," she suggested.

"That would be heavenly! Not that I'm ungrateful to Nick's folks," she added quickly. "But it would be so nice to be…"

"Alone," Kate finished for her. She chuckled at Rosa's dreamy sigh. "I'll have to discuss it with Rita first, but I'm sure she won't mind. We've been talking about hiring someone for ages, but we've just never gotten around to actually doing it." She lifted her eyebrows. "How about if I give you a call on Monday and let you know for sure?"

"That sounds great! Oh, Nick will be as happy as I am."

Rosa's eyes were still glowing when Kate and Toby left a short time later, and even Kate's heart had lightened. So much, in fact, that she felt ready to brave the lion in his den.

"Where we goin' now?"

Kate turned onto the gravel road that led to Jason's. "I thought we'd stop at the ranch for a few minutes," she told her son.

Toby bounced on the seat. "All right!" he chortled. "Maybe I'll get to ride Pete again!"

But their visit was to be even shorter than Kate anticipated.

Toby made a beeline for the corral the second after she'd pulled to a stop. She had scarcely climbed out of the car herself than Jason walked out of the barn. He spotted her immediately.

Kate couldn't quite control the rush of emotion that seized her. Did she look okay? She had to resist the urge to straighten the crease in her slacks and check her lacy white blouse for wrinkles.

His legs, long and lean, ate up the yards between them. The warm wind had feathered his hair attractively over his tanned forehead. He had unbuttoned his shirt against the afternoon heat, revealing a nest of springy dark hair at the base of his throat. He looked tired and disheveled, unquestionably masculine...and so dear to her heart, Kate felt something melt inside her.

Until she saw the expression on his face. A lesser soul would have been cringing in her shoes.

"Kate." His voice was surprisingly mild, considering the dark thundercloud on his face. "What brings you here?"

As if he didn't know! He was acting as if nothing had happened, as if they had never argued...as if they had never been lovers.

The faint coolness in his tone set her teeth on edge. She lifted her chin. "I was in town to see Rosa and Nick, so I thought I'd stop by."

He hooked his thumbs in his belt. "I see," he drawled. "How *is* the happy couple?"

His sarcasm pricked her temper. It was on the tip of her tongue to retort that if he were any kind of brother he would already know.

"You haven't seen them?"

"No." He smiled, not a nice smile at all.

She countered his coolness with a steely determination. "Rosa's fine, all things considered. They'd be much better off with a place of their own, though." Slender brows lifted questioningly. "You're aware that Nick has five brothers and sisters?"

"I'm aware." His voice was gritty.

"Nick wasn't there." She went on boldly. "He was working."

Surprise flickered in Jason's eyes for just an instant. Then they were cool and guarded once more.

Kate pressed her lips together. "He's pumping gas at a gas station." Again he said nothing. His apparent indifference irritated her more than his anger. "Well?" she finally snapped. "Don't you have anything to say?"

"Nothing you'll want to hear."

His eyes were riveted to her face. He wasn't giving so much as an inch, she noted furiously. "Try me," she said tightly.

His shoulders lifted in a shrug. "I don't feel sorry for Rosa, if that's what you want me to say."

Her eyes narrowed. "She made her bed and now she can lie in it. Is that what you mean?"

"Exactly." His gaze bit into her. "She didn't have to marry Nick, but she did. And if marriage to him isn't the bed of roses she expected—" he shrugged "—that's life. Maybe it's time she had a taste of it. It was her choice, Kate."

Kate stared at him. Was this hard, distant man the same one who had made such tender, passionate love to her? "You gave her no choice," she accused in a low voice.

But Jason was having none of it. "Why?" he demanded. "Because I told her how it would be? Ever since she met him, she's been blinded by dreams of happily ever after. She couldn't see Nick for what he really is and now it's too late. I was trying to protect her, but neither you nor Rosa seem to see it that way!" His jaw thrust out. "I'd like to know how Nick is going to make a decent living for her pumping gas!"

"That wouldn't be a problem if *you* hadn't fired him!" She flung the words back at him. "If you believed Nick was so terrible, why did you hire him in the first place?"

"For Rosa's sake, I was prepared to give him a chance. But look how he paid me back!"

"By marrying your sister. Jason, there's nothing wrong with that. You're acting just like my father. Can't you see that?"

He scarcely gave her a chance to finish. "No, I can't. I'm not interfering like your father did, Kate, and you damn well know it!"

"Not anymore you're not." She heaved a frustrated sigh. She agreed, but only to a point. "You're closing them out, your own sister for God's sake! And in my mind that's just as bad, maybe even worse, than what my father did."

He glared at her. "We can't seem to agree on anything today, can we?"

Kate closed her eyes. Rosa was right. Jason had a blind spot where Nick was concerned. Discussing the two of them with him was pointless. Hopeless! Yet for Rosa's sake, she had to try.

Unthinkingly she laid her hands on his forearms. "Jason, he loves her. And she loves him. They deserve the chance to be happy—to make their marriage work. Rosa loves you, too, and what you're doing to her isn't making things any easier for her."

Before she had a chance to say anything further, his mouth twisted. "Sometimes love isn't enough, Kate. We should know. Look what happened with us. Besides, I'm not convinced that Nick doesn't think of Rosa simply as an easy meal ticket. And a fun one at that!"

But just because their own marriage had failed didn't mean that would happen to Rosa and Nick. Didn't he see that? Kate wanted to argue with him, to plead with him to understand. Yet his reminder of their own failure kindled an icy chill deep inside her. For a moment Rosa and Nick were forgotten.

Jason's voice was that of a stranger, a voice that pierced her clear to her soul. But he was still as stubborn and unyielding as ever. *Oh, please,* she prayed silently, *don't let it end like this. Not again....* Once more th promise he'd made in Mexico flashed through her mind. *We'll start all over,* he'd said. But how could they? They were trapped by the past, unable to go forward. There was no hope for them. No hope at all, she realized bleakly.

Her hands dropped from his arms. There was a world of despair and misery churning away inside her, but she forced herself to meet his hostile gaze.

"What's happened to you?" she murmured. "You've changed, Jason. You're so hard."

His eyes sharpened on her face. "So you don't like what I've become."

"No," she said slowly. "I'm not sure that I do." Her eyes searched his. "You're not the man I thought you were," she finished very quietly.

He stiffened, then gave a harsh-sounding laugh. "This time you can't lay the blame totally on my doorstep, Kate. If I've changed, it's because of you."

Oh, she knew. She knew only too well, and that made it much harder to bear.

There was a heartbeat of silence while they stared at each other. There was an aching constriction in Kate's throat. In another few seconds she wouldn't be able to hold back the tears that stung her eyes.

"Just so you know, I've offered Rosa a job in the shop." She turned away so he wouldn't see her weakness. She took a deep steadying breath, then called Toby to the car.

Jason was at her side in an instant. "You're leaving?"

"There's no point in staying." Her voice was as clipped as his.

When Toby ran up, she hustled him quickly into the car. Jason waited until she'd closed the passenger door for Toby and walked around to the driver's side.

"What about us?" he demanded.

This time she couldn't meet his penetrating gaze. "I don't know." Her tone was one of quiet resignation.

"You're going to let this thing with Rosa and Nick come between us?"

It was almost laughable that Jason's jealousy of Greg hadn't driven them to this point. And it wasn't so much that they disagreed over Rosa and Nick, either. But the issue had revealed a side of Jason that Kate wasn't sure she could accept.

She gestured vaguely. "It changes things," she said in a low voice.

"It doesn't have to."

"No?" Her smile was sad. Happily-ever-after was something that only happened in fairy tales, not to Kate McAllister and Jason Davalos. The emotional distance between them had never been greater. "I'm not so sure."

She wasn't prepared for the hurt that flashed in his eyes. Didn't he know that this was tearing her apart as well? She wanted to reach out, to touch him and soothe his pain, yet she didn't dare.

"Damn it, Kate!" His fingers seized her arm. "Are you saying this is goodbye?"

Gently but firmly she withdrew from him. She gathered her tumultuous emotions around her like a cloak. If Jason touched her again, she felt she would shatter into a million pieces.

"I think it's best," she said very gently.

She didn't look back as she got into the car and drove away.

CHAPTER SEVENTEEN

LIFE DID GO ON, Kate discovered. Once again, she heard nothing from Jason, and after the first few days had passed, she really didn't expect to. The break she had made with him two weeks earlier was clean. Just as she'd told him, it was best this way. But she had little time to really think about it, and for that she was thankful. Unfortunately, she was certain that soon she would emerge from the blessedly numb state that had been her only salvation. And when that day finally came...well, the truth was that she dreaded it, even though she knew that she had the inner strength to cope.

But for now, at least, she had plenty to occupy her time and her thoughts. Toby was excited about beginning first grade, and there was the usual rush to buy school clothes. Rosa had started to work at the boutique, and both Kate and Rita were involved in her training. Kate was delighted with the decision. Rosa had quite a knack for pleasing even the most discriminating customer, and when it came to the window displays, she was a natural in choosing clothes for the mannequins and creating backgrounds for an eye-catching exhibit. Kate had given her an advance on her salary, and she and Nick had rented an apartment midway between Dallas and Bradley.

Things were going well for Greg, too. He had kept his word and informed a customs official of his smuggling

activities. And, when "Mike" had come to claim his delivery, Greg had assisted the agents in exposing him. Luis
Valasquez had been arrested in Mexico as well, and in
exchange for his help, Greg had been granted immunity
from prosecution. He was lucky, very lucky, but at least
the book was closed on the whole affair.

He'd been out of the hospital for several weeks now,
but his left arm was still in a sling, and Kate had half
expected Greg to play on her sympathies, but so far he
hadn't. He wasn't flying at the present time, though his
days were spent at the office. But to Kate's surprise, since
he wasn't out of town as often, he had been spending
more time with Toby.

Toby was thrilled with the attention he received from
his father. Greg had made so little time for his son, even
when they'd been married, and Kate was glad that he was
getting to know his son at last.

It was on a warm Friday afternoon, the week after
school had started, that Greg stopped by the shop to pick
Toby up after school. The two of them planned to go to
dinner and then to a movie.

Rosa was busy in the back room, but Rita was
straightening the stock on the selling floor during his
brief visit. Her eyes narrowed thoughtfully as she
watched Greg and Toby leave. "You know," she re-
marked to her partner, "Greg seems...oh, I don't know.
Different, I guess."

"Different? How do you mean?" Kate's reply was
automatic. Her mind was on the trip she'd made to the
doctor's office this morning. She was still waiting to
hear...

The other woman hesitated. "Promise you won't be
mad?"

Kate finally looked at her. "Of course not."

"He doesn't seem to be so egotistical."

That was quite an admission, coming from Rita. But Kate had thought the same thing herself many times since Greg's discharge from the hospital.

"You're right," she admitted to Rita. "It may sound odd, but I think the kidnapping changed him. Maybe he finally decided to take a good look at things—what he's accomplished and where he's going. Remember he planned to expand the company, open up some more offices here in Texas?"

The petite blonde nodded.

"He's put it on hold for the time being, and he's canceled the Mexico City run permanently."

Rita raised her eyebrows. "Well, whatever brought about this change in him, it's bound to be an improvement!" The phone rang and she picked it up. "It's for you. Dr. something-or-other." She extended the receiver toward Kate.

Kate's palms were suddenly damp. Her heart thudded erratically.

Rita frowned. "Hey, you're not hiding something from me, are you? You said you went in just for a check-up."

"It was." Oh, Lord, what if... "I'll take it in the office," she said quickly.

Fifteen minutes later, Rita opened the door to the office. Her concerned eyes immediately found the slender figure sitting motionless in the chair behind the desk. "Well," she prodded softly. "What's the verdict? You gonna make it through the next fifty years?"

Kate lifted her head to look at her friend, suddenly not sure whether to laugh or to cry. "Oh, I'll live," she said, summoning a wan smile. "I'm fit as a fiddle, in fact." For a pregnant woman...

KATE FOUND IT truly amazing how well she functioned that night. She fixed a light dinner for herself, then settled down to watch some television. She was pregnant, yet her mind seemed curiously blank and detached. It was almost as if it had happened to someone else.

Greg brought Toby home about nine, and the youngster handed her a huge foil-wrapped candy kiss. Just what she needed for a waistline that would soon be expanding without benefit of chocolate. They talked for a while, then Kate put Toby to bed.

It was also amazing that Greg knew something was wrong. He had two cups of hot tea waiting when she returned to the living room.

"Well." She pasted a smile on her face and sat down beside him. "I really rate tonight."

"I thought you might like to talk," he said quietly.

Her phony smile vanished.

He regarded her steadily. "I have the feeling something's bothering you. And you look like you need a friend. I know it's a bit late—" he gave an odd little laugh "—probably years too late, but I'd like to be that friend." He hesitated. "You went out on a limb to rescue me in Mexico, and even though I know it's not the same thing, I... Well, for once I'd like to be there for you."

When was the last time—if ever—that she'd heard such sincerity in his voice? It brought an unexpected pang to her heart.

She reached out to curl her hands around the teacup. Her lips curved in a tiny self-deprecating smile. "If I told you what's bothering me, you'd never believe it," she murmured.

His sandy brows lifted. "Try me."

It was a long, long time before she finally blurted, "I'm pregnant."

Greg sucked in a sharp breath. "But . . . how on earth . . ."

"How? I don't think I really need to tell you that." Her hand was shaky as she replaced the cup on the table. She attempted a laugh, but somehow the sound emerged as more of a strangled cry. Then all of a sudden, a tear beaded down her cheek, then another and another.

"I'm sorry," she choked out. "I'm not usually so emotional."

"I know." He handed her his handkerchief and added dryly, "Except when you're pregnant." He sighed. "I suppose I'm lucky you're not slamming the cupboard doors."

The reminder earned a reluctant smile. Reluctant, but at least genuine. "Jason?" he asked after a moment.

She nodded, her throat too tight to speak. She could tell from his tone that the question was merely a formality. He watched as she dried her cheeks and took a deep, calming breath.

"Does he know?"

The pain returned to nip at her heart. "No. I just found out today."

"What are you going to do?" he asked very quietly.

She closed her eyes helplessly. "If I tell him, it'll be just like it was before." Her voice caught painfully. Her lungs burned from the effort it took to stop from bursting into tears. "I don't think I could stand it if he married me again just because I was pregnant."

"The idea of marriage never came up?"

She hesitated. "It might have. But it all happened so quickly," she said haltingly. "And there was you, and then Rosa and Nick when we finally did get home. . . ."

At his frown, she told him of Jason's anger over their marriage, and her inability to accept or understand his bitter reaction.

Greg was quiet for a long time when she had finished. "I can't tell you what to do," he said finally. "And where Jason is concerned, I'm probably not the person to ask. To tell you the truth, I've been doing a lot of thinking. I'd even started to hope that you and I..." He gave a little sigh. "But I doubt that's possible now."

He studied her gravely for a moment. "You love him, don't you?"

Her eyes filled with tears. There was no need to answer.

There was a hint of pain in his eyes. For a moment he was silent, lost in sad and wistful thoughts. "I've made a lot of mistakes in my life," he said finally. He thrust a hand through his blond hair, then looked at her. "But I think the biggest mistake I ever made was letting you go. I took you for granted, and I never even realized it until now."

"Oh, Greg," she whispered. "I did love you but—it didn't work." The words were painful, but they had to be said. "I've known that for a long time. There's really no point in even trying again."

"Maybe. Maybe not. But we all have to take a gamble sooner or later, Kate. Don't let the chance for happiness pass you by. For some of us, one chance is all we get." He laid his hand over hers. "I want this to work out for you, Kate. I really do. I want you to be happy. But if it doesn't work out, or if you need anything, let me know. Okay?"

It took a few seconds before she could speak. Then she kissed him gently on the cheek. "I will," she promised softly.

JASON WASN'T LOOKING forward to the night ahead. Tomorrow was Sunday. Two long weeks since he'd seen
Kate. Two long weeks since he'd seen those beautiful
green eyes shining up at him. Two long weeks since he'd
heard the sound of her laughter, that sweet, pure sound
that made him feel as if a beam of sunlight had unfolded
deep inside him.

But Kate hadn't been laughing then. And her eyes had
been filled with frustration, and disillusionment...and
so much pain. As much pain as he was feeling now.

He'd been so angry when she had left that day. It was
so much like before that he'd known a bitter fury unlike
anything he'd ever felt.

But there was no anger left in him, only a gnawing void
of darkness. He felt hollow inside! He couldn't go back
to a life without her; he couldn't even face the thought.

He shoved back the wad of papers on his desk, wondering irritably why he'd even bothered. But the truth
was that he'd neglected the paperwork and it had reached
a point where he had no alternative but to contend with
it. It hadn't been by choice, though. With Nick gone,
there had been so much more to do himself...

At the thought, he sighed heavily and wandered over
to the window. As he stared out at the dusky evening
light, he found himself admitting just how valuable Nick
was. He was a hard worker, strong and capable. He
shouldered responsibility well, and accepted it willingly,
even eagerly. And until that moment, Jason hadn't admitted to himself just how much he missed Rosa as well.

The future suddenly loomed before him. His home
really wasn't a home at all, he realized bleakly. It was
barren and stark, as empty as his heart. There would be
no children's footsteps running down the hall, no squeals
of laughter bouncing off the walls. He was alone.

He had no one to blame but himself.

Kate had been right all along. He had acted selfishly, and stubbornly, just like her father.

Most people were able to grow and learn from their mistakes. But him? His mouth twisted. He had only repeated his mistakes. Was it pride that kept him from admitting he might have been wrong about Nick? Pride that kept him from going after Kate and proving to her once and for all that they belonged together?

She was his, he thought with a fiercely masculine show of possession. He'd been foolish enough to let her go once. He wouldn't be so stupid again. Damn it, he wouldn't!

It was then that he spotted a car coming up the drive. He frowned, not recognizing the vehicle. It wasn't until a tall figure stepped out and began to walk toward the house that he recognized him.

Greg.

What the hell was he doing here? His footsteps carried him across the floor. Jason threw open the front door. "What do you want?" He didn't bother with a greeting, nor did he ask Greg inside. He knew he wouldn't be staying long.

Greg didn't bat an eyelash at his coldness. "I came to talk to you," he said firmly.

"We have nothing to say to each other," Jason countered shortly.

"I think we do," the other man said very quietly. "I came because of Kate."

Kate! His eyes blazed fiercely, but suddenly there was a knot of dread in Jason's stomach. Had Greg come *because* of Kate, as he claimed, or *for* Kate. Was Greg here to tell him that he and Kate had finally patched things up?

"What about her?" His eyes were dark with suspicion.

"I want to know how you feel about her."

Jason's expression tightened at the blunt demand. "That's none of your business. You're not married to her anymore, remember?"

Greg's smile held no mirth. "I remember. But I may want to make it my business—" his pause was very deliberate "—depending on how you feel about Kate. Because if you don't want her..." He let the sentence trail off.

Jason didn't pretend to misunderstand. Greg's meaning was clear. He wanted her back. But if he was preparing to draw new battle lines between them, this time Jason was ready. And this time he intended to fight back.

"I love her," he said in a low but furious voice. "I've always loved her. And *you've* always known it."

Greg didn't say anything for the longest time. Then he said very softly, "You're right. And I think Kate's always loved you." For a second, a look of disappointment flashed in his eyes. "Even when she was married to me."

Jason's mind reeled. The statement was hardly what he'd expected. He'd spent too many years feeling he'd been betrayed by the man that stood before him to push it all aside, but suddenly he couldn't forget that there had been a time when he and Greg had been as close as brothers.

He closed his eyes, and when they opened, he didn't care that they showed all his hurt and frustration and disillusionment. "That's why you hated me? So much that you left me to die when we were in Nam—"

"I never intended for that to happen, I swear. I knew you were hit, but I didn't think it was bad. I guess I thought I'd scare you a little, just to get back at you. Hell, I don't know what I thought!'' Greg shoved a hand through his hair, his movements harried. ''But then I panicked. I was afraid I'd end up in the stockade if I went back for you and someone found out I'd left you behind in the first place. Christ, I didn't know what to do!''

He shook his head, as if he couldn't believe what he had done. It was a moment before he resumed. ''I knew Kate had never really gotten over you. She never said so, but somehow I knew.'' He paused. ''I guess we realized at the same time just how much pesky little Kate Anderson had grown up, but you were the only one she had eyes for.''

Jason watched him, his face expressionless.

''But it wasn't just Kate,'' he finally admitted. ''Oh, I was jealous because she hadn't forgotten you, but I'd been jealous of you for years. My folks always thought you were such a great kid. It didn't matter what we did— football, homework, fooling around with a car engine— they always raved about you.'' There was a moment's hesitation. ''I guess I felt like I could never compete with you.''

Greg rubbed the back of his neck with his free hand. His face was lined and drawn. ''I'm not proud of what I've done,'' he said in a low voice, then his eyes met Jason's directly. ''For what it's worth, I'm sorry.''

The seconds ticked by. Though the pain Jason had endured all these years was still there, the bitter edge had dulled. It came as something of a surprise. But it was time to let go, he realized. Time to put aside the hatred and resentment.

Still, there was something he had to know. ''Did you ever love Kate?'' He posed the question quietly, but his gaze was piercing. "Or did you marry her just so you could feel you were one up on me?"

There was a moment's silence. "I loved her." Greg's gaze swung away for a moment. "But it's too late for me," he added. There was a slight pause. "Maybe not for you, though."

No, Jason echoed silently. Kate's image swam in his mind's eye. He ached with the need to hold her in his arms, taste the dewy softness of her mouth. No, he thought again, and his blood began to surge. With any luck, it wasn't too late.

"There's something else you might want to know."

At the sound of Greg's voice, Jason's mind snapped back to attention. "What?"

"I'm thinking of moving."

He frowned. "Moving? Where?"

"Alaska. I spent some time up there a few years ago...well, I'm thinking of relocating the business there." Greg smiled slightly, his eyes on Jason's face. "In fact, I think I've just made up my mind." With that, he turned away.

It wasn't until he was at the end of the sidewalk that Jason spoke his name.

Greg turned, but stayed where he was.

Jason hesitated. The words came with difficulty, but he spoke them nonetheless. "Good luck," he said softly.

AN ETERNITY PASSED from the time Jason left the ranch to the time he arrived at Kate's. It wasn't all that late, shortly after ten, but he saw that the only light came from the other end of the house. Kate's bedroom, he recalled. His hands were sweating as he reached for the doorbell. He was scared. Scared and excited and so damned afraid....

The door swung open. Kate stood on the other side, dressed in cotton shorts and a pale yellow T-shirt. A matching ribbon at the nape of her neck held her hair away from her face. She was barefoot, and somehow that only made her look younger and more vulnerable than ever.

Neither one said a word. They simply stared at each other, for what was probably the longest moment in each of their lives.

Kate swallowed. The sight of him kindled a thousand unwanted responses. She longed to sweep back the unruly black hair that clung to his forehead. She yearned to smooth the deep grooves etched beside his mouth. He looked so tired, and there was a hint of uncertainty in the dark gold of his eyes.

Oh, Lord, why had he come? she agonized. She'd already said her goodbyes. She wasn't up to another encounter. Her heart was still raw and bleeding from the last time.

It was Jason who took it upon himself to step inside. The door clicked silently shut behind him.

"Marry me," he said without preamble.

Kate stared at him. She had moved back so they were separated by perhaps four or five feet. She gave a tiny shake of her head, as if to clear it.

"You heard me right. I want you to marry me, Kate." He needed desperately to hold her in his arms. He instinctively started to reach for her, then abruptly checked himself.

She still hadn't spoken. At the tense, waiting silence that suddenly descended, she moistened her lips. "Oh Jason," she whispered achingly. "I want to. I want it more than anything in the world." She thought of the iny life she carried inside her, a life that sprang from the man before her.

She couldn't hide the thread of need in her voice any more than she could hide the torment in her heart. "I want to believe it could work this time. But you said it yourself. Sometimes love isn't enough—"

"No." He stopped her with a look and a word. "I was wrong, Kate. *Wrong*. What we have is very precious, too precious to let go so easily. And I truly believe that what we've been through has only made it stronger."

Her breath caught in her throat. The utter conviction in his voice stunned her. Jason was such a proud man. What had it taken for him to cast his pride aside and admit that he was wrong? Yet, oddly, the admission appeared to have cost him little. He looked almost relieved.

Jason watched her closely, his expression intent. "Greg came to see me this evening."

Her heart leaped. Oh, Lord, was that why Jason was here? Why he had asked her to marry him? Because Greg had told him about the baby?

No. She could sense that Jason didn't know. She clasped her hands nervously in front of her. "And?"

A faint smile curved his mouth. "He left in one piece, if that's what you want to know."

In a way, perhaps it was. An answering smile touched her lips, but she waited for him to continue. His face was suddenly grave.

"I don't think it's possible for Greg and I to ever be friends again," he told her quietly. "But I think it's safe to say that we're no longer enemies, either." He paused. "He told me he's thinking of moving to Alaska. Do you know why?"

Kate shook her head, her mouth dry.

"Strange as it seems, I think he wants to leave the way clear." His gaze snared hers. "For us, Kate."

Some distant part of her mind acknowledged that he was probably right. And maybe the fact that Greg hadn't told Jason that she was pregnant was his way of making up for all the heartache he'd caused them both. Because if Jason had asked her to marry him a second time simply because she was pregnant...

But he hadn't. He wanted to marry her because he loved her... He loved her!

She couldn't look away from his eyes, those eyes that could burn warm and clear as a bright, sunny day or turn cold and hard as stone. But right now, they were like dark gold velvet as they slid over her face and body.

"Come here."

Breaching the small distance between them was at once the easiest and the hardest thing Kate had ever done in her life, but she moved forward wordlessly. When she stood before him, Jason took both her hands in his. She was trembling, he realized.

"I stopped in to see Rosa and Nick tonight. I was surprised to find out they had their own place already." He lifted his eyebrows. "It's not bad for an apartment, but if I were them, I wouldn't get too used to it."

Her eyes began to blaze. From the look on her face, Jason didn't doubt that, had her hands been free, she might have shortened his life by a few years. He suppressed the urge to grin at her predictable reaction.

"Don't you want to know why I went to see them?" Only the pressure of his fingers around hers kept her hands where they were—and away from his neck.

She opened her mouth, then her jaw clamped together. "By all means," she consented politely.

"First, I told Nick not to be late for work Monday afternoon." He deliberately kept his voice very bland. "Oh, by the way, don't expect Rosa at the shop until after lunch, either."

It was obvious that something was up. Kate wasn't sure exactly what Jason was getting at, but the shroud of darkness that had surrounded her the past few weeks was almost gone.

"Oh?" Her attempt to glare at Jason never quite materialized. "And why not?"

"Because they'll both be in my attorney's office while I transfer the deed to some property. There's a spot in the northwest corner of the ranch—just a few acres—but it's a perfect spot for a house." He couldn't conceal his smugness. "I thought it would make a nice wedding present."

The astonishment on her face was something to behold. "You didn't," she breathed.

"I did." He took advantage of the moment and smiled his satisfaction. Then his teasing vanished, and he tipped her chin up to his. "I love you," he said, his voice low and urgent. His eyes were burning with an intensity that left her weak. "*Now* will you marry me?"

She was laughing. She was crying. She was in his arms, and nothing had ever felt so right. "Yes," she choked out, marveling that she could even speak at all. "Oh, yes!"

His desperate embrace nearly crushed the breath from her, but Kate reveled in the contact. They clung to each other, a silent communion that was more eloquent than words could ever be.

It was Kate who finally drew back. There was a warm, inviting glow in her eyes as she took his hand and led him down the hall.

Jason glanced at the door that opened into Toby's room. "Toby's not here?" he asked in surprise.

Kate shook her head and stepped into her bedroom. "He's spending the night at a friend's."

"Dennis the Menace across the street?"

She nodded, shakily conscious of the smoldering awareness on Jason's dark features.

His mouth curved. "Maybe he's not such a bad kid after all," he murmured. "As long as he doesn't wake us up again at eight o'clock tomorrow morning." He pulled her into his arms.

It was Kate's turn to smile. "You'll probably be awake anyway."

"Probably," he agreed, then grinned. "Awake and otherwise occupied." He eased her down onto the bed, then lowered himself beside her. His hands slid beneath her T-shirt, tracing the slender outline of her rib cage before disposing of her shirt and jeans.

His fingers were reaching for the clasp of her bra when suddenly he raised his head and stared across the room. "What on earth is all that?"

Kate glanced back over her bare shoulder. In the corner was the small trunk she'd hauled from the spare room earlier in the evening. She'd been sorting through the contents when he arrived. Strewn across the carpet, or the small table in front of the window, were dozens of infant sleepers, booties, tiny undershirts and diapers.

"Baby clothes." She gave an embarrassed laugh. " kept all of Toby's things after he outgrew them."

Jason's eyes came back to rest on her face. The gleamed provocatively. "Wishful thinking already? I' be happy to oblige," he offered lightly.

She bit her lip. "You already have," she murmured.

Distracted by the tempting lines of her body, Jason had begun to smooth a hand over her back to pull her closer for his kiss, but suddenly he drew away.

"I already have?" he repeated blankly.

She nodded, not quite certain of his reaction. "I'm pregnant," she clarified further when he continued to stare at her.

His gaze slid down her body at the same time his hand came around to splay across her abdomen. He stared down at her belly, still smooth and flat, as if to seek confirmation. His fingers moved ever so lightly across the tender hollow, his touch almost reverent.

But he still hadn't said anything. She watched him, almost afraid to interpret the myriad expressions that flitted across his face. "I thought I was okay." Lord, how lame that sounded. "But I must have miscalculated...Do you mind?" she finished quickly.

"Mind?" He laughed, the sound shaky. His eyes came up to hers. They darkened when he discovered her anxiety.

He reached for her, remembering that beautiful, glorious night in Mexico City.

"Lord, no," he whispered. "It's all I ever wanted, babe. You, me, our baby..."

The depth of feeling in his voice made her throat tighten. "And Toby," she murmured.

Jason smiled down at her. "And Toby," he echoed. "I'll love watching him grow up along with his brother or sister. He's a part of you, Kate, as much a part of you as this baby." He bent his head and gently kissed her belly.

Kate's heart was so full she could hardly speak. When he raised his head to gaze at her tenderly, she touched his face. "Love me," she pleaded brokenly. "Please love me."

His heart melted. A fierce joy surged within him. His hands shook as he shed his clothes. Kate had turned on her side to watch him, lovely and tempting beyond reason. Her hair rippled enticingly over her shoulder. The lamp on the dresser cast bewitching shadows on her honeyed skin. Sheer silk and lace screened her breasts and hips from his avid gaze, but the shape and texture of her was burned into his memory forever. He knew how perfectly her breasts filled his hands; how sweet and velvety her nipples tasted in his mouth.

He burned for her, but when he came down beside her, he wrapped his arms around her and pressed her close, savoring the wonder of simply being able to hold her once more.

She tested his control severely when her hands began to roam the heavy satin of his skin. He moaned with pleasure at her aggressiveness, then slipped his hands into her hair and sought her lips.

"You're mine," he whispered between each scorching, soul-wrenching fusion of their mouths. "Mine, Kate, no one else's. Mine now, mine forever. I love you...."

She thrilled to his possession, drawn into a heated, shattering world of spinning sensation. Their lovemaking had never been so fierce, so joyous, nor so achingly tender. She couldn't look away when Jason at last came into her. His eyes seared into her soul with a hot, golden fire. Together they resealed a vow made long ago, each slow, sure thrust a new commitment, a solemn promise of love.

It was a long time later that Jason drew a light blanket over Kate's naked shoulders and resettled her head against his chest.

"Kate?"

She stirred sleepily. He took unfair advantage and kissed her awake—not that she protested much. Not at all, in fact.

"When will you marry me?"

She pushed the hair from her eyes and peered up at him through the silvery darkness. "Soon, I think. We probably shouldn't wait long," she murmured. Her head dropped back on his chest. "Not with the baby on the way."

"No," he agreed. His hand drifted idly down her arm. "How soon?"

"I don't know." She was so tired, so blissfully tired. "A week, maybe." Her voice trailed off. She smothered a huge yawn.

A week? He couldn't wait that long. He felt a purely primitive need to bind them together in every way possible, as soon as possible. An involuntary laugh rumbled deep in his chest. The sound was so unfamiliar that he did it again, feeling oddly pleased with himself.

"What's so funny?" Drowsy green eyes opened to glare at him balefully.

"Nothing. Go to sleep." He tucked her head beneath his chin.

Kate's head lifted unexpectedly. "We better make that two weeks," she murmured with a frown. "We'll probably need that long to make the arrangements. I don't want anything fancy, but let's do it right this time." Her smile was sleepy but dreamy. "Flowers...lots of flowers, and a church wedding. You understand, don't you?"

Jason understood completely. But two weeks! Such a wait was mind-boggling. She might as well have said two years.

But he smiled contentedly and kissed her temple. "I'll take care of everything," he promised.

THE CEREMONY took place three days later. Jason had allowed only for the necessary blood tests, and time for Wade to fly up from Mexico to be his best man. But unlike the first time, when they had stood in a sterile room before a disinterested judge, Kate and Jason were married in the tiny, flower-bedecked church in Bradley. Nick and Rosa had stood beside them and renewed their vows as well. It had been a simple ceremony, attended only by those closest to the two couples, but neither bride had ever been happier.

Even now, almost a year later, Kate felt she would burst with joy whenever she thought of her wedding day.

"Owww! Mom, she's got me again!"

Toby's plea for help mingled with a sweet, bubbly gurgle of delight. At the sound and sight, Kate bit back a smile and quickly moved to where her two children played on the living room floor. Toby had been blowing gustily against his four-month-old sister's bare tummy, and the two had been thoroughly enjoying the game up until now. Gently but firmly, Kate loosened the surprisingly firm grip that ten chubby fingers had gained on Toby's hair, but not before Lisa gave another lusty tug.

Toby howled.

It was this scene that greeted Jason when he walked into the house that evening.

As though sensing his presence, Kate looked up. Their eyes met over Toby's head, and she experienced the same melting sensation she always did when she looked at him. A slow smile crept across her lips as she bent her head and resumed her task.

Jason's gaze was soft with love and laughter as he moved across the room. The minute Toby was free, a hard pair of arms went around Kate and lifted her to her feet. He pulled her back against his chest, inhaling her clean, fresh scent and relishing the feel of her soft body against his. He didn't think it was possible for him to love anyone more than he loved Kate.

Kate turned, her face already lifted for Jason's kiss. It was slow and lingering, and hinted at dormant fires deep within. They both knew that if it weren't for the presence of two small children, the spark would have exploded into a fiery flame that burned hotter and brighter and stronger than ever.

Toby rolled his eyes, grinned and switched on the television, not at all bothered by the familiar sight.

Lisa let out a disgruntled yell, apparently irritated at being ignored for so long. Jason reluctantly released Kate's mouth, then glanced down at the baby. Her tiny legs and arms went wild when she saw that she finally had her father's attention.

His touch was immeasurably gentle as he picked up his daughter and moved to the couch. His big hands cradled her head, then smoothed the silky black curls that covered it. Lisa had inherited his hair, but her eyes were the same incredible green as Kate's.

Kate sat down beside him, watching as he settled the baby into the curve of his arm. Lisa's hands immediately clutched his shirtfront, intent upon the buttons.

"She's perfect, isn't she?" His eyes found Kate's. "Just like her mother."

Kate smiled. The question didn't require an answer.

"Fifteen years from now, she'll be gorgeous and irresistible. Toby and I will be tearing our hair out, trying to keep the boys away—ouch!" He glanced down to find that the baby's hands had crept into the vee of his shirt and eagerly grasped a handful of chest hair.

"By then the two of you may not have any hair left!" Kate laughed and once more pried the baby's fingers free from the dark tangle on Jason's chest.

Lisa began to wail. Jason produced his keys, usually a surefire deterrent to a tantrum, but the baby continued to fret.

He gathered her in his arms and rose to his feet. "You're tired, aren't you, sweetheart?" he crooned, already on his way to the nursery. Kate remained where she was, knowing that the baby was in capable hands.

Moments later he returned with Lisa still tucked in the crook of his arm. She was newly diapered and snapped into a lightweight sleeper. He handed the child to Kate, and Lisa was only too willing to exchange the fist she'd stuffed into her mouth for her mother's breast.

Jason slipped his arm around his wife and daughter. They had been through the same ritual many times before. He loved taking an active part in the care of his daughter, but the sight of Kate nursing his baby never failed to send a rush of tenderness through his veins.

Toby went to bed an hour after his sister was laid in her crib. "Can we go to Uncle Nick's tomorrow and help with the house?" he asked, crawling between the sheets.

The house Nick and Rosa were in the process of building was almost finished. Jason had left right after dinner to help with the roof while it was still light outside. Toby had been busy with Pete in the barn, and hadn' asked to go along.

Kate raised her eyebrows and looked at Jason. She knew Toby was sometimes more of a hindrance than anything, but neither Jason nor Nick ever complained when he wanted to "help."

As usual, Jason's consent came readily. "I don't see why not. But I told Nick I'd be there bright and early. Sure you can handle not watching Saturday morning cartoons?"

"Cartoons are for kids!" he said disgustedly.

Kate smothered a laugh when they closed the door. "Next he'll be telling us he wants an expensive sports car for his birthday." Jason's tone was indulgent.

"You don't look as if you'd protest too much." She led the way toward their bedroom.

Jason shrugged, then smiled. "I sure missed him the month he spent with Greg in Alaska. Let's hope he doesn't ask right after he comes home one of these times. I'd probably have a hard time saying no."

"I don't doubt it for a minute. You certainly never say no to me!" In their bedroom, she slipped her arms around his waist, reveling in the lean strength of his body.

His warm gaze rested on her face. "Would you like me to say no tonight?"

She shook her head fervently. "Not tonight or any other night," she told him breathlessly.

He chuckled and drew her closer, but she knew he was pleased by her words, even though they were teasing. She also knew the pleasure he derived from the physical expression of their love, a pleasure that was by no means one-sided.

"I have some news you might be interested in."

"Right now the only thing I'm interested in is you." Her tone was playful, her touch tormenting as she slowly drew his shirt apart, raking his skin lightly with her fingertips.

"I think you'll be interested in this."

His voice had the eagerness of a child anxious to tell a secret. Kate reluctantly abandoned her exploration of his body and gave him her full attention. "All right," she sighed. "What is this news you're so anxious to give me?"

"Rosa's pregnant."

Her eyes widened. "She is? Oh, I'll bet she's bursting at the seams!"

He chuckled, amused by her choice of words. "Not quite yet, Kate."

She merely wrinkled her nose at his chiding. Rosa was undoubtedly thrilled—ecstatic! "I'll bet by Monday she'll have a whole line of maternity wear picked out for the shop!" She laughed delightedly, then hugged him hard.

That Jason was just as pleased was obvious. He was almost as possessive about his sister as he was about his own family, but there had never been any need to worry about the way Nick took care of Rosa, as he had discovered during the past year. Jason's acceptance of Nick couldn't have pleased Kate more, or Rosa, for that matter.

"Do you think Nick will be the same doting father you are?"

Her fingers resumed the task she had already started. Jason nearly groaned when she pushed his jeans off his hips and down his legs. He needed no urging when her hands came back up to his naked chest.

He took her with him onto the bed. "I think," he said very softly, "that Nick will like being a father just as much as I do." He smiled against her lips. "But I like being a husband even more."

Harlequin Superromance

COMING NEXT MONTH

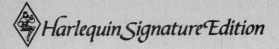

◆ *Harlequin Signature Edition*

Penny Jordan

Stronger Than Yearning

He was the man of her dreams!

The same dark hair, the same mocking eyes; it was as if the Regency rake of the portrait, the seducer of Jenna's dream, had come to life. Jenna, believing the last of the Deverils dead, was determined to buy the great old Yorkshire Hall—to claim it for her daughter, Lucy, and put to rest some of the painful memories of Lucy's birth. She had no way of knowing that a direct descendant of the black sheep Deveril even existed—or that James Allingham and his own powerful yearnings would disrupt her plan entirely.

Penny Jordan's first Harlequin Signature Edition *Love's Choices* was an outstanding success. Penny Jordan has written more than 40 best-selling titles—more than 4 million copies sold.

Now, be sure to buy her latest bestseller, *Stronger Than Yearning*. Available wherever paperbacks are sold—in October.

What the press says about Harlequin romance fiction...

"When it comes to romantic novels...
Harlequin is the indisputable king."
—New York Times

"...always with an upbeat, happy ending."
—San Francisco Chronicle

"Women have come to trust these
stories about contemporary people,
set in exciting foreign places."
—Best Sellers, New York

"The most popular reading matter of
American women today."
—Detroit News

"...a work of art."
—Globe & Mail, Toronto

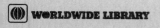

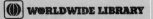